"I always knew it
smugly.

When Shawna breathed, she could feel her breasts moving against his chest. It was hopelessly erotic and hopelessly exciting. "Knew what?"

His arms tightened around her. "That you'd fit."

"How far back is 'always'?" She half expected him to say something about "forever." But she didn't want Murphy mouthing lines like an ordinary Casanova. She wanted him to be special. Because what she was feeling right now was special. Unique.

"That's easy. Since I opened my eyes in the emergency room and saw three of you."

Desire throbbed, demanding tribute. But doubt began to raise its head again. The emergency room. His injury. "I—" she began.

Murphy seemed to see Shawna's thoughts forming and laid a finger lightly to her lips. "No, no shop talk. Not tonight." He melted her protests with just a look. "Tonight is meant for loving."

Dear Reader:

Welcome to **Silhouette Special Edition**…welcome to romance. Our aim this summer is to continue bringing you deeply emotional stories you'll be sure to love!

And this month we're certainly fulfilling that ambition as we start three new mini-series. Look out for THIS TIME, FOREVER, HOMETOWN HEARTBREAKERS and THE BLACKTHORN BROTHERHOOD. We're sure you'll enjoy these sets of linked stories by popular Silhouette writers.

Also in June, we'll be giving you a unique THAT SPECIAL WOMAN title from Marie Ferrarella and two terrific books from new authors Elizabeth Lane and Elyn Day.

THIS TIME, FOREVER, a wonderful new trilogy by Andrea Edwards, begins now with *A Ring and a Promise*. Ancestral passion pledged with a ring and an unfulfilled promise guides two modern lovers towards each other.

The first of Susan Mallery's HOMETOWN HEARTBREAKERS, *The Best Bride*, is a lovely, warm story about a sexy lawman who thinks he's destined to fail at marriage. It'll have you desperate for the follow-up novel, coming in July, so that you can pay a return visit to the town of Glenwood. How can so many gorgeous men live in any one place?

Finally, don't miss Devon Monroe's story—and his secret—in *The Adventurer* by Diana Whitney—the first book in THE BLACKTHORN BROTHERHOOD.

Happy reading!

Jane Nicholls
Silhouette Books
PO Box 236
Thornton Road
Croydon
Surrey
CR9 3RU

Husband: Some Assembly Required

MARIE FERRARELLA

SILHOUETTE

SPECIAL EDITION

*First published in Great Britain in 1995
by Silhouette Books, Eton House, 18-24 Paradise Road,
Richmond, Surrey TW9 1SR*

© Marie Rydzynski-Ferrarella 1995

*Silhouette, Silhouette Special Edition and Colophon are
Trade Marks of Harlequin Enterprises B.V.*

ISBN 0 373 09931 2

23-9506

Made and printed in Great Britain

To Helen Conrad,
the greatest best friend
God ever created

MARIE FERRARELLA

lives in Southern California. She describes herself as the
tired mother of two overenergetic children and the
contented wife of one wonderful man. She is thrilled to
be following her dream of writing full-time.

Other Silhouette Books by Marie Ferrarella

Silhouette Special Edition   *Silhouette Sensation*

It Happened One Night   *Holding Out for a Hero
A Girl's Best Friend   *Heroes Great and Small
Blessing in Disguise   *Christmas Every Day
Someone To Talk To
World's Greatest Dad   * *Those Sinclairs*
Family Matters
She Got Her Man
Baby in the Middle

Books by Marie Ferrarella writing as Marie Nicole

Silhouette Desire

Tried and True   Foxy Lady
Buyer Beware   Chocolate Dreams
Through Laughter and   No Laughing Matter
   Tears
Grand Theft: Heart
A Woman of Integrity
Country Blue
Last Year's Hunk

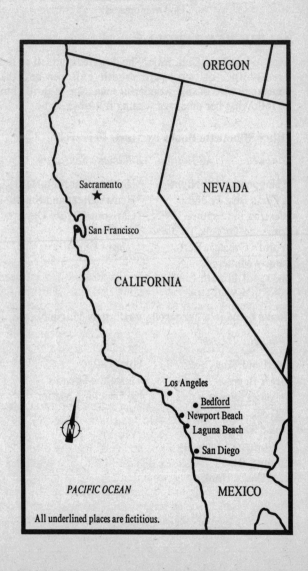

OREGON

NEVADA

Sacramento
★

San Francisco

CALIFORNIA

Los Angeles

Bedford

Newport Beach

Laguna Beach

San Diego

N

PACIFIC OCEAN

MEXICO

All underlined places are fictitious.

Chapter One

It caught her attention as soon as she walked into the bedroom. Shawna stopped toweling her hair. The red light on her answering machine was blinking spasmodically, winking at her like the bloodshot eye of a sailor on shore leave.

Dr. Shawna Saunders frowned as she impatiently rotated her shoulders beneath the light yellow terry-cloth robe. The telephone must have rung while she was in the shower. She fervently hoped it wasn't an emergency. Her mind wasn't functioning yet. Alertness was still a filled coffee cup away at this hour of the morning. Her entire body felt achy, protesting the only way it could against the long hours she kept and the little sleep she accumulated.

Striding across the room, Shawna blew out a breath as she resumed toweling her long blond hair. She'd stayed at the clinic longer than she had anticipated last night. But there'd been no real choice in the matter. The other physician who usually volunteered his services on Tuesdays hadn't come to relieve her. Something to do with a birthday party.

Shawna had understood, and opted to remain. The other physicians on the rotating dais that provided services for the inner-city clinic had families they shared things with, occasions they cherished. She had her work.

Besides, Shawna hadn't wanted to leave the clinic with only Carolyn to handle the walk-ins. Caro was certainly competent, but it seemed an unfair burden to leave the young nurse alone to cope with everything until closing time.

On the other hand, it wouldn't have been fair to close early, either. So Shawna had remained. Remained despite the fact that she'd already put in an eight-hour day at her practice in Newport Beach before driving over to the rundown downtown L.A. free clinic that so badly needed the services of *any* physician, specialist or G.P.

Lucky thing she'd hung around, Shawna mused as she circumvented her bed to get to the answering machine. That had been a nasty head wound she'd sutured for the last patient. It had taken Caro and the girl's mother to hold her down while she worked. Shawna hated to think what might have happened if she had gone home instead, the way her body had begged her to. It wasn't as if that section of the city had readily available medical care on every street corner.

Shawna smiled to herself, though the smile was hollow around the edges. It was her way of making a small difference. Her way of attempting to outrun the memories that shadowed her.

There were times, such as last night, when she almost succeeded. Exhaustion anesthetized her. But she was never too tired to remember. Never too tired to grieve.

Still, she could try.

Shawna pressed her lips together and jabbed an unpolished fingernail at the Play button. The machine laboriously wound and then rewound its tape. Shawna began vigorously toweling her hair again. She had a cataract surgery scheduled at seven-thirty at the hospital. That didn't give her much time to get ready.

A bright, cheerful voice filled the room.

The towel slipped from her fingers to the floor as she listened, foreboding winding a steel coil around her heart.

"By my watch it's six o'clock in the morning in California. Where are you, Shawna? I hope you're not answering because you're wrapped up in the arms of some adorable hunk, too full of passion to speak to your mother." A deep sigh followed. "But knowing you, you're probably immersed in some medical journal. Or you've already left the house to cure twelve people before breakfast."

Shawna groaned. Her mother's casual tone made her career sound as important as delivering newspapers.

"Anyway, I just wanted to tell you that I'm coming into town soon. And have I got a surprise for you!" The secretive announcement was followed by a throaty chuckle. "Don't try to call me, because I've moved. Bye."

The connection broke abruptly.

Shawna sagged against the wall and sighed, suddenly feeling incredibly tired.

"Oh, God, Mother, now what?" She stared at the answering machine accusingly as it fell into silence. "It's a man, isn't it? Again."

Her mother usually called when she was involved with a new man. Sally Rowen was never happier than when she was in love. Or thought herself to be. The last one had been a rock climber twelve years her junior. Ten broken fingernails later her mother had decided that their love wasn't meant to be.

With a deep sigh that unconsciously emulated her mother's, Shawna pushed the Rewind button and stalked into her kitchen. Her immediate need for revitalizing coffee had passed. What she needed now, after being given Hurricane Sally warnings, was a soothing cup of tea instead. And perhaps a couple of aspirins to chase away the headache that was forming behind her eyes.

Maybe he should get a dog. One that could be trained to yank him out of bed by the leg like a cartoon character when the alarm clock went off in the morning. Murphy Pendleton mulled over the idea as he glanced at the hands on his wristwatch, willing them to retreat. They remained steadfastly glued to their present position, at least for the moment, before moving on.

Eight-thirty.

Damn, he should have been up and out of here at least half an hour ago. If he did eighty all the way and the traffic lights stayed frozen on green, he'd make it to the office with about a minute to spare. Otherwise, he was going to arrive late. For the third time in as many months. Not exactly an admirable record.

He had too much to do this morning to be late, Murphy thought as he pushed his arms into his light jacket. He knew that Kelly would cover for him, but it wasn't fair to put his sister on the spot that way. And there was that meeting he was supposed to attend at nine.

Murphy picked up his briefcase. It was full of work he'd meant to get to but hadn't. He supposed that he could always say he was late because he'd stayed up till two working on a case.

Catching a glimpse of himself in the mirror, he smiled as he brushed a long red hair from his jacket. There was no way he could classify what had happened last night as work. Not by any stretch of the imagination. It had been a very unexpected, enjoyable evening. The kind he liked. Fast, fleeting, with no strings on either side.

No, he was just going to have to face the music.

Or the firing squad.

As pleasurable as last night had been, that was no excuse for being late this morning. He had obligations, and he prided himself on living up to them. It was just that he wasn't a morning person. He never had been.

He needed to place his alarm clock out of reach, he decided. Right now it was entirely too easy to lean over and shut it off without even realizing what he was doing. Just as he had done this morning.

Murphy detoured to the kitchen. His coffeemaker, far more dependable than he obviously was this morning he thought ruefully, had been programmed for seven-thirty. The coffee was brewed and tantalized him with its aroma.

He poured a full ration into the traveler's mug Kelly had presented him with, thought longingly of an English muffin heaped with raspberry jam and knew he'd have to pass. Maybe someone had brought in doughnuts this morning.

Switching off the coffeemaker, Murphy hurried into his garage. He tossed his briefcase onto the passenger seat of his red convertible and got in. He depressed the button on his garage-door opener and used the momentary respite as he waited for the door to open to take a long sip of his coffee. It tasted like hot, black ashes, just the way he liked it.

Revitalizing coffee coursing through his veins, Murphy could feel his system coming to attention as the garage door yawned open. He set his mug down and backed out, then pressed to close the garage. The coffee sloshed as he took a sharp turn out of the cul-de-sac. There was nothing coming in either direction. He patted his pocket to make sure that his tie was there, then took an immediate right.

Maybe he could get Jack to postpone the morning meeting till after lunch. It was worth a try, he mused, forcing himself to slow down. He couldn't very well fly out of the development. There was always that stray cat or dog to watch out for. With his luck, there was probably a parade of ducks crossing the street somewhere up ahead, on their way to the man-made lake.

To his relief, the tidy streets of the suburban development where Murphy lived were all but deserted as he drove by. Apparently everyone had either already left for work or school, or was safely nestled inside, watching "Sesame Street" or doing housework. Everyone was where he was supposed to be, he thought, turning down another block, except for him.

The dark cloud hanging overhead like a scowling black brow captured his attention immediately. It bobbed and wove just beyond the heads of the Italian cypresses.

Was something burning?

As Murphy drove past where he normally turned out of the development, the question answered itself. Bright red and yellow flames were just beginning to emerge out of the two-story house at the end of the next block.

Murphy grabbed his car phone and punched 911 on the pad.

The response was immediate. "Hello. This is 911. What seems to be the problem?" a woman's voice asked.

He felt as if he was in the middle of one of those re-created television dramas his sister Kimberly found so entertaining. Murphy told the dispatch operator about the fire and rattled off directions to the development.

The woman on the other end thanked him for his help, but her words were addressed to no one. Murphy had already brought his car to a screeching halt and had bolted from it.

It was the sound of a small, terrified scream coming from the house that had prompted him to leap out of the car.

More than once, Murphy had seen a little girl of about five or six playing on the front lawn as he passed on his way home. He was convinced that the scream had come from her. He wasn't about to stand about speculating if he was right.

The front of the house was already being eaten away by flames as Murphy dashed up the front walk. Everything was eerily quiet around him, save for the sound of the flames crackling and snapping as they devoured the two-story house. All Murphy could think of was thank God it wasn't windy the way it had been yesterday. A Santa Ana condition would have had half the development in flames in no time.

Murphy tried the door. The knob, hot, wouldn't give. The house was locked up tight.

Another scream came, then turned into a frightened whimper. There was no time to go for help, no time to wait for the firemen to respond. By the time they arrived it might be too late. Murphy yanked off his jacket and wrapped it around his arm and hand. Swinging hard, he rammed his fist through the front window and broke the glass.

A curtain of heat met him as he climbed through the opening he'd created. His foot came in contact with something soft. There was a sofa against the window. One end was already burning. He jumped off. The fire was spreading rapidly.

He could feel his heart racing as he scanned the large living room. "Where are you?"

Smoke and flames joined invisible hands to engulf him. He'd heard the cry, he was certain of it. It hadn't been just his imagination. The child had to be in here somewhere.

Murphy tried to keep his voice calm. He didn't want to frighten her any more than she already was. "I'm here to help you, honey, but you have to tell me where you are."

His lungs were beginning to pulse and ache and his eyes were smarting. Murphy strained to hear a telltale sound. The curtains against the dining-room window were an entire sheet of flame.

This was insane. What was he doing here? He wasn't a fireman, he was a lawyer, for heaven's sake. What did he know about dashing into a burning building and saving someone? Especially when there was no one to save. Maybe he *had* imagined the scream. Murphy stumbled toward the window again. The scream was probably from someone's television or—

"Here. I'm in here."

Murphy swung around. The muffled sob was coming from the closet.

Oh, God, the closet. Even Daffy Duck told children not to hide in closets during a fire. Where were this girl's parents?

Praying it wasn't too late for both of them, Murphy hurried past burning sections of rug and yanked open the closet door.

A blond child in coveralls was huddled on the floor, her eyes huge with terror. She held a ragged rabbit pressed to her small chest.

Relieved and apprehensive at the same time, Murphy scooped her up into his arms. "We're going to be fine." It was a promise he fervently hoped he could keep.

Pressing the child against him, as if that could somehow protect her from the grasping yellow fingers that were all around them, Murphy began making his way to the door. A room that had once been warm and friendly was now a flaming obstacle course. Was he leaving someone behind? The question throbbed through his brain.

"Is there anyone else here?" he asked, raising his voice.

The child never moved her head, never looked up. He felt her words vibrating against him. "My mama went out. She told me not to, but I played with them. I didn't mean to, but I did. I'm sorry." She began to cry. The bunny's hard nose was burrowing a hole into his chest.

Matches, he thought. The little girl had played with matches. But this was no time for confessions or lectures. Everything but survival was put on hold. He had to get her out of here. His head was already spinning from the smoke he'd inhaled.

"It's okay," he soothed. "It's okay." Keeping his eyes focused on the door, Murphy fought his way to it, so close in distance, so far when measured in flames.

He thought about climbing back through the window, but the sofa in front of it was completely engulfed in flames. It was the door or nothing.

Just as he reached it, there was an ominous crack to his left. Murphy looked up to see the drapery rod above the sofa come swinging down, one side severed by the slice of the fire's sharp tongue. As if it was a baton being hurled by an overly zealous majorette, one end of the rod caught him on the side of the head.

He saw more colors than he could identify, then a sheet of pulsating white passed over his eyes. For one awful moment he thought he was going to pass out just short of the threshold with the child still clutched in his arms.

Everything shimmered and then blurred. He heard screams and vaguely realized they were coming from his arms. The child. She was still there. Oh, God, he had to save her.

Instincts and something far more basic than he was conscious of took over, forcing him to set one foot after the other. He felt the hot doorknob radiating under his hand, though he wasn't certain how it came to be there. The next moment he was turning it, pulling the door wide open.

Air, cool and sweet, hit his face. Behind him another beam groaned and fell, a curtain of fire trailing after it.

More screams. Someone was calling out a name. He thought it was "Suzanne," but couldn't be certain. He was too busy sucking in air, too busy attempting to fight off the darkness that was reaching out to him.

Something against his chest was whimpering piteously, "Mama, Mama." Murphy felt someone prying at his hands and realized that they were clenched around something.

The child. Of course. They were taking her from him. There were more voices, noises all around him, yet Murphy felt alone. The borders of the world were shrinking, drawing closer and closer together around him until they had completely, effectively, squeezed out the light.

He felt himself tumbling forward, unable to stop, praying that he wouldn't fall, face first, into the fire.

Murphy heard a siren screaming somewhere in the distant background and thought that he'd left the television set on again. After that he didn't think at all.

"Dr. Saunders, thank goodness I found you."

Shawna looked over her shoulder at the nurse who stood in the doorway of her patient's room. A semblance of a smile tugged on Shawna's lips.

"I wasn't aware that I was misplaced." She heard the woman in the bed laugh quietly. The nurse, Telma, merely grimaced at the humor. "What can I do for you?" Shawna finished writing the notation in her patient's chart.

With an eye on the patient, the nurse assumed a professional stance. "Dr. Scalli would like to see you in E.R. as soon as possible."

Shawna closed the chart and looked up at Telma but made no move to leave. "What's up?"

The nurse remained in the doorway. "We've got an accident victim. The paramedics brought him in about half an hour ago. He's had a trauma to the head. Dr. Scalli thinks there might be optic nerve damage."

Shawna nodded, tucking the chart into the holder on the outside of the door. On her way out she glanced over her shoulder at the woman in the bed. "See you tomorrow, Kathy. With your discharge instructions."

Shawna led the way to the emergency room. Telma had to almost trot to keep up.

"Where do you get all this energy from?" she grumbled as they hurried down a long, newly recarpeted corridor.

Dr. Shawna Saunders's schedule was a matter of record. A record that had yet to be beaten since she had come on staff a year ago.

"Clean living, good food and overactive genes," Shawna quipped, stepping into the elevator. She pressed for the first floor. "Auto accident?" She tried to keep her voice moderate. It was the first thing she thought of whenever the word *accident* was mentioned. Like the devastating one that had irreparably destroyed her life.

"What?"

The door opened again and they quickly walked down the corridor past a group of workmen. "The patient in E.R. Was it an auto accident?"

Telma shook her head, lengthening her stride again. "No, he saved a little girl from a burning building."

"Oh, a hero. Don't get many of those these days."

Shawna opened the door that separated the corridor from the E.R. waiting room. A small cluster of people sat or stood around the leather-and-glass-furnished room, some watching the television that was constantly on, others merely studying their clenched hands.

So far, it looked like a light day, Shawna thought absently as she pushed open the swinging door that led into the examining area.

"Rather a nice-looking hero, too," Telma added.

"Well, then we'll really have to save him now. There's a shortage of good-looking heroes around." On either side of the large room was a long row of beds. Shawna raised an eyebrow as she turned toward Telma.

Telma pointed. "Last bed on the right." She shadowed Shawna's steps as she approached the small cubicle.

Shawna recognized the patient as soon as she pulled back the white curtain, though it had been more than twelve years since she had last seen him.

Murphy Pendleton.

Small world, she thought, once her surprise had passed. She reached for his chart.

Dr. Nathan Scalli, a tall, fastidious neurologist in his late forties, approached from behind. He was glad to see Shawna under any circumstances. Nathan nodded at the patient. "His name's—"

"Murphy Pendleton," Shawna said in a small voice as distant memories rustled the pages of her mind.

Nathan was surprised. She hadn't opened the chart. "You know him?"

She gave a perfunctory nod. "We went to school together, though I don't suspect he remembers me." As a matter of fact, she would bet on it.

Nathan looked at her for a long moment, then laughed. "I find that difficult to believe."

"Flirt with me later, Nathan." She opened the chart, perusing it. "For now, fill me in on the patient's status."

Light, harsh and invasive, was slicing through his subconscious like a saber wielded by a dueling enthusiast. It probed first one corner, then another. Murphy heard a groan and thought of the child. It was another moment before he realized that the sound was coming from him.

The stinging sensation along his hands and the left side of his face registered at the exact same moment that he began his ascent to the surface. Layer by hazy layer fell away, like an onion being peeled, until he opened his eyes.

He blinked twice. Moisture formed at the corner of each eye and slid down his cheeks.

The light didn't go away.

Someone was holding it, a pencil-thin beam that was being shone into his eyes, a prospector searching for an elusive vein of gold.

"So you've decided to join us again. Good. Hold your head still, please. This'll only take a moment longer."

The voice, soft and feminine, felt as if it was cocooning him. It would have been easy to slip away again, into a cottony nothingness. But Murphy struggled against it as he cleared the final hurdle and made it to the surface. He didn't like not being in control. Things happened to you when you weren't on top of a situation.

Everything around him was draped in white, including the woman standing over him. "Where—"

He hadn't changed any, Shawna thought. If anything, the years had been kind to him, improving on what nature had so whimsically bestowed.

"You're in the Harris Memorial emergency room."

The rest of it returned to him in a singeing flash, a kaleidoscopelike coming attraction from a movie. The fire, the girl, everything.

He attempted to prop himself up on his elbows. "The little girl?"

Shawna frowned slightly, resisting the temptation to plant her hand in the middle of his chest and push him back down. "She's fine, I'm told, thanks to you. Just very scared. She promises never to play with matches again. Her mother is thinking of building a shrine to you." Telma had filled her in after Dr. Scalli had left.

He sighed. Relief blanketed him. "That's good, about the girl, I mean."

Murphy's head felt as if it was spinning off. Groaning, he held it, aware of the small bandage at his temple. He sank down on the bed again. There was no pillow beneath his head and the mattress was completely horizontal. He felt awkward and tense, lying there. And decidedly miserable.

Concentrating, he looked at the woman beside his bed. Her image was slightly shimmery.

A minute smile lifted a corner of her mouth. "I thought you'd like to get that out of your system by yourself," Shawna said, answering the question in his eyes. "Now maybe you'll lie flat the way you're supposed to."

He wasn't happy about it, but at the moment there wasn't anything he felt up to doing.

Murphy suddenly remembered his meeting. Damn, but he was late. He blinked furiously, trying to clear the blurriness from his eyes. "Where's the doctor?"

Shawna watched his eyes. He was having trouble seeing her. Scalli might have had something, she thought, though her initial probing had shown nothing.

"You're looking at her. Or attempting to," she amended. Shawna leaned over him. "How many of me do you see?"

His vision might have been fuzzy but not so fuzzy that he couldn't see she was an exceptionally attractive woman. When she leaned over him like that, he caught a whiff of very faint, very sensual perfume.

He attempted to smile. The effort hurt his head. "Enough to fill my dreams."

Shawna shook her head. "You haven't changed any."

Did he know her? No, he would have remembered someone like her. He glanced for a name tag, but there wasn't one. He probably couldn't have made it out right now, anyway.

He tried to think. That hurt, too. "Excuse me?"

Shawna realized her slip. She retreated. "Nothing. I was just reminded of something."

But there was something about her voice that nagged at the corners of his mind. He *did* know her, but from where? A former client? Someone at a party? Where? It all remained obscured. "You look vaguely familiar."

Shawna picked up his chart again and scanned it once more to quickly reinforce her decision. She flipped to the X-ray report. "I bet you say that to all the E.R. physicians."

Murphy narrowed his eyes. The milky borders diminished when he did that. He struggled to remember, to place her. His mind was a frustrating blank, wrapped in pain. "No, this is my first time in an emergency room."

She stopped writing and glanced up. He was going to need an M.R.I. "First time at playing hero, too?"

His mouth curved with just a shade of cynicism. He'd been one hell of a scared hero. "Yeah."

She watched the way he massaged his forehead. That had been some blow he'd received, though fortunately, no stitches had been required. Just a butterfly bandage. "Head hurt?"

He lowered his hand and looked at her again, responding to the sympathy in her voice. "Like a thousand devils marching in double time."

She made a notation about his medication. "That'll pass." She flipped the chart closed and laid it at the foot of the bed. "You have a mild concussion."

He groaned. "Doesn't feel very mild."

Shawna nodded. That was to be expected. He'd been lucky, at least at first glance. There was a huge lump on the side of his head where he'd been struck, plus a mild burn on his fingers. The preliminary X rays, taken while he was unconscious, showed nothing. But she liked being thorough.

"I'm having you admitted for observation. We'll check you out."

Murphy frowned. "No."

He just had a headache, albeit a really bad one. And maybe things were a little blurred around the edges. But under the circumstances, that was to be expected. Murphy didn't like hospitals and wasn't about to remain in one if he could help it.

Based on the Murphy she knew from years ago, Shawna had expected some snappy retort, not a refusal. "Excuse me?"

Someone had draped him in a blue-and-white flowered hospital gown. He wondered where his clothes were and who he'd have to bribe to get them. "I have a meeting to go to."

A stern look entered her eyes as she bent over him, pushing him back down on the mattress. There was little physical resistance, which reinforced her point.

"You have a room to go to." She lifted his hand by the wrist and held it up as if it was exhibit A. "Your hands, luckily, are not badly burned." She released it again. "But you do have a mild concussion, and I am concerned that the blow to your head might be affecting your vision." She drew herself up, looking for all the world like a staff sergeant issuing orders to a green recruit. "We'll both feel a lot better if you're admitted for a day."

She assumed that was the end of it. Shawna wasn't accustomed to having her judgment questioned.

"There's only one way I'd feel a lot better about remaining in a strange room," he told her in a voice that wasn't as loud as he would have liked. If he raised it above the present low level, it throbbed in his head as if every syllable was a physical entity equipped with pointy edges. "And that's if the room was in the Hyatt Hotel. With you to hold my hand."

She wondered how hurt he'd have to feel not to flirt. "Mr. Pendleton, I don't think you really appreciate the gravity of the situation." She didn't have time to stand here, debating with him. Her appointments began at nine-thirty, and it was already ten past that now.

He wasn't up to arguing, but there seemed to be no other way out of here. "And you probably don't appreciate just how hard my head really is."

Shawna eyed him as she shoved her hands impotently into the pockets of her smock. There wasn't anything she could actually do if he demanded to be released. "I'm beginning to get the idea. Well, Mr. Pendleton, I can't keep you here against your will. I can only make suggestions."

He smiled, though he didn't get up immediately. A couple of seconds more on the bed wouldn't hurt, he told himself. "I'm not unreasonable. I'm always open to suggestions."

And the smile on his face told her exactly what kind of suggestions he was thinking of. Or perhaps she was just reading something into it, remembering his reputation in high school.

She crossed her arms before her. "I've been known to get rough with patients."

"Stop, you're exciting me," Murphy muttered, his teeth clenching as a sudden sharp pain creased his forehead like a lightning bolt. His eyes momentarily fluttered shut as he attempted to absorb the brunt of it.

He was in no condition to waltz out of here, she thought angrily. What was he trying to prove? "Hurt?" she asked dryly, as if her point had been validated.

Murphy slowly opened his eyes again. He needed an economy-size bottle of aspirin. And perhaps warm, willing fingers to massage his brow. "If I say yes, will you nag me about staying?"

She pulled no punches, especially since she already considered the bout won. "Yes."

He set his mouth stubbornly. The pain was already mercifully receding. "Then the answer's no."

Shawna sighed. "Have it your way."

"I generally do."

Yes, I remember.

Chapter Two

Murphy began to rise. Shawna placed her hand lightly but firmly on his shoulder, holding him in place. He raised his eyes to hers questioningly.

She couldn't, in good conscience, just let him walk out without attempting to convince him to at least have another test done. "Are you up to a compromise?"

A smile curved Murphy's lips, instantly turning him into the boyish football hero Shawna had secretly sighed about while poring over her physics textbook. "Such as?"

She roused herself, pushing aside the fleeting memory that had slipped through her mind. "Stay here long enough to have a cranial M.R.I. done. I can arrange for one to be taken this morning."

Shawna was hedging. She had no idea what the imaging lab's schedule for the morning was like. She was gambling that once Murphy agreed to the test, he'd remain in the lab waiting room until it was his turn.

He didn't want to stay in the hospital a minute longer than necessary. "I'll see your compromise and raise you a visit."

Shawna frowned as she looked at Murphy. "Excuse me?"

He sat up slowly and was pleased that his head wasn't spinning around like a basketball on the tip of a Harlem Globetrotter's finger, the way it had before.

"I go home now and then come by your office for a visit. Officially," he added when he saw her skeptical expression. "You can poke and prod me to your heart's content."

Despite the situation, Shawna felt a smile rising to her lips. "Don't ever say the word 'poke' around an ophthalmologist."

"Sorry." He grinned and faint hints of dimples lightly indented both cheeks. It gave him an endearing look she was certain he had to be aware of. "How about it, have we got a deal?" Murphy put his hand out toward her.

Since he appeared to be focusing well enough, and his pupils weren't dilated, she mentally capitulated. Rather than place her hand in his, though, Shawna took out a card from her smock pocket and put that in his palm instead.

"I suppose I have no choice. I just hope you don't regret yours." She nodded at the card. "Call my nurse for an appointment. Tell her I said to squeeze you in any time."

Murphy would have rather that the doctor did her own squeezing. She was as impressive and attractive a woman as he'd met in a long time, he mused, slowly running his finger and thumb over the card. If the action smarted a little, because of the tenderness of his digits, he didn't show it.

Shawna watched the way he rubbed the card and was struck by the sensuality of the minute motion. Sometimes, she thought, loneliness had a way of taking a bite out of her when she least expected it.

"On the outside chance that you come to your senses, here." She wrote out a prescription for the M.R.I., then handed it to him. "Just call the imaging lab for an appointment."

"Are you all right?"

Shawna and Murphy turned almost in unison to find Thomas Sheridan standing just to the right of the curtain he had pulled back. Concern was etched across his chiseled, broad features.

Murphy attempted to appear nonchalant. "All my parts seem to be moving in the right direction." He wiggled his toes beneath the sheet and winked, not at his brother-in-law, but at Shawna. The simple action seemed to echo through his system, whispering faintly of pain. He concentrated on Thomas. "What are you doing here?"

Thomas made his explanation half to Murphy, half to the woman at his side. "Kelly called and asked me to check up on you since she wasn't getting an answer at your house and you hadn't arrived at the office yet. I didn't have to be at the university until eleven today, so when you didn't answer my call, I swung by your house."

Thomas shoved his hands into his pockets as he recalled the sudden wave of nausea he had experienced when he'd seen Murphy's red sports car parked crookedly at the curb before the partially gutted building, with Murphy nowhere in sight.

"There was still a ring of people around that house where you played fireman." Thomas saw the question rise in Murphy's eyes. "I saw your car parked there and started asking if anyone had seen you. They told me the paramedics took you to the hospital. And that you were unconscious."

His tone was casual, but they had been friends since childhood. Murphy didn't need to be told that Thomas had been really worried.

Murphy lifted a shoulder and then let it fall again. "They probably blew it all out of proportion. You know what a placid, boring city Bedford is. People magnify any little bit of excitement."

Thomas looked at the butterfly bandage across Murphy's temple. A jagged circle of blood had seeped through to darken the middle. He turned toward Shawna, knowing better than to expect a truthful assessment of the situation from Murphy. "I'm his brother-in-law, Thomas Sheridan. Is he going to be all right?"

Brother-in-law. So they had made the friendship official. Shawna remembered Thomas, too. He and Murphy had been inseparable in high school, and while it was Murphy she had had the crush on, it was difficult to forget someone as tall and imposing as Thomas.

But she gave no indication that she knew him as she nodded in response to Thomas's introduction. "He seems to think he is." A shot of hope pushed through the concrete. Perhaps Thomas could talk some sense into Murphy. "I'd like to keep him overnight for observation."

Thomas suppressed a smile. She wouldn't be the first woman who had uttered those words in reference to Murphy, but she'd be the first to say them with a medical intent.

"And he doesn't want to stay." It wasn't a guess. Thomas knew how Murphy felt about hospitals.

"I tell you, I'm fine." Murphy propped himself up farther. He saw the way Thomas was looking at the bandage on his temple. "It's just a little bump on the head. How many times did you bean me when we were playing catch as kids?"

"Obviously one too many times," Shawna commented. It earned her a tolerant grin from Murphy and a soft laugh from Thomas.

The laugh died slowly as Thomas took a good look at the woman attending Murphy. There was something vaguely familiar, something he couldn't quite place his finger on. He knew her. Had he run across her when he had brought Kelly here for the birth of their daughter? That would be the logical explanation, but somehow, it didn't seem to fit. Thomas shrugged mentally. It would come to him eventually.

Right now he had Murphy to worry about.

"I'm not staying," Murphy said quietly.

Thomas was well acquainted with that tone. Murphy might give the impression of being happy-go-lucky, but whenever he chose to stick with something, heaven and earth couldn't move his friend from the position he had taken. Thomas turned toward Shawna. "Can he go home?"

"It appears that there's no stopping him." Thomas, she thought, was the more reasonable one. She presented her case to him. "At the very least, I would like to see him in my office for a follow-up." Though Murphy had said he'd come, she had her doubts.

"I'll see that he gets there," Thomas promised.

Very carefully, Murphy turned and, gripping the side of the bed, swung his legs out from under the covers.

Thomas didn't bother to hide his amused smile. Murphy looked completely out of place in the hospital gown, which had hiked high up on his thigh. "Nice legs."

Murphy glared at Thomas. He tugged down the edge of the gown as far as it would go. "Where are my clothes?" Murphy looked at Shawna and second-guessed her response. She'd be the type to pretend that they had been misplaced. "Or would you rather that I streaked out of the hospital?"

Streaking was a fad that was twenty years in the past. Men with bodies like Murphy's could definitely bring back a demand for it. But she wasn't about to test him, or set a precedent at Harris.

"God forbid." She nodded toward the other curtained-off beds. "Some of the people in here are heart patients. No telling how they might respond to seeing you making a dash for the parking lot wearing only a grimace." He wasn't about to dash out anywhere, she thought as she studied him, at least not without intense pain. If nothing else, that bump on the head was giving him one hell of a headache.

Shawna pointed to the metal drawer housed beneath the foot of his bed. "Everything you came in with is right there. I expect to see you soon. Very soon." It wasn't a polite remark, but an order. To punctuate her statement, she pulled the curtain closed after her as she withdrew.

"I'm sure you will," Thomas muttered under his breath. He'd seen the way Murphy had looked at the woman. Bump on the head notwithstanding, Murphy was definitely interested. After more than twenty years with him, Thomas knew the signs.

Ignoring the doctor's edict, Murphy slid off the bed and almost continued onto the floor in one fluid motion. Thomas grabbed his arm, stopping Murphy's descent just in time.

Concern was resurrected as Thomas helped Murphy onto the bed. "Maybe you'd better listen to her and check in here."

Out of habit, Murphy began to shake his head. He stopped abruptly as the room threatened to tilt to a forty-five-degree angle. "I'm just a little dizzy, that's all,

Thomas.'' He curbed the annoyance he felt. ''I'd like to see how you'd take a drapery rod coming down on your head.''

''Lying down.'' Thomas bent and fished Murphy's clothes out of the open-faced drawer. They were neatly folded and tucked into a blue-and-white plastic hospital bag. ''In a hospital bed.''

''That's because you have Kelly to nag you,'' Murphy observed. He indicated the closed curtain. ''Make sure nobody comes in.'' He pulled open the bag and dumped the contents onto the bed.

Why did they have to take your clothes off if you had a head injury, he wondered, annoyed as he struggled into his trousers.

His back partially to Murphy, Thomas stood sentry, watching as shadows representing nurses and orderlies hurrying to other beds filtered through the white curtain. ''Kelly would nag you about this, believe me.''

''It's not the same thing.'' Murphy closed his belt and felt infinitely better. There was something almost dehumanizing about wearing an abbreviated, flapping gown. ''Besides, she doesn't live with me.''

Thomas thought about inviting Murphy over for a few days, just in case. ''That could be arranged.''

Murphy looked at him. He knew exactly what Thomas was thinking. But he didn't want to stay with them and have Kelly fussing over him.

''Thomas, be a friend and don't argue. I had enough of that from the good doctor.'' An image of Shawna, crisp and cool as she peered into his eyes, crossed his mind. ''Funny thing.'' Murphy slipped into his shoes as he rose from the bed, a little more steadily this time. ''I couldn't quite shake the feeling that I know her from somewhere. But how could I forget someone who looked like that?''

He picked up his jacket and decided against slipping it on. Instead, he slung it over his shoulder.

''The bump on the head?'' Thomas suggested innocently.

Murphy was in no mood for levity. Or harassment. ''Very funny. Spring me out of here, Thomas, or I'll thumb a ride and my sister'll never forgive you.''

Thomas sighed. "You always did know how to phrase a threat." Thomas took his arm. Murphy gave him a malevolent look, but Thomas didn't release him. "Humor me. It'll be a lot more embarrassing for you if you do a pratfall in front of everyone in the waiting room."

Too weary to argue, and feeling just the slightest bit wobbly on his feet, Murphy acquiesced.

He remained silent until he got into the passenger side of Thomas's car, as if talking would somehow sap the strength away from his legs. Once in the car, Murphy leaned back and strapped in, breathing a sigh of relief. That blow to the head had affected him more than he was willing to admit, even to himself.

He turned and looked at Thomas as the latter started up the car. "What time is it?"

"Almost eleven. I've just got enough time to get you home and get to the campus to prepare for my class."

Thomas debated calling the department and asking someone to take over his history class, but he knew Murphy would look upon his sticking around as baby-sitting.

Murphy had stopped listening to the rest of the explanation. "Home?" he echoed.

"You know, that place with the curtains and the bed? A few blocks away from the scene of your derring-do?"

Thomas's suggestion was unacceptable. "I can't go home. I've got to get to the office."

"Talk sense, Murph."

As far as Murphy was concerned, he *was* talking sense. "I've got to review a case this afternoon. I've already missed the morning meeting." Nothing that couldn't be made up, of course, but he hated thinking of himself as vulnerable.

"You should have thought of that before you decided to play hero." Looking at him out of the corner of his eye as he took the off ramp, Thomas saw Murphy's mouth harden. "Besides, you can't go to the office wearing that." He waved at Murphy's clothing. "It brings new meaning to the term 'smoking jacket.'"

Murphy looked down at his clothes, consciously seeing them for the first time. They were sooty and badly in need of cleaning. He slumped in his seat, resigned. As usual,

Thomas was making perfect sense. He could see how that could irritate his sister. "All right, you win. I'll go home."

Murphy smiled to himself. "Don't see how you have much choice in the matter." He turned to look at Murphy as they came to a stop at a light. "I'm driving and I'm bigger than you are." He saw the small, rigid line of pain and the clenched jaw. "How's your head?"

There was no reason to lie. "It feels as if someone used it to punt with and everything's a little fuzzy around the edges, but I'll be all right."

Annoyance at the situation crept into his voice. He didn't think of himself as superhuman, of course, but neither did he see himself as being capable of being injured. It got in the way of how he viewed himself. He'd played three years of football in high school and four more years in college with little more than a scratch and some strained muscles. This was his first brush with mortality and he didn't like it. "Just give me a little while, okay?"

The light changed and Thomas resumed driving. "I can give you as much time as you want."

Murphy frowned. He hadn't meant to snap at Thomas like that. This wasn't anyone's fault. "Figure of speech. I didn't mean to get surly with you."

"Apology accepted."

Frustrated, Murphy looked out the car window. Everything *was* slightly blurry, but he had only to blink his eyes several times to get everything back into focus. No big deal. It would pass, he told himself. No need to have a doctor hovering, poking and prodding him.

The word *poking* brought the emergency-room doctor back to him. "Damn, but I can't get her out of my head."

Thomas didn't have to be told who Murphy was thinking about. "Must be crowded in there for her, what with all those tantalizing memories you keep tucked away."

Murphy bit his lower lip thoughtfully. "No, I mean, I really think I know her, but..." He lifted his shoulders and let them fall again. "I just can't place her."

That made two of them. She had to be someone they both knew, which narrowed the scope somewhat. "What was her name again?"

"Shawna something." Murphy felt chagrined at his oversight. And then he remembered. "But hey, wait, she gave me her card." He fished the stone gray card out of his shirt pocket.

The small black letters seemed to squeeze together in a football huddle, defying him to discern one from the other. He felt his exasperation mounting.

"Here, you read it." Murphy practically slapped the card into Thomas's hand.

It wasn't a good sign. Murphy normally had twenty-twenty vision. Thomas glanced at the card. The writing wasn't particularly small. "You can't make out the letters?"

Murphy didn't answer him.

Thomas curbed the urge to turn the car around and head back to the hospital. Instead, he looked at the card as he eased the car to another stop. "Her name's Shawna Saunders."

Murphy turned the name over slowly in his mind. "Doesn't ring a bell with me." He looked at his brother-in-law. "How about you?"

Something clicked as Thomas repeated the name aloud and thought of the woman in the E.R. "Not Saunders." He handed the card back. "But we went to school with a Shawna."

Murphy tried to think, but concentration was out of the question. The war party in his head forbade it. "We did?"

"We did. High school," Thomas clarified. "Shawna Rowen." A clearer picture began to form in his mind as he remembered. "Quiet, shy, braces, glasses. Straight-A student. She was in our biology class and a couple of others, I think, although I wouldn't swear to it." He remembered her because their seats had been alphabetically arranged and he'd sat behind her.

Murphy leaned back, trying to think. Thomas's verbal sketch was bringing her to life for him. He began to vaguely remember. "You think—?"

Now that he was describing her, Thomas was almost certain that the two were one and the same. Besides, how many women named Shawna were there?

"I think," Thomas confirmed. He slowed as they passed a school area. "She's the right age and coloring. Give her contact lenses, straightened teeth and a different hairstyle and presto. It's her. Otherwise, why would she look so familiar to both of us?"

It made sense. Murphy let out a low whistle. "Talk about a late bloomer..." The Shawna Rowen he vaguely recalled had been on the plain side.

Thomas took the turn that eventually led into Murphy's development. "I'd rather talk about what the late bloomer said."

Thomas could talk about it all he wanted to. Murphy's mind was made up. "I'm not going back to the hospital."

Thomas shook his head. "No, I meant the visit to her office—and the test."

He'd already forgotten that she'd said anything at all about that. What was it that she wanted him to have? An R.I.M. test? No, an M.R.I. test.

Murphy frowned. "You know I hate tests."

Thomas laughed. "You won't have to cram for this one."

Murphy sighed. He could tell he was going to get no peace about this. "Anyone ever tell you that you're a nag?"

"Only you, but I forgive you." Thomas grinned broadly. "Kelly tells me that nagging means you love someone."

Murphy leaned back in his seat. "Kelly'd be the one to know."

Thomas retrieved Murphy's car from in front of the partially gutted house after he had brought Murphy home. Extracting a promise from his brother-in-law that he would stay put for the day, Thomas hurried off to the university.

Murphy began going stir-crazy as soon as he had shut the door. It wasn't as if there weren't things he could be doing. There were. He just didn't feel like doing any of them.

And he certainly didn't want to lie down. Somehow, doing that, even in the privacy of his own home with no one around, would be tantamount to admitting his own vulnerability. He wasn't willing to do that.

So instead, he roamed about his living room like a freshly trapped tiger who took no interest in his new surroundings.

When the telephone rang some fifteen minutes later, Murphy sprang to answer it, grasping the receiver as if it was a lifeline being thrown to him in a tempestuous sea. "Hello?"

"Thomas tells me that you're a hero."

Murphy grinned and settled back on the sofa next to the telephone. "Hello to you, too, Kelly."

"Thomas just called me from the university with all the lurid details."

Although she was aiming for a casual tone, Murphy could hear the underlying tension in her voice. He blew out a breath. "After twenty years I find out that he's a tattletale. What a disappointment that man turned out to be."

"This isn't funny, Murphy. You could have been killed."

The last thing he wanted was a lecture. "But I wasn't. I'm fine."

"Not from what Thomas told me."

Murphy didn't want to be babied or fussed over. He wanted to get back to work. He enjoyed work almost as much as he enjoyed life. Being put on hold for any amount of time annoyed the hell out of him. He'd never been one to be able to lie in bed with a cold, either. "Thomas exaggerates."

Kelly laughed shortly. "When pigs fly. Thomas is the most understated man I know. Call the doctor."

Murphy tucked the telephone against his neck, amused. "What shall I call her?"

He might be her older brother, but there were times when Murphy needed a keeper. "Don't get cute on me, Murphy. I want you examined thoroughly."

He grinned and felt better for the first time. "So do I, but not the way either she or you might have in mind."

"Thomas told me about that, too. He says we all went to high school together."

"Thomas is getting too gossipy in his old age."

"That's your opinion. I'm finally breaking him in properly so that I can find out what's really going on in your life." Her tone grew serious. "I'll take over your cases here. You do what you have to to make sure everything's all right. I'll drop bv tonight to look in on you."

Murphy groaned. "Please, spare me the Florence Nightingale routine. Use it on Thomas, instead."

"Okay." She played her ace card. "I could always call up Kimberly or Mom and have them come over instead."

Kimberly would revert to lectures on safety and his mother would probably be even worse. "You always did play dirty."

Kelly laughed. "I'll take that as a compliment. Are you going to call the doctor for an appointment?"

He'd already made up his mind to do that, but he didn't like being bullied into it. "If I start to feel bad after a day or so, I'll call."

"Not good enough."

Because his eyes and his head were still giving him trouble, Kelly's insistence made Murphy just a little irritable. "Kell, I'm a grown man. I can make up my own mind about things."

She let out a long breath. "I have to hang up now and call Mom."

He knew what that meant. The end of peace as he now knew it. "Uncle."

Kelly laughed, victorious. "I thought so."

He let his exasperation drain from him. She was, after all, only worried about him. He couldn't fault her for that. Exactly. "I taught you too well."

"And I appreciate it. Now be a good boy and do as I say. Call the doctor and then go to bed. I'll see you later."

"Bye."

Murphy hung up and then frowned. Where was that card Shawna had given him? He searched his pockets and found it just where he had tucked it in before, his shirt.

He laid the slightly bent card on the counter and looked down at it. The letters were no longer huddling together. He could make them out clearly. A vindicated feeling wound through him. He'd known it all the time. There was nothing wrong with him that an aspirin and a good night's rest couldn't cure.

Murphy smoothed out the card thoughtfully. Still, this would give him an excuse to see the doctor again and relive old memories.

And perhaps, eventually, make a few new ones. Nothing serious, of course. He'd gotten serious only once in his life. With Janice. And that had eventually left him with a rather large hole in his heart, not to mention the one in his pride. It had been enough to teach him not to take relationships any deeper than surface level.

He wondered, as he pressed the numbers on the telephone keypad, if Shawna remembered him. She was still only a vague memory, a name he remembered being called out occasionally by the teacher. A shadow he'd brushed by in the hall as they left the classroom.

He decided that he'd really like to add a touch of depth to that shadow.

There was one last patient to see for the day and then Shawna could go home. It felt as if she'd put in a forty-eight-hour day.

She stretched in the privacy of her office, where she'd gone to take a call from another doctor. One more patient and then she'd treat herself to a hot bath and turn in early for a change. She could certainly use the rest. It felt as if she had been running since she'd gotten up this morning, especially since she'd been launched with that phone call from her mother.

She definitely couldn't say she was looking forward to the visit. It wasn't that she disliked her mother; it was that they had nothing in common. Not even, she thought sadly, memories. Her mother had always been far too busy with her own life to really attempt to forge a path in Shawna's.

No, there was no need to rehash that now. She'd have plenty of time for thoughts of her mother once Sally swept into town. Right now she had a patient to attend to. And then a bubble bath with her name on it to meet.

With any luck, Shawna thought, she'd have a dreamless night. A swift shaft of pain pierced her soul as she recalled the last dream she'd had. They were theme and variations of the same thing.

She sighed, pushing it all out of her mind. Taking the brand-new chart from the holder on the door, she didn't look at the name as she turned the knob and walked into examination room number three.

And saw her new patient sitting there.

Murphy.

He turned and smiled at her. "You said you could squeeze me in."

Chapter Three

Feeling an uncustomary flutter of nerves that had its roots in the girl she had once been more than a decade ago, Shawna dropped her eyes to the folder she held in her hand. Mechanically she glanced at the name written across the tab on the file before opening it.

There were only two sheets in it. Her assistant's notations were on the right. Neatly clipped to the left leaf was a patient history Murphy had filled out not fifteen minutes ago.

It looked, Shawna thought, particularly sparse. There wasn't anything in the space reserved for the name of his family physician. A host of ailments had been left blank or checked "no." Either Murphy Pendleton had a phobia about going to doctors or he was incredibly healthy.

Shawna mused that it was probably a combination of both. Except for the bandage on his temple, he certainly looked healthy. Almost *too* healthy, if there was such a thing.

She closed the folder and held it against her chest as she crossed to Murphy. Her heels gave off a rhythmic cadence as they hit the highly polished wooden floor. "I must say that you surprise me."

The lady looked even more attractive now than when he had first seen her in the emergency room, Murphy mused, successfully burying his restlessness about being here. Yes, a great deal more attractive. And just a tad defensive, he noted. Or was that his imagination?

"Why?" The grin came easily to his lips as he tried to make himself comfortable in the padded chair. "I haven't done anything yet."

"But you have." Shawna saw his brow quirk slightly above eyes the color of particularly exquisite turquoise jewelry. It took effort to keep her gaze steady, linked to his and still remain free of the almost hypnotic effect they had. "You came in much sooner than I thought you would." She would have easily bet that she would never see him again.

His amusement deepened the curve of his mouth. Shawna summoned an expression of professional concern to mask any extraneous thoughts she might have in reaction to it. It was best to get down to the business at hand as quickly as possible. Judging by his lack of patient history, he wasn't the type of man who entered a physician's office casually or often. He had to be deeply motivated.

She looked intently into his eyes, searching for signs. "Has the pain increased?"

It had, for a short time, right before he'd made the call. But now that it had receded he felt almost emasculated admitting the momentary panic when a cloudy curtain had descended over his left eye.

"No. Actually, except for one small incident, if anything it's probably gotten a little better."

Her eyes narrowed as she picked up the nuance in his voice. "Probably?"

He lifted a shoulder and let it fall carelessly. She was looking at him as if he were something squirming beneath a microscope. "I'm not paying strict attention to it."

Shawna was having a difficult time following him. Her hectic pace, she thought, was catching up to her and muddying up her mind. "And why is that?"

Her eyes looked like bright blue pebbles lying at the bottom of a very shallow spring with the morning sun shining on them. He vaguely recalled that she'd worn nondescript glasses in high school. Or had that been someone else? "Well, I've been busy..."

He didn't strike her as a workaholic, but she had been wrong before. "As I remember, you were supposed to take it easy."

Murphy held up his hand. "Before you castigate me, there was no physical labor involved." He saw a line of impatience deepen between her eyes. Despite her calm exterior, if he didn't miss his guess, the lady took life a little too seriously. "I was busy racking my brain, trying to remember who you were."

So he did recognize her. Well, there was nothing to be gained by a stroll down memory lane. "The ophthalmologist who examined you in the emergency room."

She didn't remember him, he guessed, which probably was to be expected. Twelve years was a long time. "Before that," he prompted.

She didn't want to discuss the past. Her life was here and now and she preferred it that way.

"Before that, I was who I am now." She squared her shoulders stubbornly. "A slightly harried doctor who has a very busy schedule, so let's get on with this, shall we?"

If he didn't know any better, he would have said that she was deliberately shying away from him. "Your nurse told me I was the last patient of the day."

Shawna flipped open his folder again. There were a few notations on the snow white page Jeanne had clipped in. Her assistant had done a preliminary visual fields test on him.

"She's my assistant," Shawna corrected. "And when did she tell you that?" She asked the question casually without looking up.

The room was small, windowless and as cozy as a room could be with an army of lenses sequestered in neat rows along a small wooden cubby on the left and an assortment of instruments used to probe the accuracy of a patient's vision on the right.

She looked so terribly solemn, he thought, studying her expression. She was also taking an inordinate amount of time looking at a few scribbles. "In between the third and fourth row of letters on the eye chart."

Shawna ran her fingertip along the last line of writing. "Speaking of which, you have twenty-twenty vision in your right eye." She looked up at him. "You didn't score as well with your other eye."

He shrugged. She wasn't telling him anything he didn't know, but he had every confidence that it would clear up soon. "I'll study harder for the exam next time."

Shawna dropped the folder onto the small side table as she sat down on the three-legged stool. He was obviously reluctant to discuss his problem. But if that was the case, then what was he doing here? This was certainly a great length to go to for a flirtation.

She was misreading the signs, she told herself, and tried again. Taking a breath, she studied his face for a moment. "You didn't get the test I prescribed, did you?"

He had toyed with the idea for a moment, then dismissed it. It had been a bump on the head, nothing more. No reason to panic and overreact. "No."

She struggled to curb her impatience. People didn't realize just how precious eyesight was. And how quickly and easily it could be lost. "Do you plan to?"

He could smell a lecture coming on. "If I have to."

Shawna counseled herself to retreat. She wasn't responsible for everyone. What this man did was his own business. She could only advise him.

"Meaning?" Shawna leaned back to adjust the dimmer.

Shadows took over the room, swallowing up the light. The projection of the eye chart on the back wall became more visible again. He'd been in the darkened room with Shawna's assistant a few minutes ago, yet it seemed somehow far more intriguing being in the semidark with the very serious Dr. Saunders.

It took a beat to unscramble his thoughts. "Meaning that if it gets worse, I will."

Shawna paused and pressed her lips together. "Worse. That means it's not good now."

He was a lawyer. Words were his stock-in-trade. He knew the value of weighing them and the penalty of carelessly misusing them. He frowned at his own error. "That means I have a headache and a slight blurriness of vision, which, under the circumstances, I believe you would say was warranted."

The man had a silver tongue, which undoubtedly served him well in court. And in the bedroom. But she was too busy for games. Shawna crossed her arms before her, momentarily abandoning the tools of her trade. "Then why are you here?"

It was easy enough to fall back on the excuse he'd given himself. He'd come to see her. If the woman who had caught his attention also happened to be a doctor and could say a few words to assuage the slight unease he felt about his condition, so much the better. But first and foremost, she was an attractive woman who had definitely aroused his interest. *That* was what had brought him here.

Murphy leaned forward. "I wanted to find out if I was right about who you are."

She wasn't buying his reasons. Perhaps a remote part of her was leery of buying it. "And that's all?"

No, but that was all he'd admit to at the moment. Leaning back in the padded examination chair, he linked his fingers before him and studied her face. He attempted to relate the woman before him to the girl she'd been and couldn't quite succeed. Still, Thomas wasn't usually wrong and there was a faint, nagging memory in his mind, as well.

"That's all," he assured her. "So, are you Shawna Rowen?"

There was no point in denying the truth. He could find out easily enough if he really wanted to, although why he would want to bother didn't seem logical to her. It wasn't as if they had dated, or for that matter had even been friends back then.

"Yes."

He grinned. Score one for Thomas. "You don't remember me, do you?" He thought it prudent to refrain from mentioning that he didn't exactly remember her, either. At least, not vividly.

"Oh, yes, I do." He might want to play games, but if he was going to sit here in her chair, she was going to go through at least a minimal exam. If nothing else, it would satisfy her own concerns.

Shawna swung the arm of Murphy's chair forward, bringing around a small examining device that looked like a cross between a head brace for people who'd broken their necks and a miniature guillotine.

"Rest your chin here." She indicated the small, tissue-covered chin rest. "And lean your forehead here." Shawna tapped the horizontal metal bar above it. It amused her that there was a flicker of hesitation in his eyes. "Don't worry, it's not lethal."

Following her instructions, Murphy leaned forward. He didn't much care for the sensation sitting here like this generated within him. He felt like a prisoner looking through bars. "I don't like not feeling in control."

"Not many of us do." There was a shade more feeling in her voice than she had intended. To Shawna, control was everything. And fate enjoyed stepping in every so often to taunt her with the knowledge that it held all the cards and she none.

Shawna realized that Murphy was looking at her oddly. She shook off the feeling that was threatening to take hold of her and reached for the ophthalmoscope.

"Look straight ahead," she instructed as she shone the blue-and-white light into his left eye.

Murphy strained to keep his eye open as lights seemed to burst upon him. "What did you mean by that?"

"Look straight ahead? I rather thought it was self-explanatory." She switched positions, peering into the other eye. "Look straight ahead with the other eye, please."

He tried not to blink, but it was damn hard. Murphy could feel his eyes begin to tear. "No, when you said you remembered me."

Shawna peered intently. Everything looked fine, yet instincts nagged at her, contradicting what she saw. "That I remembered you."

No, there was more to it than that, he thought. "You said it with a bit more feeling, as if you knew something about

me that wasn't entirely flattering.'' He'd searched his mind
for any encounters that they might have had and had drawn
the proverbial blank.

She wanted him to have that test, but doubted if she could
bully him into it. With a sigh she shut off the beam and
leaned back. A hint of a smile curved her mouth as she allowed herself to think back to when life was, if not simple,
at least less complex.

"*Flattering* was probably a good choice of words. As I
recall, you were 'flattered' by every girl who came your
way.''

She had a nice smile, he thought. Too bad she didn't show
it more often. He winced lightly as she turned the lights back
up. The accompanying pain surprised him, but he managed to keep it from registering on his face.

Murphy raised his hands as if to ward off the accusation.
"Innocent until proven guilty.''

He was flirting with her, she thought. Actually *flirting*.
What man in his right mind would pay for an office visit in
order to flirt with his doctor? "Your guilt or innocence is
not the question here. I have no interest in your activities as
long as they don't affect your medical condition, which, I
might add, is still very much up in the air.''

He stubbornly clung to the belief that he was all right. The
time he'd been tackled by Rod Parnell on the football field
in his junior year in college and had had the wind knocked
out of him, he'd seen two of everything for more than a day.
In comparison, this was a walk in the park.

Leaning forward again, he summoned his most persuasive smile. "How about dinner tonight?''

Talk about a fast worker! Shawna thought. But then, he'd
had a reputation for that. A ladies' man who had managed
never to antagonize a single girl he'd gone out with in high
school. No easy feat, she'd imagine. Still, it didn't change
anything. "I don't date patients.''

Murphy nodded. "I can see how that might complicate
things. All right, you're fired.''

It took Shawna a moment to realize that her mouth was
open and nothing was coming out. The world she dealt with,
while not usually immersed in life-and-death matters, was

still etched in seriousness. She just wasn't accustomed to Murphy's sort of laid-back attitude. "Is everything a joke to you?"

He paused for a moment and his expression became so grave that Shawna almost doubted that he was the same man. "No, injustice isn't a joke. Destruction isn't a joke. Hurting someone isn't a joke." And then, just as quickly, he smiled again and the twinkle that had glimmered in his eye returned. "But I find that humor sees me through a great many of the rough spots that seem to have a nasty habit of popping up in life." If he was any judge, the lady could use a little laughter in her own life. Maybe more than a little. "The way I see it, if you can't laugh, you're dead."

Shawna inclined her head. "An interesting philosophy, but . . ."

She was going to say no and he didn't want her to. Whether it was male pride or something else that pushed him on, he didn't know. But he did know that he would regret the opportunity lost if he let it slip away.

"I thought we'd catch up on old times, nothing serious." His tone was light, as if to underline his assurance.

Things probably did get serious with Murphy, Shawna mused. For possibly an hour. Or two. But no more than that. She was definitely not in the market for that brand of "seriousness." She wasn't in the market for anything at all.

"We have no old times." She smiled again, more to herself than to him. She'd been a mouse of a girl back then, given to daydreams and secret hopes in between her studies. "You probably couldn't even pick me out of the yearbook."

"Sure I could." Then, in case she thought him too cocky, he added, "Everyone's labeled."

His manner had her smiling even though she knew better. All charm, no substance, wasn't that the way it always was with incredibly good-looking men? Her mother had certainly been through enough of them to teach her that, if nothing else. "You're very persistent."

It came with the territory. "I'm a lawyer." But he would have been persistent even if he'd been a bricklayer. It was his nature. Persistence covered with a blanket of laissez-faire.

"And I'm a very tired physician," she countered. She realized that she hadn't risen to her feet, even though she'd ceased examining him.

That wasn't the reason she was saying no, he thought. If it had been, she would have at least paid lip service to a rain check. But he played along.

"I promise I won't make you run laps before dinner." It seemed only natural to take her hand. "I won't even take you dancing. That way you won't even have to stand up."

She'd bet even money that he did most of his entertaining horizontally. Twelve years ago she would have been tempted. Tempted? If she was being honest with herself, she would have said yes immediately at the first hint of an invitation, and breathlessly so. She'd been shy, awkward and eager then. As introverted as her mother was extroverted.

But twelve years had passed. And a lifetime with them. Two lifetimes, she amended silently.

Politely but firmly she extricated her hand. "Sorry, no."

Murphy glanced at her hand. Long, slender fingers capped with unpolished nails. And completely without the twinkle of jewelry. "You're not married."

"No."

It wasn't that he couldn't believe a woman would turn him down. It was that something in her manner suggested her reluctance was for reasons other than taste. "Taken?"

Yes, she thought, she was. Taken by a memory, but she wasn't about to explain that to him. Lying was easier. "Yes."

He was pretty astute when it came to reading body language and nuances. She wasn't being honest, not completely. "You know, one of my eyes *is* a little blurry." He tapped the folder on the table. "But as your assistant noted, I have perfect vision in the other."

"Your point?"

"You hesitated."

"I was taking a breath." He was crowding her and she didn't appreciate it. "Counselor, you're heading for a mistrial here."

Shawna reached into her lab coat and took out an almost depleted prescription pad. Without looking at him, she wrote out instructions for the imaging department. Again. With a flourish she tore the paper off and held it out to him. "Now, about your eye. We'd both feel better if you'd have that test done."

He took the paper from her. "I don't know about that, but one of us would feel a great deal better if we could get to know the doctor."

She stuck the remainder of the pad into her pocket and rose to her feet. "I'm listed with Harris Memorial Hospital and with the AMA. Either will tell you all you want to know."

He fingered the prescription thoughtfully before slipping it into the back pocket of his jeans. "I sincerely doubt it."

She had no idea how he managed to create such an intimate air between them out of absolutely nothing. It was probably his talent. And it was wasted on her. "Those kind of answers you're not about to get from anyone."

He rose. "Don't you know better than to challenge a lawyer?"

Shawna ignored his question as she stopped in the doorway. "I trust you have someone to drive you home."

He shrugged. "I'll manage."

Shawna frowned. The man was an idiot. "You drove here yourself, didn't you?"

"I do have one twenty-twenty eye," he reminded her glibly.

She could only shake her head as she retreated into her office. There were more pressing matters awaiting her attention than a daredevil, irresponsible lawyer with a killer smile.

It wasn't until after she closed the door to her office that Shawna acknowledged the fact that her pulse was just a wee bit accelerated. In addition, there was a very amused smile on her lips. She wasn't really conscious of the latter until she saw her reflection in the glass of the curio she had in her office.

It came as a surprise.

As if to assure herself that it was her own face, Shawna ran her fingertips lightly over her lips, bemused. The man was a hopeless flirt.

He had flirted with her, she thought, and she had responded. It had been a long time since she had done anything so lighthearted.

It felt good.

The next moment Shawna shook her head, as if that would erase something so trivial from her system. She had no business flirting with anyone. No business, she thought, even being alive.

God, where were all these thoughts coming from, so fresh after all this time? It was as if seeing someone from her past had unearthed everything all over again.

Shawna ran her hands over her face, wearied beyond words.

She had walked away from the car accident with a three-inch scratch on her arm and a mile-long gash across her heart.

Tears sprang to her eyes as she looked at the framed photograph on her desk. Doug holding Bobby. Her heart constricted even as their names whispered across her mind. She'd taken that photo just two weeks before the accident. They'd been at the Grand Canyon. They had gone together, one of those rare holidays that Doug had permitted himself.

Usually he was so busy at the hospital that the only time she saw him was when they passed each other in the halls or consulted over a patient. Douglas James Saunders had been a widely respected neurosurgeon, at the top of his field.

She closed her eyes. The tears still managed to squeeze through.

He'd been so like her in temperament it had been almost scary. It was as if they had been carbon copies of each other, only with different faces. They'd had the same tastes, the same likes, the same thoughts. Life with Doug, when she'd had a chance to see him, had been blissful. No waves, no traumas. Predictable. And so terribly soothing and comforting.

She'd never had to ask him how he felt about something—she knew. In all the time they had been together, they had never disagreed on a single thing.

Except driving.

She loved it. He hated it. So she had been behind the wheel that horrid day the world ended.

Shawna squeezed her eyes tighter, but the tears still wouldn't retreat.

The slight rap on her door startled her.

She cleared her throat twice before she trusted herself to say anything. With the heel of her hand she pushed aside the telltale streaks on her cheeks and then sniffed twice.

"Come in."

But when she turned her head to look, it wasn't Jeanne she saw in her doorway. It was Murphy.

Murphy strode into the room at her invitation. "I just— hey, are you all right?" He stopped abruptly, hesitating, then quickly crossed to her. He took her hand, and there was something infinitely warm and comforting about the way he held it.

Still, she was embarrassed at being caught this way. Shawna nodded her head a bit too rigorously. "Yes, I'm fine."

The hell she was. "You're crying," he observed gently.

For the second time that day she withdrew her hand from his. Annoyance cloaked her embarrassment. "I just hit my shin against the corner of the desk." She shrugged. "Brought tears to my eyes."

It wasn't a very convincing story, but he let it slide. Instead, he merely smiled in response. Let her have it her way.

Indignation reared. It was better than accepting sympathy. "I don't see why that strikes you as amusing."

"It's not. It's just nice to know you're human like the rest of us."

What kind of signals was she sending out to him? Whatever they were, they couldn't be all that flattering. She squared her shoulders and sat up a little taller. "I never pretended to be anything else."

He grinned at her and inclined his head. "There was a little walking on water back there."

She assumed he meant her attitude about not dating her patients. Did he find that aloof? Maybe it was at that, and maybe it was a good thing besides. "That wasn't walking on water, that was separating doctor from patient. That, Counselor, is ethics.''

"I know all about ethics." Murphy leaned a hip against her desk, as much for comfort as for support. He wasn't about to admit it, but he wasn't feeling entirely confident about the reliability of his equilibrium. It hadn't really bothered him until a moment ago. But there was no reason to tell her that, just as there was no reason to admit that he had driven the short distance from his house to the medical complex with his left eye shut in order to clearly see the road.

"The trouble with ethics, Shawna, is that you have to keep a tight rein on them. Otherwise, they might turn you into a holier-than-thou kind of person."

Shawna's sigh was a mixture of exhaustion and exasperation. He wouldn't take her advice, he wouldn't take no for an answer, and now he seemed bent on taking her dignity. "Mr. Pendleton—"

"Murphy," he prodded genially. "We have a history together, remember?"

The man was incredible. Despite the fact that he was confounding her, he was also managing to amuse her. "We don't have a history together," she corrected. "We *took* history together."

"We did?" He laughed softly to himself. The momentary dizziness had receded and he felt infinitely better. "Thomas recalled only English and bio."

He lit up a room when he laughed, she thought, struggling not to let it undermine her. "I have things to do. Why did you come back here?"

"To see if I could change your mind about dinner." He raised his brows innocently at the first sign of mounting annoyance in her face. "Can't right now, huh?"

She shook her head. "No."

As he moved away from her desk he accidentally knocked over a photograph. Murphy caught it before it fell over and before Shawna had a chance to catch it herself.

He righted it carefully. "Nice family."

"Yes."

Hers. Judging by her reaction, she was divorced. Recently, he guessed, and probably leery of rebounds. Murphy smiled to himself. He could readily understand that, probably better than most.

He looked down at her, not ready to leave just yet. "Want to swap sad stories?"

There was a note of sympathy in his voice. It surprised her. Shawna raised her eyes to his. "I thought you believed in humor."

"I do. *Because* of the sadness. Remember?"

"Oh, yes, the philosophy." There was just the smallest smattering of regret as she turned him down this time, but that was a holdover from the distant past. "I'm not interested in any stories just now."

That wasn't aloofness in her eyes, he decided, it was sadness. He had a weakness for sad eyes. "Even if I have an M.R.I. done for you?"

He still wasn't taking any of this seriously, was he? The immortal jock. "If you have it done, it would be for you, not for me." She looked at him squarely, something she wouldn't have had the courage to do years ago. "And why are you so interested in going out with me?"

That, he mused, was the million-dollar question. But there was no denying that he was interested. A man could do a lot worse than be interested in a sensual, willowy blonde with sad blue eyes. Besides, he wanted to see her smile again. Genuinely. With feeling.

"I told you, I love a challenge."

That was his problem, Shawna thought. The only challenges she was up to were found in patients' folders. "Then I'd suggest that you go climb Mount Everest—when your vision is better."

The smile on his face told her that he was taking her flippant advice in an entirely different context. "I think I just might do that." He crossed to the door, then looked at her over his shoulder. "Yes, I just might do that," he repeated.

The man had a Casanova complex. She didn't know why she was smiling. Annoyed with herself, she turned her chair away from the doorway. "Don't forget to close the door behind you," she murmured.

Very deliberately, Shawna picked up the closest file on her desk. But though she scanned it, she didn't see any of the words before her. She was too busy listening for the sound of the door being closed.

When she heard the reassuring click, Shawna shook her head and let out the breath she had been unconsciously holding. The man was completely irresponsible. As irresponsible as he had been in high school. Back then she had found it charming.

Now it was simply irritating.

Chapter Four

Kelly Sheridan turned the knob and eased open the door to her brother's office. Her three o'clock appointment had canceled and she thought she'd take the opportunity to look in on Murphy. He'd been out of the office the entire morning and had returned less than ten minutes ago.

He shouldn't even *be* here, she thought. Murphy gave a whole new meaning to the word *stubborn*.

Kelly barely knocked as she entered his recently redecorated office. The faint smell of varnish still hung in the air and teased the senses.

"Hi, Murph. Heard you blew them out of the water today in court." She crossed to his desk. Above objections, he had gone in to conclude pleading a client's case. And skillfully gotten the man acquitted. "The word 'partnership' is being bandied about in the halls even as we speak."

Damn, why hadn't Kelly waited a few minutes before she came in like gangbusters? He had wanted a little time alone to pull himself together, to shake off the clammy hand of fear that had clamped onto his soul. Right in the middle of his first cross-examination this morning, the courtroom had suddenly become veiled in an opaque curtain. Mercifully, that had cleared up almost immediately. But then, just before he'd left court, it had happened again. This time he'd seen only ghostly shadows through his right eye, and nothing through his left.

It had scared the hell out of him.

But it had passed, just as it had previously. He just needed a minute to compose himself, a minute to push aside the tendrils of anxiety that were swaying around him.

Murphy slowly took in a deep breath and turned his swivel chair to face her. Try as he might to talk himself out of it, he was unnerved and didn't need someone else adding to his tension right now.

"Really?" He forced a glib smile to his lips. "A partnership? Certainly took them long enough." The sound of his own voice, robust and confident, did a great deal to calm him.

"Well, you know how these rumors have a way of spreading like wildfire, sometimes entirely without any foundation." Kelly perched on the edge of his desk, her long legs dangling casually over the side. She couldn't quite keep her artificial smile in place. He looked awful. Kelly dropped the act. "Murphy, are you all right?"

The concern in her voice was as thick as molasses in January. He didn't want it aimed in his direction. Even as a boy he had never felt comfortable being on the receiving end of sympathy, only on the giving end.

The grin on his face deliberately widened. "Haven't you heard? I'm perfect."

The man gave mules a bad name. "I wasn't talking about your overbloated ego or the pitifully underdeveloped women you choose to associate yourself with." As her anger with him heightened, the tempo at which she swung her legs increased.

Amusement slivered through him. He raised a brow. "Underdeveloped?"

She was tempted to wipe the smirk off his face physically. She was being serious and he was doing his best to throw up a smoke screen. "I was referring to their mental capacities. Or lack thereof."

He had to admit that ever since Janice, the women he'd seen socially had been on the light side as far as mental prowess went. But there had been a reason for that. It decreased the danger of entanglement.

The expression on his face was deliberately lascivious. "I don't debate world politics with them."

It broke Kelly's heart that Murphy had been hurt the way he had and that he had retreated from a world that she knew in her heart he wanted. "Maybe you should."

Thoughts were scrambling in his brain and he wasn't up to sparring with his sister. "Isn't there a tax audit you should be looking into or something more productive than nagging me?"

Kelly leaned closer. She didn't have to scrutinize him very hard. "You're pale."

He lifted a shoulder carelessly as he turned from her and turned on his computer. "Just means I need to get out into the sun more."

"It means you should stop playing cat and mouse with me."

He had absolutely no idea what screen he was pulling up on the computer. Exasperated, he glanced at Kelly over his shoulder. The room threatened to tilt a little before it righted itself.

"Look, Kell, I've got a few things to catch up on." He gestured toward the computer. "That little unexpected holiday of mine the other day threw me off schedule."

She hated it when he was so glib. "It wasn't a holiday and you're an idiot to come back so soon." She fairly spit the words out.

"I'm fine," he insisted, struggling to maintain his good humor. "And besides, as you noted, I had to be in court."

He was good at twisting things around. "I said you *were* in court, not that you had to be. I was prepared to take that case for you. I told you that yesterday." She'd stayed up half the night reviewing the case, only to discover that Murphy had gone to court anyway.

The grin on his lips purposely teased her. "You wouldn't have been as brilliant."

Kelly laughed shortly. "Nothing wrong with your ego, I see, though it might do with some downsizing." She placed a hand on his shoulder and silently cursed him when she felt it stiffen. Why was he being so defensive? Why couldn't he be sensible when it came to himself? "Murphy, talk to me. What's wrong?"

He shrugged off her hand before he could think better of it, his temper flaring for a moment. He was fine, just fine. All he needed was a little peace and quiet. And maybe some rest. "Nothing," he snapped. "I'm fine."

She knew him better than he knew himself. "In a pig's eye."

A glint of humor returned. "I wouldn't fit."

She was through debating this. Kelly slid off his desk and picked up the telephone receiver. "All right, what's her number?"

He drew his brows together and was relieved that the automatic action hadn't spawned an accompanying sharp stab of pain the way it had earlier. That was a good sign, right?

"Which 'her' are we referring to?"

Kelly fisted her other hand on her hip to keep from hitting him. "The 'her' who obviously didn't do her job in examining you."

That brought back an image of Shawna and the interest she had aroused in him. And a trace of mischief to his smile. "That was not for lack of trying on my part."

Violence wasn't going to solve anything, though right about now it might have felt good. Kelly made a conscious effort to curb her temper. The receiver slipped from her fingers back into the cradle.

She took his hands in hers. "Murphy, it's me, remember? You can lose the love-'em-and-leave-'em act. I was at the church, I shared the pain." She looked into his eyes and saw that it was still there, a pain that had nothing to do with the blow he had received to his temple. A pain that wouldn't go away until the right woman picked up the pieces and helped Murphy put his life together again. "You don't have to be the world's greatest playboy with me."

He squeezed her hands in mute gratitude, then let them drop. He wouldn't accept sympathy, not even from her.

"You're my sister, Kell. They have laws against that in every state in the union."

Kelly moved restlessly through the elegantly furnished room. If she ever ran into Janice Wilson she was going to cut the woman's heart out. Just the way Janice had done to her brother.

Sympathy tugged at her the way it always did whenever she thought of Murphy being literally left standing at the altar. The strains of "Here Comes The Bride" had just begun to fade into the huge church as Janice's older sister had come running up the aisle to Murphy, her face a mask of anxiety. Janice had called the officiating priest to say that the wedding was off, that she was marrying someone else.

Stunned, Murphy had appeared to recover quickly and had made a joke out of it. He'd invited everyone to attend the reception anyway, since the tab had been paid for. He had gotten royally and roundly drunk that night, but not so drunk that she couldn't see his broken heart.

Kelly sat down, sorry the topic had been dredged up and that she had been the cause of it. "It was a case of cold feet creating a huge mistake."

"Yeah." He laughed shortly. He'd been a fool to believe in happily ever after. That only happened to a chosen few. And he wasn't one of the chosen. "Mine."

"No," Kelly insisted adamantly. "Hers. It was her mistake. She missed out on a hell of a guy."

Kelly might have her shortcomings, but lack of loyalty had never been one of them. "It probably wouldn't have worked out."

"No." She agreed with him wholeheartedly. "It wouldn't have. She turned out to be a flake." Shifting to the edge of her chair, Kelly pinned him with a look. "Nice try, Murph, but you're not getting me to forget the subject. Jennings said that while you were very good in court today, you looked a little under the weather. Taking a look at you, I'd say that Jennings was given to making understatements."

"Flatterer."

He wasn't going to bait her twice. "I'm not interested in flattery. I'm interested in you." She rose again, unable to sit still for long. "Something's wrong, Murphy. I can feel it."

Concern etched lines above eyes that were the mirror image of his. "Don't lie to me and say it isn't."

Turning from her, Murphy squinted as he focused on the blinking cursor on his screen. Just took a little concentration, that was all. The world would remain in focus soon. He'd just gotten scared in the courtroom. And who could blame him? Everyone around him was hell-bent on being pessimistic.

"The good doctor didn't find anything." He thought it unnecessary to add that she had wanted him to go in for further tests.

That wasn't good enough for Kelly. "Then the good doctor needs to be replaced by a better doctor."

Murphy sighed. He couldn't let Kelly place the blame on Shawna when it was his fault. "No, she's just fine."

Her face was a mask of skepticism. "Fine, like you?"

Murphy laughed softly as he leaned back in his chair. For a moment he rocked as he thought of the way Shawna had looked in her office when he had walked in and surprised her.

"Funny you should put it that way. I think there's something bothering her." He didn't realize that, for a moment, he had let his guard slip, alluding to the fact that they had this in common, that there was something inherent bothering him. He had never admitted to anyone that he had been the least bit affected by what Janice had done, except to be supremely relieved.

Kelly frowned doubtfully. "Probably malpractice suits."

Murphy shook his head. "No, there's a sadness in her eyes that—"

He was doing it again, trying to divert her. "I'm interested in *your* eyes, Murphy, not hers." She moved until she was directly in front of him. "Are you having trouble seeing?"

Kelly didn't pull any punches. And while he might evade, he never lied. "Yeah." Murphy dragged his hand through his dark hair and struggled to compose his features. He didn't want anyone else concerned about this. It was his problem. His. And maybe not even a problem at that.

Maybe they were just making mountains out of molehills.
"But, hey, that'll pass, Kell."

"And if it doesn't?"

He spread his hands wide, surrendering. "Then I'll call
her. Fair enough?"

She closed her eyes, summoning patience. She didn't believe him for a minute. Men could be such idiots sometimes. "Murphy, let me take you to the hospital."

He looked up and studied her for a moment. She was
completely, exquisitely clear. It was going to be all right. All
it needed was a little time. "If it was you, would you go?"

She fisted her hands at her waist. "We're not talking
about me."

That was her way of saying no and they both knew it. She
hated hospitals as much as he did. Murphy leaned back,
resting his case. "See?"

Kelly sighed, consciously working at cooling her temper.
"Yes, I would go, because I don't believe in sticking my
head in the sand." She saw the surprise on his face and
continued, picking up steam. Giving him reasons. Giving
him the truth. "Because it's not just me anymore, it's Harmony and Thomas."

There was more than a trace of envy in his eyes as he
looked at her. "You're lucky."

Damn, she shouldn't have led off with them. "And the
rest of you." She nodded toward the framed photograph on
his desk. It was a group shot, taken last Christmas Eve.
"You and Mom and Kim and company." She was pleading
with him now. "You've still got that. You've always had
that." She took a breath. What she said next was something she believed down to the bottom of her soul. "And
someday, you'll have the rest." She arched her brow. "*If*
you listen to your sister and get yourself checked out," Kelly
added with emphasis.

"Sure." He nodded as if she had just told him to renew
his subscription to a popular journal. "Now beat it, brat."
He tapped the computer monitor. "I need to finish this."
Whatever the hell "this" was, he added silently. All he
wanted was a little time to himself.

And silence.

Kelly crossed to the doorway, then turned and looked at him. "You make me crazy."

He gave her a reassuring smile. The reverse was true as well, but there was no doubting the love that went between them. "I'm your brother, it's in my job description. Look it up."

His smile lasted until she left the room.

Once she closed the door, Murphy sank back in his chair, his limbs feeling oddly liquefied.

It cost him to admit that he needed help of any sort. That wasn't what he was about. He was the big brother, the best friend, the man of the family ever since his father had died. He was the caretaker, the care giver, not the one who needed to be taken care of.

If you admitted to that, he thought, it left you vulnerable, and he knew where that led.

A cryptic smile played on his lips. Yes, he knew where being vulnerable led. He'd been there once and the pain and humiliation had taught him that wasn't a place he wanted to return to, not even for a brief visit. If that meant sacrificing a dream he'd briefly entertained, well, those were the breaks. Dreams were not one-size-fits-all, anyway. Some dreams just weren't meant to be.

The one he had laid out for himself with Janice certainly hadn't been. What hurt most was that, all that time, she'd been seeing someone else and he hadn't even had a clue.

His telephone buzzed. Murphy turned his attention to things that he could control.

She couldn't get him out of her mind.

Try as she might, Murphy Pendleton and his empty folder kept cropping up in her mind at the least opportune moments, filling in the tiny spaces that the day had allotted to her mind.

He confounded her. Professionally speaking. It irked her beyond words that he was so cavalier about his eyesight. Where was the harm in having a simple M.R.I. done? It wasn't as if they were going to draw and quarter him. All he had to do was remain perfectly still in a cylinder for half an hour. A child could do it.

A mature child, which Murphy Pendleton obviously was not.

She couldn't let go of it.

The blurriness he'd grudgingly admitted to could very well be nothing. But then again, it might be an indication that the blow to the head had caused some damage to the optic nerve. Symptoms weren't something to be lightly shrugged off, like snowflakes during a light flurry. Granted that from her exams, both in the E.R. and in her office, it didn't appear that there *was* any damage, but it was better to be safe than sorry.

Shawna upbraided herself as she pulled in to her carport. There was no good reason to be obsessing this way, just because she'd once known him. It wasn't as if she didn't have other cases to take up her time. If anything, she had too many cases.

She turned off the engine and sat there for a minute, thinking. Perhaps it was just nothing.

And perhaps it wasn't.

Instincts, something that couldn't be picked up from a textbook, told her that there was something wrong.

His problem, not hers, she told herself. She could do only so much.

Shawna got out of her car and locked the door behind her. There was a bubble bath with her name on it lurking in the not-too-distant future, and a book she'd been reading—a page at a time, for over two months—that begged to be finished.

It was time to indulge the inner woman, time to relax just a little. She'd more than earned it. It wasn't her night for the clinic and there was nothing pressing that required her attention.

It was time to let herself be human.

Before her mother descended on her, she reminded herself, which was going to happen all too soon. She had better take advantage of her privacy while she still had it. She'd grown very used to it, attached to it and held prisoner by it at the same time.

Nothing but silence greeted her as Shawna unlocked the door of her small apartment. She'd lived here a little less than a year and a half. Shawna dropped her purse on the floor near the front door and stepped out of her shoes as she walked into the tiny living room. Tiny. It suited her. The house in Maine had seemed too large, too full of memories for her after the accident.

Everywhere she'd turned, everywhere she'd looked, memories had popped out at her, good memories that made her feel bad. Memories she couldn't cope with.

So she had sold it, sold the house she and Doug had fallen in love with. Remembering that she had once been happy in Bedford, she'd applied for a position on the staff of Harris Memorial. She desperately needed a change of scene. Within a week she had packed up, pulling up the only real roots she had ever known, determined to transplant herself away from the pain.

It had followed along in the U-Haul.

The apartment could easily have fit into her old house three times over. It was cramped with her belongings. She hoped that perhaps somewhere in this crowded jumble she could lose herself.

And not think.

The telephone rang, shattering the silence before she had a chance to cross to the bedroom.

Please let it be a wrong number. Just this once.

She stared at it and debated not answering it. Ethics had her picking up the receiver on the third ring. The book and the bubble bath began to drift off into the realm of fantasy.

"This is Dr. Saunders."

It was her answering service. "I have a call from a Mr. Murphy Pendleton. He told me to tell you that it was urgent."

I bet. Didn't the man ever take no for an answer?

Habit had her reaching for the pad and pencil she always kept next to the telephone.

"Give me his number." Shawna scribbled it down as the woman rattled off the numbers. Shawna put the pencil down and cradled the receiver against her ear and shoulder for a moment. "Did he happen to say just what the trouble was, Myra?"

"Not exactly." There was a pause as the woman glanced at the notes she had taken. "Only that he's ready for that M.R.I. now."

"All right, thank you."

Shawna hung up the telephone, then stood staring at it. Was that a cryptic message he was passing on to her, referring to their last conversation, or was he finally admitting that there was really a problem?

Only one way to find out.

Looking at the telephone number she'd written down, Shawna tapped it out on the keypad. Mentally she went over her Hippocratic oath. Mailmen, she mused, had it easy. They only had to contend with sleet, rain and snow, and not even that here. They didn't have to convince ex-jock types that their masculinity remained intact even if they admitted to having a medical problem.

Murphy answered on the second ring. "Hello?"

His voice was deeper, more resonant transmitted over the telephone. He sounded sensual. Like a predatory cat. A cat who had been sitting on the telephone, judging by the way he'd picked up so quickly.

Shawna's survival instincts took over. "This had better not be a false alarm."

He recognized her voice immediately and laughed at the accusation, tickled. "Shawna. You called."

Was that a note of relief she heard beneath the glibness? Shawna straightened and took the receiver back into her hand, as if that could help her direct the course of the conversation.

"My answering service said you told her it was urgent." When he didn't answer her immediately, she thought it rather unusual. Had he lied and was now having the decency of experiencing second thoughts. "Urgent as in a bottle of champagne chilling on ice, or urgent as in something I would be interested in?"

She bit the tip of her tongue, realizing that she had unintentionally fed him a straight line. But she wasn't used to trading banter. She was used to serious, professional people, and patients who sought her out because they wanted to be helped.

This wasn't easy for him. God knows he'd tried to hold out before calling her, but he wasn't an idiot, either. His vision hadn't improved as he'd hoped it might. It had done the reverse. "The other eye's being affected."

He sounded serious. And possibly just a little unnerved. In any case, she couldn't take a chance that he wasn't on the level. She shook her head, hoping that if he was telling her the truth, he hadn't allowed something irreparable to happen by being stubborn.

She looked around for her shoes and saw them in the corner. So much for a quiet evening at home.

"Damn, but you macho types make me angry." Holding the long telephone cord, she walked over to her shoes and slipped them on. "Can you get someone to drive you to the hospital tonight?"

He glanced out his window. It was still light outside, even though it was after six. "Yeah, sure."

He was lying again; she could tell by the cadence in his voice. It was too quick, too flippant. She recalled the address she had seen written down on his patient history. He didn't live that far away from her. She toyed with an idea as she blew out a breath. "How badly affected is the other eye?"

He'd always been good at describing things. This was not so easy. "It comes and goes."

Was he deliberately trying to be evasive and exasperating, or did it come naturally to him? "*What* comes and goes?"

"The cloudiness." His voice picked up speed as denial reemerged. "And it doesn't last very long. I'm probably just making something out of nothing." It was Kelly's fault. If she hadn't badgered him, he probably would have just shrugged this off and turned in early tonight. Maybe he could still do that. He was beginning to feel like a fool again. A pathetic, whiny fool. "Listen, I'm sorry I bothered you—"

He knew just how to reel someone in, didn't he, she thought. He'd spun this out just enough, then retreated, knowing she was bound to follow up. Whether he knew it or not, and she suspected he did, he was good.

"Oh, no, you don't, Counselor. You've come this far, I'm not having you back out now." She picked up her purse and slung it over her shoulder. "I'm only about five miles away from your house. I can come by and take you to the hospital myself."

"A house call?" She could hear the smile in his voice. "Isn't that a little unorthodox?"

Look who was talking about unorthodox. "I don't always play by the rules, especially when something precious is involved." She was already searching for her car keys, impatient to be off.

He laughed. "Why, Shawna, I didn't realize you cared."

Warning signals went off in her head. "I care about all my patients, and for your information, I was referring to your eyesight." She checked her watch. She'd been home five minutes. Not bad for downtime. "I can be there in fifteen minutes. Oh, and Murphy?"

He'd almost hung up. "Yes?"

She thought it only fair to warn him. "If this *does* turn out to be a ploy of some sort, I hope your insurance is paid up."

"Health?"

"Life."

With that she hung up.

Chapter Five

Shawna pulled up the hand brake on her car and got out. As she walked up the driveway to Murphy's front door, she did a quick sweep of the surroundings. It was a nice house, a house where laughter was welcomed. Where it was invited, she thought with a sudden, unexpected smile.

The smile left just as quickly. She was here in a professional capacity, nothing more. If this turned out to be a giant hoax at her expense . . .

Well, she would feel sorry for Murphy if that was the case. His ears would be ringing for a week after she finished boxing them. She pressed the doorbell. The door opened almost instantly.

He looked a little uneasy, she thought. She doubted if her presence had anything to do with it. Either the man was a consummate actor, or he was really worried about his condition. And trying hard not to show it.

It was, as far as she was concerned, the first sign of intelligent life residing between his ears.

She looked formal, he thought, wondering if she ever kicked back. She was dressed in a two-piece strawberry suit with the hint of a beige blouse peeking through. The best way to describe the aura she exuded was distant. Her bed-side manner needed work, he thought. It was something they could work on together.

Murphy gestured behind him, taking a step back. "Do you want to come in?"

That was the last thing she wanted to do. Just in case this *was* a ploy and the man *was* a good actor, she was not about to step into the spider's parlor like a dim-witted fly.

"No." Impatience etched across her face. "C'mon, let's go." The sudden sensuous grin that curved his mouth froze Shawna in her tracks.

"You wouldn't believe how many beautiful woman have said that to me."

"Yes, I would." One look at him would tell her why. Butterfly bandage notwithstanding, he was drop-dead gorgeous. That much hadn't changed.

But her daydreams definitely had.

Murphy couldn't tell from her expression whether or not she was joking. He hoped she hadn't taken that the wrong way. He was just trying to make them both feel a little more comfortable with this situation. God knows he wasn't. He felt awkward and dumb, and she didn't look all that comfortable, either.

"Are you flattering me, Shawna, or putting me in my place?"

Her smile was enigmatic. "You figure it out."

He sincerely doubted if he could. She was a puzzle, and he had always liked puzzles.

The door was still open at his back. "Sure you wouldn't like to come inside?"

That was just the problem, something whispered within her, she wasn't one hundred percent sure. The slight touch of ambiguity had her stiffening defensively.

"This isn't a social call, remember? You used the word 'urgent.' If it's not, I'll go." Murphy was wearing the most polite, conscientious look she'd ever seen, but she would bet her soul there was a smirk lurking beneath it. She hated being played for a fool. Her face was deadly calm as she took a step toward her car. "I'm a very busy woman."

She was going to leave. Without thinking, Murphy clamped his hand around her wrist.

"You must be." His voice was casual, as if he was carrying on a conversation in his living room with an old friend rather than with a doctor who had come rushing to his aid. "You don't look as if you even changed."

She looked down expectantly at his hand. He dropped it to his side. "I didn't. I took the call from my answering service as I walked in."

He felt guilty. He hadn't meant her to drop everything and come running over. Murphy locked the door behind him. "I could have waited."

He was hedging again. *Not this time, Counselor.* "And waited and waited." The fact that she was onto him pleased her. She wasn't aware of the fact that she was smiling as she turned and led the way to her car, but Murphy was. "No, I think that whatever made you sensible for a minute is already beginning to fade. I'm not about to let this opportunity pass."

He found himself admiring her legs as he followed her. "Dedicated."

She couldn't tell whether he was playing up to her or mocking her. "That's the word for it." Murphy stood staring at her car even after she unlocked the passenger side for him. "Now what's wrong?"

He looked at her uncertainly before his gaze returned to the small vehicle. They didn't make this model anymore. There were a couple of small rust spots threatening to break through the faded white paint. The car appeared to have all the comfort of an early torture chamber.

"*This* is your car?"

A deaf man could have heard the surprise in his voice, and Shawna wasn't deaf. "Yes."

It seemed inconceivable to him that anyone in her position would be driving something so worn looking. It was a car begging to be towed. "Haven't your patients been paying you?"

"Not that it's any business of yours, but yes. Most of them," she amended. The ones at the clinic paid her in gratitude. The way she saw it, she got more than she gave. "Why?"

He circled the car slowly. There was a dent on the side, another on the hood. It would be an easy matter to take them out. All he'd need was a free Saturday.

"It's pretty old." He said it in the same tone people once had uttered the word *leper*.

She arched a brow in his direction. "Very astute, Counselor."

Murphy shoved his hands into his pockets, still scrutinizing the car. Old cars were of special interest to him. Well-preserved, kept-up old cars. "Shouldn't someone in your position be driving something, I don't know—"

"A little flashier?" she suggested as she got in on the driver's side.

Murphy got in quickly as she started up the car. He shrugged and felt his shoulder brush against the side of the car. "For lack of a better word, yes."

Shawna backed out of the driveway and headed toward the freeway entrance two miles away.

"Why?" She ran her hand along the steering wheel. There was a shimmer of affection evident that was not wasted on Murphy. She'd had the car for eleven years and seen the mileage indicator go around the odometer twice now. "It gets me to where I want to go." There was also a more practical reason she drove the car, if that was what he was after. "I work at a free clinic in a rough neighborhood in downtown Los Angeles two to three evenings a week. I wouldn't want to drive temptation into their midst."

Shawna changed lanes, getting out from behind a slow-moving car. She wanted to get this over with as fast as possible. She'd called ahead and had someone waiting for them at the radiology department. She was sure the technician wanted to go home as soon as he could.

"Is that safe?"

"What?"

"Driving in downtown L.A. at night."

It was a rhetorical question and she resented his patronizing her. "Driving is. It's the stopping that might not be. To get back to my car," she said forcefully, "I'm sentimental about it." A nostalgic smile slipped over her lips. "It was the first large purchase I ever made. It wasn't new at the time, either."

She remembered the way her hand had shaken when she had signed the papers. And the swell of pride that had overtaken her as she'd driven the car from the lot. Hers, completely hers. It had felt good.

Murphy ran his hand along the black dashboard. "They're not that reliable."

So she had been told. But she had lucked out. "This one is." He seemed inordinately interested. "Are cars a hobby with you?"

Murphy settled back as she eased the car onto the freeway. He preferred being in the driver's seat, but there was nothing he could do about that. Besides, if he was, she wouldn't have been here tonight. "A passion, actually. My sister calls it an obsession. I've been working on restoring an old '57 Caddie for the last three years."

So he didn't spend all his time just going from woman to woman in his off-hours. "Why so long?"

He enjoyed working on his car. It relaxed him. He thought it prudent not to say that he worked on the vehicle the same way he made love to a woman—slowly, languidly, with feeling. Savoring every nuance. That was where the correlation stopped. His relationship with his car had outlasted any that he had had with a woman.

When he had bought the car it had been little more than a heap. He'd spent the past three years working on its exterior. Now he was attempting to get the engine to come to life. It was a labor of love.

He shrugged. "Busy." He turned his head slowly in her direction, afraid of making a sudden move that would bring on another dizzy spell. "And parts are all hard to come by." She should be home after a long day at work, he thought, not chauffeuring him around. "You know, you really don't have to be going out of your way like this."

He sounded as if he meant it. Her attitude toward him softened. She laughed quietly, unaware that the sound wafted over him as seductively as a spring breeze. "I have a feeling that you won't go for the M.R.I. if I don't take you there myself.''

He grew silent for a moment. It had gone beyond where he could just shrug off the matter. ''I don't know about that.''

''Oh?'' Shawna glanced at Murphy as a motorcycle whizzed by them on the left. ''Tell me what made you change your mind.''

She was his physician, and who better to talk to about this? Still, he couldn't get comfortable with the topic, or with the admission that something might really, really be wrong. ''Better safe than sorry, right?''

That would be the sensible, cautious approach. It wouldn't be his approach. ''You don't seem like the type to think that way.''

Her observation amused him. ''What type do I seem like?''

She turned her face forward. Rush-hour traffic was choking off the road. ''Irresponsible.''

Murphy winced. ''Ouch.''

She supposed that did sound a little harsh. And there were other factors to take into consideration, besides his persistence in hitting on her. She sighed, revising her diagnosis.

''But then, you did save that little girl. Irresponsible men don't risk their lives for strangers.'' She looked at him as she thought of something. ''Or was she someone you knew?''

He began to shake his head, then stopped abruptly as pain whispered along his brow from a distance, threatening to consume him. He hoped Shawna didn't detect anything in his voice.

''Only by sight,'' he told her. ''And irresponsible men take all sorts of risks without thinking about it,'' he observed. ''That's the basis of irresponsibility, Doctor. Foolish risks.''

She knew without knowing why that he hadn't taken a foolish risk. It had been a calculated one. A selfless one. He deserved his due, no matter what else she thought about him.

''I stand corrected,'' she amended softly. ''I don't think you're irresponsible, Murphy.'' She cast a side glance at him. "Flippant and irreverent, maybe, but not irresponsible."

Murphy concentrated on the dialogue and told himself that his head didn't hurt. "Ah, an upgrade." As he drew a breath, he could catch a faint whiff of her perfume. Gentle, sultry. It probably cost more per ounce than the car did. "Does this mean you'll go out with me?"

Shawna felt herself smiling and bit her lower lip to hide it. "You can consider this our date."

He took the ball that had been passed to him and ran for the goalpost. "Our first date?"

She gave him a reproving look. "Our *only* date. Now stop flirting with me long enough to answer my questions seriously." The end of the freeway was up ahead and she eased off the gas pedal a little. Cars were queuing up for the exit. "What changed your mind about the test?" She heard his intake of breath and raised her hand in a solemn oath before he could say a word. "And I swear if you give me one more vague, cute answer, I'll stop the car right here and have you walk home."

She would, too, he thought. The idea that she was a tough little cookie tickled him. The woman next to him was light-years away from the quiet, mousy young girl he was beginning to recall.

"Heartless."

Shawna lifted her chin. The exact opposite was true. She had too much heart. And all of it ached, but she wasn't about to share that with him. Or with anyone. "That's me."

Murphy had to make a conscious effort to steel himself as he spoke. "All right. While I was in court this morning, everything looked as if it had been dropped into a bowl of soup, all hazy and distant." It gave him a chill just to remember. "Through both eyes."

Damn, she thought. There were times she hated being right. She glanced at him as they came to a stop before a red light. "But it cleared up?"

"Yes, almost immediately." And he had been overwhelmingly grateful when it had.

Shawna nodded thoughtfully as she took her foot off the brake. "Is that all?"

He would have been happy to say yes, but there was no sense in lying. "No. It happened again just before I left court. Except that this time the haziness was just in my right eye."

He had been complaining of trouble with his left eye previously. "The other eye was unaffected?"

Murphy stared straight ahead at the road. When he spoke, his voice was low, emotionless. "I couldn't see anything out of it."

She looked at him incredulously. "And you waited to call?"

He didn't care for the accusing tone she used. The experience had momentarily unnerved him. "I waited to get myself under control again." To downplay the situation, he flashed a smile. "I don't like having something wrong with me."

There was that ex-jock mentality again. "You'd be a masochist if you did."

"If I'm going to be flat on my back, being pampered, I want to be able to enjoy it. I don't want to need it." He shifted, restless. He'd never thought about having anything seriously wrong with him before. He didn't want to think about it now. The world around him was slowly getting dark. Was darkness in his future? "I've never really been sick before."

"You had a perfect attendance record," Shawna recalled absently before she could catch herself. She saw his quizzical look and shrugged, a hint of embarrassment coloring her cheeks. "So did I. I noticed you were never out."

If she knew that, then she had to have been around a lot more than he actually remembered. "Were you always in my classes?"

Traffic had thinned out and the hospital loomed just ahead. For a moment she let her thoughts drift back. "I was always in at least one of them every semester for four years."

He laughed self-consciously. "You know, I really don't remember you all that well."

At least he was honest. "I'm not surprised." She'd been shy. And still was. "I tended to blend in with the scenery a lot."

As they drew closer to the hospital, his restlessness increased. "No chance of that happening now."

Shawna made a left turn and slowed down to five miles an hour as she entered the hospital grounds. "Don't get predatory on me now, Murphy. I was just beginning to relax around you."

"Do I make you nervous?"

"No." The denial was automatic. Her guard snapped into position like a switchblade that had been suddenly pressed into service.

Her response was too adamant. "Then why do you need to be on constant alert?"

"Because I don't like leaving myself open for things," she replied matter-of-factly. And that included charming men with nothing on their minds but an evening of hot sex and passion. With his jet black hair, brilliant eyes and chiseled good looks, Murphy Pendleton no doubt ran with that pack—if he didn't lead it.

She pulled her car into the physicians' parking section directly in front of a modern-looking building.

"That makes two of us." His voice had dropped. Murphy wasn't looking at her; he was looking at the hospital.

He was afraid, she suddenly realized. Without thinking it through, Shawna reached over and placed her hand over his in mute comfort. Turquoise eyes turned toward her in surprise.

"It's a harmless test." Compassion swelled in her voice. "All you have to do is lie still for half an hour. Forty-five minutes, tops. It doesn't hurt at all."

It wasn't pain he was worried about. It was what the test might find. As long as he didn't know, he could pretend everything was fine. "Piece of cake."

She gave his hand a squeeze. Then, as if the contact had suddenly penetrated, Shawna withdrew her hand. "Exactly."

Murphy got out of the car, but remained next to it, looking at the hospital as if it were an opponent to be faced in a duel. "So why do I feel like a defenseless little kid?"

"Easy." She flipped on the security alarm on the car, something she had added since she had begun traveling to the clinic. "Peter Pan *was* a little kid."

"Peter Pan." So far, the image he seemed to be projecting to her wasn't all that flattering. "Is that what I seem like to you?"

Actually, yes. But then, she had always loved Peter Pan. Her mother had taken her to see the feature-length cartoon. It had been one of those rare instances when her mother had actually acted the part. It was nestled in among Shawna's fondest memories.

If she told him that, she knew she would regret it.

"Let's forget about my impressions of you, Murphy. They have absolutely nothing to do with your condition." The first thing a physician learned to do was separate personal feelings from professional ones. Why was she having trouble remembering that?

She led the way to the entrance a short distance away.

Murphy fell into step beside her. "Exactly what do you think my condition is?" It was the first time he had asked. The first time he had dared to.

Now that he was finally asking, she was almost reluctant to discuss it until she saw the results of the test. "That's hard to say."

He'd been here many times before for various reasons, but only once as a patient. The trip to the E.R. had permanently colored his reaction to the hospital. The halls felt forbidding. "I won't sue for malpractice for an educated guess."

They turned left in the hall, following the arrows that ultimately led to the radiology department. "All right. Your symptoms match a variety of conditions."

So she was telling him that she didn't know. "That's reassuring." Visiting hours, in effect all day, were winding down. The halls were relatively empty. He wanted to turn around and leave.

She ignored the sarcasm she heard. "But my cursory exam doesn't indicate a tear of any sort or any outstanding damage to the optic nerve." She wished she could give him good news, but she couldn't lie. He knew there had to be something wrong as well as she did. "It might be some sort of hematoma. A small clot behind your eye, pressing against it."

That would explain the pressure he felt off and on. Murphy stopped before the darkened gift shop. "If it is, what are my options?"

"Surgery."

The single word felt like a concrete blanket draped over him. "You?"

"Me." She didn't want him to think she was pushing him into anything. All her patients were always encouraged to get as many opinions as they needed to make them feel confident. "Unless you want someone else."

Murphy shoved his hands into his jeans, studying her. She looked as if she would be more at home doing needlepoint than holding a scalpel in her hand.

"I don't know. How good are you?"

She was relieved to see his humor returning. Relieved and oddly comforted, as well. More than that, she could feel something kindred stirring within her. "I'm very good. I graduated near the top of my class."

The one thing he did recall clearly about her was that she had been one of the studious ones. "Can I request a print-out of your transcripts?"

She laughed. "If it comes to that." And maybe, just maybe, if he was lucky, it wouldn't. That was for the M.R.I. to determine. "Not very trusting, are you?"

"I'm a lawyer. I'm not supposed to be trusting."

"C'mon." Though she was not a physical person, somehow it seemed natural to thread her arm through his. "I have a spot reserved for you."

Murphy smiled as they began to walk. He glanced down at the link between them. It was a start. "Too bad it's in an imaging lab."

Shawna merely shook her head as she led him down another corridor.

He didn't like it.

It was like being swallowed up by a large silver cylinder. The technician, a large-boned Hawaiian with an incredibly gentle manner, was very genial. But it didn't negate the fact that Murphy didn't want to be here. The sound of the machine, muted but steady, was getting on his nerves.

As promised, he felt nothing as photo after photo was taken of his cranium. Nothing except restless and apprehensive, as if he were in a lighthouse tower, waiting for a storm to hit.

When it was over he couldn't get up fast enough. The best part was that Shawna was sitting on the sofa in the outer room waiting for him when he emerged.

Shawna rose as soon as he walked through the parted electronic doors. The vicarious tension she felt refused to slip completely away. "See, painless."

It might have been painless, but he still didn't like being subjected to it. He left the room quickly. "Now I know what a hot dog feels like, lying in a bun and wrapped in aluminum foil."

She had to stride quickly to stay abreast of him. "Very colorful."

It took less time to retrace his steps to the hospital entrance than it had to reach the imaging department to begin with. He took a deep breath of the evening air. It felt good.

So did having her stand next to him. "I'm just glad I'm not claustrophobic."

He probably didn't realize what a problem that presented with some patients. "We can be grateful for small favors."

Now that it was over, he was reluctant to return home. Instead, he stood there, letting his senses enjoy the small things, like the sound of crickets calling to each other.

Like watching the lights from the hospital play off her hair. There were too many things left to see. Too many things he'd always want to see. "Okay, how soon will we know anything?"

Most patients said "I," not "we." She didn't know if she liked being lumped together with him this way. Distance was always best, but in his case it somehow kept slipping from her. "I've put a rush on it. I should have the results before noon tomorrow."

He wanted them sooner. And never.

"I can swing by your office around lunchtime." Murphy looked at her and decided to make the best of the situation. "Maybe I can take you out for a bite to eat." He saw the protest forming before it ever emerged. "You do eat, don't you?"

She was quick to dismiss the invitation. "On occasion, but since I really don't want you driving, I'd much rather someone brought you by." Turning, she began to walk toward her car.

Murphy caught up to her in two strides. "Three on a date is awkward."

She stopped and he bumped into her. On purpose, she thought. "Murphy, this is getting tiresome."

He was more than ready to agree. "I know." He could see suspicion rising in her eyes. "Say yes and I'll stop."

She had no idea what possessed her to play along. "All right, yes." She deactivated the security alarm and unlocked the car.

"Great. When?"

She swung around to look at him. "I thought you were going to stop if I said yes."

The expression on his face was boyish and yet unnervingly sensual at the same time. She felt its effects before she could set up proper barriers against it. For a moment she felt just the way she had in high school.

But she wasn't in high school, she reminded herself. And hadn't been for a long time.

"I lied." He wanted to put his arm around her shoulder, to pull her close to him. There was something about her that made him feel safe. Comforted. But he knew he would scare her off if he made any moves. "Besides, now we have to decide on the particulars." He smiled at her. "I am a nice guy, you know."

Something stirred. Something that had to be kept dormant. "Yes, I suppose you are, but I'm not in the market for a nice guy."

That was her divorce talking, he guessed. He wasn't in the market for anything permanent, either. But a pleasant evening or two in the right company held a definite attraction. "In that case, I could give being a rogue a shot. Just don't ask me to burn, pillage or plunder. I haven't done that since college."

She really didn't want to laugh, but she couldn't help it. He made it too difficult to resist. "Let's just get through this, all right?"

By "this," he knew she meant the test. He folded his arms and leaned gingerly against the car. "I'd really rather have something else to think about besides my medical condition, whatever that might turn out to be."

She could sympathize with that, with needing something to take your mind off what was bothering you. "Don't you have cases to work on?"

Work couldn't be all she thought about, Murphy reasoned. She was far too young to bury herself like that. "All work and no play..."

Suddenly Shawna was too aware of standing beside him. Of his breath against her face when he spoke.

Shawna turned away. "I've forgotten how to play."

He wasn't going to let her off the hook that easily. "All the more reason to go out with me. I'm offering a refresher course."

Shawna could almost feel herself being reeled in. Like a prize fish. "You are incorrigible."

He wondered if it was unethical to kiss his eye doctor in the hospital parking lot. He knew he wanted to. "I'm also inevitable, like the tide."

She placed a hand against his chest, just in case he was getting any ideas. "Well, ebb out for a while and I'll get back to you. Now get into the car and let me take you home."

Since she was getting into the car, he had no choice but to do likewise. "If I do, will you promise to have your way with me?"

Shawna didn't know if it was the man, the moonlight or the mood. Whatever it was, she couldn't help herself. She began to laugh, completely and without restraint. When she finally stopped, she had to admit it had felt good, despite the silliness that had prompted it.

"My way with you," she managed to say, drawing in air as she started up the car, "would be very boring."

He had a feeling she wasn't giving herself enough credit. In any event, he wanted to discover that for himself.

"I'll be the judge of that." He paused, wondering what would set her at ease. The more he was around her, the more he wanted to get to know her. Kelly, he mused, would definitely approve. She always had something disparaging to say about the women he brought to family gatherings, usually murmuring something to the effect that they had IQs that would make a pair of shoes seem intelligent.

That certainly wasn't the way with Shawna.

"Do you remember Thomas Sheridan?" he asked suddenly as they left the parking lot. "You know, the man who came to pick me up at the hospital."

"Yes." That had come out of the blue, she thought, wondering where he was going with this.

Murphy was easing into this slowly. "He married my sister, Kelly. They have a little girl now."

And I had a little boy, once, Shawna thought as a sudden pang rose up and seized her.

He sensed the change in her and hurried on. "Anyway, they're having a birthday party for her, and I was wondering if you'd like to come."

She didn't mingle well. "I don't—"

"You'll be safe," he promised, guessing at the source of her reluctance. "I'll be doomed to remain on my best behavior." He could just make out her skeptical look. "My mother will be there."

Mother. "I can't. My mother's coming to town." Although when was anyone's guess, he didn't have to know that.

Murphy remained undaunted. "Great, bring her along."

That was like asking her to bring her own personal natural disaster. Her mother flirted with every male she encountered under the age of ninety, though she preferred them young. "My mother's not the type you bring along to family parties." It would be like bringing Auntie Mame into a monastery.

"Why?" It was an innocently posed question. "Does she chew with her mouth open?"

Laughter had vanished from her life more than a year ago. It felt odd having it make a reappearance so abruptly. Yet he had made her laugh three times in the space of an evening, each time more than the last. "No, she doesn't chew with her mouth open. Murphy, I can't laugh and drive at the same time."

He placed his hand on the wheel to steady it. "Then stop driving. I think you need to laugh."

She didn't like being analyzed, especially not when it hit the mark so well. It made her feel vulnerable. "I think I need to get you home."

His smile blossomed. "My sentiments exactly."

She could see exactly what he was thinking. "Your home. Alone. In the shower, with the water on cold." She put in as many qualifiers as she thought were necessary. "Maybe frigid."

Her reluctance goaded him on, but there was no sense in pushing the matter right now. He surrendered. Temporarily. "You're behind the wheel."

"Yes, I am."

And she most definitely intended to remain that way. Behind the wheel and plotting her own course. While it was tempting, driving down the path that Murphy was suggesting so persistently could only lead to problems.

She didn't need any more of those. She had accumulated more than her share as it was.

Chapter Six

The traffic along Newport Boulevard and the Newport Freeway had lightened considerably. It took Shawna almost no time to drive back to Murphy's development.

A pang of regret wafted across her. She dismissed it the next moment.

She turned to Murphy as she guided her car down the main thoroughfare. He hadn't said very much on the way back. Suddenly she became concerned. "Are you feeling light-headed?"

Murphy had been pensively examining his options, dealing with the hoary what-if scenario. What if the M.R.I. showed that he had a blood clot and he had to have an operation? Or possibly something worse? He willingly abandoned that terrain. "Yes, but only because you're near me."

And here she was being worried. "I know that was meant to be charming, and perhaps in a different context, it might be." She saw the ready grin curve his mouth. He was clearly aware of his effect on women. "But I'm asking as your doctor."

She was making that infinitely clear. "As your patient, the answer, actually, is no." Though he was being guardedly optimistic, he went a little farther for her benefit. "Whatever I was experiencing earlier, it seems to have subsided." Murphy shrugged. "Maybe I overreacted before."

Maybe, but she doubted it. "Hang on to your optimism until we get the results in. Maybe it'll prove you right."

She just missed the light. A single red eye glared down at her as she came to a halt before the crosswalk. The man on the radio was playing up the joys of new car ownership. She switched to another station.

He was looking at her, she could feel it. Shawna refused to turn her head.

She had a regal profile, Murphy thought, fine boned and delicate. He felt an urge to lightly run his fingertips along her face, much the way a sculptor did when he was caressing his finished product.

"Now can I answer as something other than your patient?"

Her hands tightened a little on the steering wheel as she turned into the development. She had a feeling she knew exactly what was coming. "No."

Shifting in his seat so that he could look at her more easily, he studied her expression. It gave nothing away. "Why?"

She made it a point not to begin something she had no intention of finishing. "I'm really not interested."

He wondered if she meant that, or just thought she did. "In me or in friendship in general?"

She glanced in his direction, skeptical, "Is that what you're offering? Friendship?"

He had to admit that he had something different in mind, but there was something about her that was drawing him out on a number of levels. He liked her company.

"Under the circumstances, yes. Thomas tells me that, on occasion, I make a very good friend." He leaned a little closer toward her. The seat belt dug into his shoulder. "Or is the position already filled?"

No, it wasn't filled. She had no friends, no time for friends. Friendships took energy to cultivate, and all of hers went toward her patients. And to surviving. "I'm too busy."

That was a load of freshly cultivated fertilizer, he thought. Everyone needed a friend, someone to talk to. "Too busy for friends?"

The pace she forced herself to keep up was almost breakneck. "Too busy for breathing, actually."

He was beginning to believe her. Which was a shame. "Very necessary thing, breathing. You should keep it up." His expression grew serious. "So's friendship. Necessary, I mean." Murphy paused, weighing his next words and the wisdom behind uttering them. But he sensed distress beneath the surface layer and he was a sucker for a damsel in distress. "Is it because of your divorce?"

She was just picking up the hand brake. She jerked it as she turned to stare at him. "What divorce?"

Was she trying to keep it a secret, or had he just made a twenty-four-karat, gold-plated mistake?

"I just assumed…I saw the photograph on your desk and the fact that you weren't wearing a ring…" He licked his lips and came to a skidding halt. "I'm putting my foot in my mouth, aren't I?"

He looked so sincerely contrite she couldn't readily fault him.

"I'd say you were going in for a second helping." She might as well tell him. Shawna had a feeling that Murphy would find out soon enough. "I'm a widow." Why did that hurt so much every time she said it? She would have thought she'd have gotten used to it by now. "My wedding ring is buried with my husband."

Well, he'd certainly made a mess of that. "I'm sorry. Really sorry." His expression was compassionate. "If you need a shoulder to cry on…"

He meant it. He wasn't just paying lip service to a line. But it didn't change anything. This was something she kept under lock and key. Something she didn't talk about. To anyone. "I don't cry anymore."

Ordinarily, that would have meant that she had gotten over the initial impact. But he doubted it. There was something in her manner that indicated otherwise. He knew the signs. She was very much *not* over it.

"Well, if you do need a shoulder, mine are both wide."
Murphy paused, trying to find some way to smooth over his
unintentional mistake. She had come to his aid and he'd just
raked over her heart with a rusty nail. "That boy in the
photograph, is he your son?"

The sadness that rose into her eyes was overwhelmingly
evident, even in the dark.

"He was," she whispered.

Maybe he should just tape his mouth shut. "I can't make
this any worse, can I?"

He was obviously upset about bringing up such a painful
subject for her. She was moved to try to alleviate *his* feelings.

"You might find a way." Shawna smiled and placed her
hand over his. "It's okay. It's not your fault, Murphy. You
didn't know."

That still didn't negate the fact that he had brought the
subject up and hurt her. "How long ago did it happen?"

She'd never talked about it, not to anyone. Not even to
her mother. She couldn't. She didn't want to talk about it
now.

Yet, somehow, as she sat there beside him in the en-
croaching darkness, she suddenly needed to. It had been
bottled up inside her for so long she thought it was going to
explode. And take her with it.

"A year ago. Eighteen months, actually," Shawna
amended after a beat.

She spoke so softly he had to strain to hear her. "Accident?"

The nod was almost imperceptible. "Car." The single
word clogged her throat.

Shawna knotted her hands in her lap and looked down at
them. Her voice floated from her as if it was disembodied,
as if someone else was forcing the words out.

"We were driving home from a vacation. Doug hates—
hated," she corrected, still having trouble thinking of him
in the past tense, "to drive, so I was the one behind the
wheel."

She was knotting her hands so tightly Murphy was surprised her fingers didn't break. He reached over and placed his hand over hers, silently urging her on.

She could almost feel his strength seeping into her, comforting her. It helped her continue.

"It was a produce truck, going a little too fast around a curve. Or maybe much too fast. The police said he'd been drinking." She took in a breath, bracing herself against the image that came to her mind. "I swerved to get out of the way and careened into a ditch." She shrugged helplessly. The blame was heavy in her voice. "I hit my head and passed out. Someone called the paramedics. They said that Doug was killed instantly." She swallowed. The lump in her throat threatened to choke her. It refused to subside.

Shawna closed her eyes, pushing tears back. They gathered anyway, seeping through her lashes and falling down her cheeks.

"Bobby died in the hospital before I regained consciousness. He died alone." She would always regret that. That she hadn't been there to hold him, to tell her son one last time that she loved him. "My little boy died alone."

Once the tears began, she couldn't stop them.

The stick shift was between them, but it seemed like a flimsy barrier in the face of her grief. As gently as if he were taking a baby into his arms, Murphy drew Shawna to him and held her while she cried.

The sobs racked her body. She cried for all the times she hadn't. For the awful, horrible waste and for the guilt that ate away at her like the slow drip of a battery's acid.

She cried for a long time.

Murphy murmured soft words that Shawna couldn't quite make out and stroked her hair. And held her until she was empty.

Shawna straightened slowly, rubbing away the last of her tears with the heel of her hand. A slight blush of embarrassment colored her cheeks. She took a deep breath, struggling to get herself under control. Composure was still some way off.

"I'm sorry, I have no idea what came over me." She exhaled a ragged sigh. One moment she had been fine, the next moment she'd been a puddle of tears.

Though he loosened his hold, he didn't release her. He wasn't quite ready yet. It felt good to hold her, even though he would have preferred it to be under different circumstances.

"They call it being human." His voice was low, soothing. Comforting. "I've only seen it at a distance myself, but I know for a fact that it exists."

Shawna sniffed one last time. His shirt was tearstained. "You're right, you are nice."

His mouth curved. They were making headway despite his bout with hoof-in-mouth disease. And that was good, because he wanted to see her. To be with her. "Does that mean you'll come to Harmony's party?"

She was tempted, but self-preservation was strong. "I—"

"Please." He really wanted her to come. He thought it might help her get on with her life. There was something almost miraculous, watching his extended family at a gathering. Warmth was a definite by-product.

She relented. "All right." If she resisted, they could be here all night and she was leery of where that might lead. She'd been with him only a short time and had already said more to him than she had to any other living soul. She didn't want to expose any more of herself. "When?"

It took him a moment to remember. He envisioned the calendar in his kitchen, where he noted down everything that was a part of his life. "Next Saturday. Thomas is going all out and renting a pony."

She thought Murphy had said that his niece was having her first birthday. "For a one-year-old?"

Thomas was conservative by nature. Unless it came to his family. Murphy grinned; a man could do worse than indulge that group. "Kimberly's kids are old enough to enjoy riding around in a circle. So are some of the other kids who'll be there."

It sounded as if it was going to be rather a large crowd. Shawna didn't do well in crowds. She never had. "I really don't know—"

"Come," he urged. He slipped his hand over hers. "As a friend. An old friend."

For just a moment he was. "All right, I'll come."

But even as she said it, Shawna unconsciously nibbled on her lower lip, debating the wisdom of what she was agreeing to. In the past eighteen months she had withdrawn from social activities altogether. She didn't entirely feel confident about taking this kind of plunge.

She looked so vulnerable. Murphy's action was entirely automatic, just one human being offering comfort to another. He leaned over and kissed her lightly on the lips.

Shawna's eyes widened. They looked at each other, their eyes scarcely two inches apart. The startled wonder was mirrored in turquoise and blue.

He'd felt something. Something small and needy, clawing to be freed. Whether it had been within him or her, he wasn't certain. But it had been there.

And it was begging to be released.

Instincts as inbred and natural as breathing took hold. Murphy kissed her again.

She shouldn't be allowing this to happen. There were ethics to think about. And things with far graver consequences than that.

Everything within her, all her emotions, all her feelings, had been sealed away with a tight lid over them. Murphy was threatening to pry it off.

More than threatening. Succeeding.

And she was afraid.

But, oh, it felt good, so wonderfully good to be held, to be wanted. To be kissed like this and swept beyond the realm of pain. Shawna twined her arms around his neck as Murphy's kiss seeped into her soul.

Without thinking, Murphy deepened the kiss, surprised at the depth of feeling he encountered within her. Surprised and delighted, and just a little bit shaken, as well.

Because she swept him away.

He had meant to offer her a little solace and console her the best way he knew how. He hadn't been prepared for the sudden bonfire that erupted before him. That erupted within him in kind.

Murphy could taste her tears on her lips, salty and dolorous. They stirred him, aroused him, made him want to soothe her and excite her all at the same time.

He dove his fingers into her hair, pulling her closer to him. His mind had gone spinning off into oblivion, but now the stick shift dug into his abdomen, reminding him just where he was.

Blowing out a breath, Murphy pulled back and took stock of what was happening here. Took stock of himself. All in all it was just as unnerving as the incident in the courtroom had been for him.

Maybe more.

He struggled for humor as he brushed his composure in place. "They were right."

Shawna was so dazed she could barely focus on a thought. All she saw was him. It took her a second before she came to her senses. She shouldn't be doing this.

"Who?" Letting out a ragged breath, she realized that her jacket was slightly askew, not to mention the rest of her. She could fix the jacket, but . . .

He couldn't help himself. He tucked a loose hair behind her ear. Something flared in her eyes. Not anger—fear. It reminded him of something he might expect to see in a doe's eyes as she was frightened away by the scent of man approaching.

"The people who said still waters run deep." He smiled at her, trying to set her at ease. "I think I just got pulled in by the undertow."

Her lips felt as if they were throbbing. She had to concentrate to keep from shaking. What had just happened here? She felt as if she had run a marathon. She struggled to gather her thoughts together. "Under the circumstances, perhaps—"

"I'd better go in," he finished quickly before she could say anything further. He didn't want her having second thoughts about the invitation she had just accepted. Murphy's interest in Shawna had been ignited for a number of reasons, although he had to admit that the fire she'd lit beneath him just now had made the top of the list.

But it was more than that. How much more, he didn't know. He wouldn't find out if she shied away.

Murphy eased out of the car, then closed the door behind him. The tarnished handle felt loose under his hand. He crouched to look at her inside the car. "I'll come by tomorrow to get the results of the test. Maybe we can go out to celebrate afterward."

The test. She rallied, grateful for something to hide behind for a moment until she pulled herself together.

"Life is not one big, long party, Murphy." She realized that she wasn't referring to the possibility of his celebrating good news; she was chastising him for what had just happened. But it had been her fault as much as his.

A cryptic smile quirked his lips, playing with the corners of his mouth. "No, it's not." He guessed that they both knew that firsthand. "But we can enjoy ourselves once in a while." He rose again. "See you tomorrow, Shawna."

Shawna straightened her wheel as she slowly drove into the street. Her heart was hammering now like the kettledrums of an orchestra performing the *1812 Overture*.

All right, Shawna, what was all that about?

She hadn't the slightest clue. She just knew it scared her.

By the time Shawna reached her apartment complex, it was close to nine. Thoughts of bubble baths and books were shelved. All she wanted to do was go to bed and forget that the past couple of hours had even happened.

Fat chance.

She had no idea what had possessed her to talk to Murphy and even less why she had kissed him.

Yes, she did, she argued silently. Because he wasn't just some empty-headed pretty boy or predatory womanizer. There had been something there, something kind that had drawn her words out of her. She'd seen genuine concern in his eyes when she'd told him about Doug and Bobby. Concern and sympathy.

In her present state it had completely undone her, unexpectedly cracking the protective shield she kept around her heart. By being kind, by listening, he had caused the dam to break open. And the tears to come.

He was probably going to be utterly impossible from now on, she thought with a sigh. She had taken a giant step and it was going to be hard to retrace it.

Who would have thought, twelve years ago, that she would ever have kissed Murphy Pendleton?

She pulled in to her parking space beneath the clay-tile-roofed carport and shut off the engine. Murphy Pendleton. Her mother would have been overjoyed if she had seen her.

Sally Rowen had always despaired about her wallflower, bookworm daughter. A sad smile curved Shawna's mouth. When her mother bothered to notice her at all.

It wasn't a case of mean-spirited neglect on her mother's part, Shawna thought as she got out of the car. It was that her mother had never really grown up herself. She could barely take responsibility for herself, much less someone else. Sally Rowen had no business becoming pregnant in the first place. She hadn't the vaguest idea how to be a mother. All she really knew how to do was have a good time. Or look for one.

There was no sense in rehashing that now. She'd think about everything tomorrow. Her mother, Murphy, the kiss, everything.

Tonight, all she wanted to do was crawl into bed and not think about anything, least of all about the fact that for one frozen moment before Murphy's door she had completely dissolved into a nonfunctioning organism. That was something that she—

Shawna stopped and stared, her breath hitching in her throat.

There was someone on her doorstep. Sitting on a suitcase, looking as if she was posing for a travelogue. She was a young-looking woman with hair the color of darkening flame, long, well-curved legs and a skirt that hadn't exhausted the manufacturer's supply of material by a long shot. There was another suitcase next to her. A large one.

Shawna hurried over, though she was hardly aware of crossing the last few yards.

"Mother."

Except for the hair color, they looked more like sisters than mother and daughter. They well could have been. Only fifteen years separated Shawna from her mother.

Sally Rowen uncrossed graceful legs and rose to stand beside her luggage. "Hello, baby. It's about time you got in." She looked behind her daughter, hoping there might be someone behind her. No such luck. "I gather from the fact that you're alone that you're just coming home from work now."

There was absolutely no way she would tell her mother about Murphy or what had happened. "Something like that."

Sally shook her head. Her hair brushed from cheek to cheek like a lover's caress. "Oh, Shawna, where did I go wrong with you?"

Lots of ways, Mother. Lots of ways.

The next moment Shawna found herself in the midst of a quick, emotional embrace. After a beat, she returned it. She hadn't seen her mother since the funeral. And before that it had been several years. Sally drifted in and out of her life like smoke, leaving only a faint telltale scent in her wake.

"God, that felt good." Sally stepped back, her hands on Shawna's shoulders. "Here, let me get a good look at you." Sally cocked her head, studying her the way she did when she examined the integrity of an article of clothing she was thinking of purchasing. "You look tired."

Shawna's eyes swept over her mother. The smile was a little too tight, the makeup a little too heavy, hiding shadows beneath her eyes. Something was definitely up. "So do you."

Sally dropped her hands and shrugged carelessly. A little too carelessly, in Shawna's estimation. "It was a long flight."

Shawna took out her key. "From which city was it this time?" Her mother logged more miles than a nomad.

"Chicago." Sally shook her head as Shawna opened the front door. She swept into the apartment like a queen, leaving her luggage standing on the doorstep. "It doesn't have a thing on San Francisco," she announced loyally.

With a sigh, Shawna picked up the two suitcases and followed Sally in. She kicked the door closed with the heel of her shoe.

Her mother had always been partial to San Francisco. It had been only one of the many cities she had lived in as a child, Shawna remembered. By the time she began high school the number had been eight and counting. The three and a half years she had spent in Bedford was the longest period of time Shawna had remained anywhere until she'd gotten married. As always, the location was because of the man in her mother's life. Sally had been married to Fred at the time. Or was that Steve? It was hard to keep track. Each time she was divorced, she reverted back to her maiden name. Otherwise, her signature would have been longer than she was tall.

Shawna assumed that a man was why her mother was here now. She braced herself for the gush of words. The man Sally Rowen was with at the moment was always the right man. The man she wanted to be with forever. Until it went sour.

Shawna placed the suitcases just inside the door. "So, what's this big surprise you were talking about on the answering machine?"

"You're looking at it." Sally spread her hands dramatically, turning around. "Me. I've decided to come live with you. At least, until I get my own place."

Oh, God. Keeping a tight rein on her composure, Shawna dropped her purse beside her mother's suitcases. "I thought you were getting married again."

So had she, Sally thought miserably. "Nope. I'm single, fancy-free and very happy to be that way."

And where had she heard that before? Shawna stepped out of her shoes as she unbuttoned her jacket. Stripping it off, she draped it over the recliner. "You want to tell me about it?"

The brown eyes were wide with innocence. Shawna wasn't buying into it for a moment. "It?"

"It," Shawna repeated. "Whatever it was that made you pack up and leave."

Sally moved around the room, trying it on for size. It was too small.

"Wanderlust." She fingered the draperies. Expensive, she decided. "Awful word, you know." The material slipped from her fingers. "Who has lust for wandering? For men, maybe, but wandering? Uh-uh."

As Shawna watched, Sally turned in a complete circle. There wasn't much to take in. "You live here, huh?"

Here it came, Shawna thought. Criticism. But she was too old to want her mother's approval at this stage of her life. "No, my house is in the shop—this is a loaner. Yes, I live here."

Sally frowned at the sofa. She knew that Shawna had a penchant for volunteering her services. "Aren't you making any money at all?"

That was the second time tonight her salary had been questioned. Or more accurately, her tastes, she thought. "Yes, I find this suits all my needs."

"If you say so." It was obvious that Sally didn't agree with her daughter's assessment. "This was the kind of place I was always trying to get us out of."

Yourself, Mother. You were always trying to get yourself out of those places. I was just an afterthought.

Shawna felt suddenly incredibly weary. She wished she'd had a little time to herself before her mother descended on her.

"Maybe that's what I liked about it," Shawna lied. "It brought back memories."

She stood there for a moment, feeling ill at ease. She felt that way whenever her mother came to see her. And by the time she could get herself to relax, her mother would be on her way, off to follow another dream.

Or another man.

The problem was, Shawna suspected, their roles bled into one another. Her mother had always needed nurturing and Shawna had always provided it. She had never had the luxury of being a child. Her mother had that part sewed up.

Shawna looked at her now and thought that her mother looked a little lost, a little waiflike despite the glitter at her wrist and throat. Her mother collected men and jewelry, not always in that order. "Are you hungry?"

Sally started to say something, then stopped abruptly. "I've had dinner. Some tea might be nice."

Shawna was too tired to go the whole ten rounds. She wanted to cut to the chase. "So, tell me, why are you here?" By the look on her mother's face, she knew another glib response was coming. She aborted it. "Really."

Sally's smile drooped a little. "Am I that transparent?"

Because she looked so lost, Shawna placed her arm around her mother's shoulders. "We've been there before, Mother."

"Maybe I'm just having a bit of remorse for not being the perfect mother." Sally had the good grace to flush slightly.

"Maybe." Shawna paused, waiting. It didn't take long.

Sally sighed. Her shoulders slumped as she gave up the act. "He left me."

She'd been right. There was a man at the heart of this. There always was. "He?"

"Michael," Sally said mournfully.

Michael. The last man had been someone called Carl. He'd come after the rock climber. This was a new one. "And he would be—?"

"My fiancé. Michael Rockford." She saw that Shawna wanted more information. "The accountant."

A working man for a change. But his vocation wasn't the flamboyant type her mother usually gravitated toward. She was into risk takers. Daredevils. Charming bums. "An accountant? That sounds rather tame for you."

Sally sank onto the sofa as if the air had suddenly been siphoned out of her. She'd been so sure that she had made the right choice this time.

"I know. I was finally going for stability." She looked at her daughter. "I'm not getting any younger." It was a difficult thing to admit, even to herself. Age was something she had always tried to outrun. For a while, she thought she had. "I want someone to grow old with." Indignant tears shone in her eyes as she looked up at Shawna. "He told me I was too old for him."

"You'll always be young, Mother," Shawna told her. Just how young a man had she set her sights on this time? "How old was Michael?"

"Thirty-eight." Sally sniffed.

Shawna reached for a tissue from the dispenser and handed it to her mother. "I'm surprised you went after someone so old."

Sally chuckled softly. She wiped her eyes, then raised her head. Renewed determination to straighten out her life glinted in her eyes.

"I told you, I was going for stability." She balled up the tissue and tossed it aside on the coffee table. "That showed me."

Shawna laughed and took her mother's arm, ushering her from the sofa. Sally needed to unburden herself before she felt better. It was a familiar pattern they'd been following all their lives. And she was always the one who could put her mother's pieces together.

"C'mon, I'll brew us that tea and you can tell me all about it."

Sally patted her daughter's arm, letting herself be led off like a child seeking guidance. "You're a good daughter, Shawna."

Shawna smiled indulgently at her mother. "I know."

Chapter Seven

She wasn't at her best today.

Shawna had spent the better part of the previous evening and most of the ensuing night sitting in the kitchen, nursing lukewarm mugs of tea and talking about her mother's problem.

Listening actually would have been a more accurate description of what had transpired. Listening and offering words of comfort whenever her mother took a momentary respite. Her mother, usually so flamboyant and outrageous, had been like a small, hurt child last night. A child in need of reassurance that she was still lovely, still lovable. It seemed like forever before she talked herself out and finally went to sleep. Shawna gave her the bedroom.

What there was left of the night Shawna had passed trying to find a comfortable spot on the sofa.

There wasn't one.

She'd slept in tiny, fitful snatches and felt worse when she got up than when she had lain down. It brought her days in medical school and residency back in vivid colors.

Consequently, Shawna felt ill equipped to face the day. But it was there, waiting for her whether she was up to it or not.

Attempting to kick-start her system, she drank three cups of strong coffee in rapid succession, threw a handful of saltine crackers into her purse in lieu of breakfast and was out of the house before her mother, a habitual late riser, ever opened her eyes.

Shawna had no time to attempt to rouse her mother. Besides, she judged as she drove away, her mother was undoubtedly exhausted and needed her sleep. And she had a radial keratotomy waiting for her first thing in the morning.

Jeanne Hawkins walked into Shawna's office and stood quietly in the doorway, waiting for Shawna to look up. It was just a few minutes past twelve and Shawna had been on the go since she had walked in at eight-thirty.

When Shawna sensed her presence and glanced up, Jeanne shook her head. Cheeks as round as Washington apples spread wide as the woman smiled.

"How do you do it?" It was a rhetorical question. If pressed, Jeanne wouldn't have been able to think of a single person she admired more than Shawna, and she had been in medicine for the past twenty-three years. "You've had a waiting room crowded to overflowing with patients who you've managed to attend to, all before lunch. You've been going nonstop since you came in from the hospital, which is probably where you're going to spend your lunch hour."

Her assumption was confirmed by the slight smile of acknowledgment on Shawna's lips.

"And I know that tonight's your night for the clinic." Jeanne's expression was one of awed mystification. "Just how do you do it?"

Shawna never really thought about the pace she maintained, which was the blessing. That was her goal, to be too busy to think. Too busy to feel.

Last night had been an exception. "I just do."

Mechanically, as she had been doing all morning after each patient, Shawna reached for her mug and took a sip of the coffee that was always standing ready for her. She shivered and frowned, setting it aside. The coffee was beginning to taste more and more like sludge.

Jeanne was still studying her. "Maybe it's the vitamins," Shawna added.

If that was true, there would be a run on vitamins at every drugstore and market. "Remind me to order a gross for myself."

Shawna closed the patient folder she'd been making notations in. Jane McBee. She'd performed cataract surgery successfully on the woman, doing first one eye, then the other four months later. After a year Jane, a feisty eighty-year-old, was doing better than ever.

Turning in her chair, Shawna looked at her assistant. Jeanne did look a little tired. "Hard night?"

Jeanne laughed, tickled at the question. "When you've got four boys, all in different grades, all with papers due 'now, Mom,' the word 'hard' doesn't begin to cover it. Thanks to Willie, my youngest, I now know more about Wisconsin's dairy products than I ever wanted to in my wildest dreams." Despite her complaint, Jeanne fairly glowed, just as she always did when she talked about her sons. "Mind if I send over a couple of the boys to you? You at least have the energy to keep up with them."

Shawna thought of the cramped condition of her apartment. Her mother's evaluation came to mind immediately. "Sure, I'll squeeze them in."

The phrase nudged Jeanne's memory. "Speaking of squeezing, he's back." She nodded toward the hall.

Shawna rose slowly. "He?"

If the doctor was oblivious to the man she had seen a couple of days ago, the woman had no pulse. "The gorgeous hunk who told me you said to squeeze him in the other day." Jeanne's expression grew dreamy. "Wouldn't mind doing a little squeezing of my own with him."

Shawna's mouth quirked. Jeanne was almost old enough to be Murphy's mother. Unlike her own mother, Jeanne exuded motherly warmth. Her idea of an exciting time was to curl up with her husband and watch a rented movie while her sons played basketball in the backyard. "Jeanne, you're a married woman."

Jeanne's chuckle was surprisingly lusty. Murphy, Shawna mused, seemed to bring out the sensual side of every woman whose path he crossed.

"Yeah, I know, but I can dream, can't I?" She noticed that Shawna, usually a portrait of perpetual motion, was just standing there. "Do you want to see him?" Just like the last time, he'd had no appointment, but had prevailed on her to "squeeze him in" again. Because Jeanne knew Shawna had only one more patient scheduled for the morning, she figured it was worth a shot.

Did she want to see him? Shawna thought. *Yes.*

No.

Suddenly nervous, Shawna chose to procrastinate for a moment. "Sure, give me a minute to throw this out." She lifted her mug.

Like a hawk swooping out of the sky and snatching its prey, Jeanne took the mug. "Here, I'll do it for you."

Left without an excuse, Shawna followed Jeanne out into the hall. She glanced toward the front. Only one of the patient rooms had a closed door.

I'll take door number two, Monty. The phrase floated to her out of the recesses of her childhood. She'd spent hours alone, with only the television set on in the background to keep her company.

Jeanne pointed toward the room. "I put him in room two for you."

Shawna nodded, then remembered why Murphy was coming in. "Did his M.R.I. arrive yet?"

"Half an hour ago. It's on the side shelf in your office." Jeanne tossed the words over her shoulder as she rounded the corner to the tiny kitchen they maintained in the back.

Shawna retraced her steps to her office. The huge manila envelope was just where Jeanne had said it was, leaning to one side. How had she missed that?

Because she hadn't had the time to look around, that's why. The morning was a blur from this vantage point.

Taking a deep breath to steel herself, she pulled out the large, flat sheet. At first glance it looked like a ghoulish composite of undeveloped film. She placed it on the view box and flipped the light switch on the side. Muted light shone through the various negatives. There were twelve different angles of Murphy's cranium. Shawna studied each in turn and stopped abruptly as she came to the third one.

Bingo.

There was no missing it.

The fact that her prognosis had been correct didn't please her. She didn't need to read the two-page report that accompanied the films to tell her what was wrong, but she did just to be thorough.

When she finished reading, she laid the pages aside. She rubbed the bridge of her nose, trying to ease the tension. Murphy's condition didn't generate a life-and-death scenario, but it wasn't a walk in the park, either.

What was worse, she couldn't seem to divorce herself from the case, couldn't quite take the distant, professional view that had always been her mainstay. This time, she took it personally.

That wasn't good.

With a sigh, Shawna took the unwieldy sheet with its accompanying report and went to see Murphy. To tell him what they both already knew and had been hoping against.

Murphy was standing by the enameled worktable, attempting to entertain himself by looking through the various lenses that were housed along the wooden cubby. When she opened the door he turned, startled, looking like a kid with his hand caught in the cookie jar.

Very carefully he replaced the last lens and took his seat in the examination chair. His eyes never left her face.

"Hi." She looked a little tense, he observed. Was that because of last night? Or was there another reason behind the tight smile on her lips? "What's the good word?"

"Hello." For a second, as she placed the report to the side, she couldn't get herself to say anything else.

She was definitely uncomfortable. He had a feeling it was more than just last night that was causing it. "No other good words, eh?'' Crossing his arms, he resigned himself to what she was about to say. "All right, what did they find?"

Instead of answering immediately, Shawna placed the gray-and-white sheet of images against the view box. She turned on the light switch and stepped back.

Murphy rose and joined her. He studied it in silence for a long moment. "They didn't get my best side."

With the tip of her index finger, Shawna pointed to a small region just behind his left eye. There seemed to be a light dot there, no larger than a pencil point. It seemed incredible that something so minor could be the source of all this trouble.

And yet it was.

"What you have is rather unusual. That blow to the head you sustained during the fire caused a small vessel attached to the dura—the outer covering of the brain," she interjected for his benefit, "to tear. That led to the accumulation of blood between it and the brain. You have what's known as a subdural hematoma located near the optic canal. That's where the optic nerves leave the brain and run through the skull to end in the eyes. Essentially, that tiny clot is what's responsible for your dizziness and that in-and-out feeling that you've been experiencing."

So saying, she switched off the light and then laid the sheet aside. It suddenly seemed like a macabre reminder of what lay ahead.

Murphy slipped his hands into his pockets, feeling defenseless and hating it. "Any chance of it just going away?"

She knew that was what he was hoping for. Though she was suddenly tempted to comfort him, she couldn't give him false hope. "I suppose that anything is possible, but it's also highly improbable."

That was not what he wanted to hear. Despite their conversation last night, he wanted her to tell him that the clot would dissolve on its own and he could go about his life, business as usual.

Damn it, he didn't have the time to take off for an operation. Even worse, he didn't want to think of himself as being vulnerable, not this way, as well. Commitment might not be something he could place his trust in, but he thought he could rely on himself. There had to be *something* he could always rely on.

He stared out the window. "But it *could* happen."

Murphy's tone begged for an affirmation. She couldn't give it. Shawna shook her head, denying him the lifeline he was asking for. "More likely, if you don't have it taken care of—" *Taken care of.* What an inane euphemism for surgery, she thought.

He'd always been able to face things head-on before. He was ashamed of himself for looking for another route now. "Yes?"

"There's a chance that you could go blind in that eye."

He raised his chin, as if daring her to repeat her words. "But it's not a sure thing."

Why was he being so stubborn about this? This was something that could be fixed. It wasn't as if they were contemplating a degenerative disease. This damage she could alleviate. "Murphy, don't tell me you're thinking of not having the surgery."

He turned away from her, restless, stubborn, still unwilling to accept what she was telling him. "All right, I won't tell you."

"Murphy!" She raised her voice before she could think better of it. It fairly rang with the frustration and exasperation that was stirring within her.

He turned to look at her, surprised by her tone. "Do I have to have it right away?" He needed time to assimilate this, to think it through.

"Not this second, no." She was thinking of performing the surgery within a week. There were still a couple of openings left in the early-morning hours. Bids for the operating rooms went quickly.

"All right." Murphy nodded slowly. He'd been feeling better. There'd been no more spells, no more incidents since yesterday afternoon. He'd hoped, believed that he was coming around and that there was nothing to worry about. Now he had to face the fact that there was. "Then I want to think about it."

Shawna had gone into medicine because she wanted to help people. It was the one outlet she had for her passion.

His stubborn resistance was eroding her patience. "There's nothing to think about. You need to have it done."

They'd already established that. Painfully. "And I will, but..."

He was hedging. Maybe she had been misreading the reason behind it. Maybe it was her he felt unsure about, not the diagnosis or the procedure. The thought stung, but she could certainly live with it. The bottom line was to get him to have the surgery. Ego had no place in medicine as far as she was concerned. Only helping did.

"If you wait a minute, I can give you a couple of referrals to other doctors."

Is that why she thought he was hesitating? He didn't want another doctor. He wanted her. He just didn't want to rush into it.

"You didn't let me finish," he said sharply, stopping her before she could continue. "I want you to do the surgery. I already told you that yesterday. It's just that I want to get comfortable about this, all right?"

It was a reasonable request, as long as he didn't take too long. The fact that he had faith in her felt oddly reassuring and flattering. She drew herself up. "How long do you think that's going to take?"

Murphy dragged his hand through his hair. How long did it take for a man to come to terms with the fact that he wasn't immortal? That things could happen to him just as easily as to everyone else? It wasn't a matter of ego, just a case of rampant optimism. He'd never had to deal with anything like this before. It made him feel weak, as if he had no control. After his experience with Janice, he couldn't afford not to be in control. "I'm not sure yet."

"I wouldn't advise waiting too long, Counselor."

There was a knock on the door before he could reply.

Jeanne stuck her head in. She smiled at Murphy before addressing Shawna. "Doctor, I'm sorry to interrupt, but there's a call for you on line one."

"Take a message." Shawna thought it odd that Jeanne hadn't done that automatically, the way she usually did.

The cherubic expression on Jeanne's face was understanding and apologetic at the same time. "It's your mother. She insists on speaking to you."

She might have known. Sally Rowen wasn't accustomed to waiting, not where her daughter was concerned. Shawna frowned. "All right, I'll take it." She glanced at Murphy. "I'll be right back."

He'd seen the momentary flash of impatience, mingled with distress. It aroused his curiosity. But he gave no indication as he spread his hands innocently. "I'm not going anywhere."

Shawna didn't bother commenting as she hurried out. One day in town and already her mother was disrupting her life. She wasn't feeling overly friendly as she lifted the telephone receiver.

"Hello, Mother. I'm afraid you're going to have to make this quick. I'm with a patient."

"A good-looking one, I hope."

Shawna could feel her patience fraying instantly. There were far more important things in the world than looks. If her mother had learned that, perhaps she wouldn't be here now, lost and alone, fearfully awaiting the ghost of Christmas Future, afraid of what it had in store. "I didn't notice."

There was a cluck of sympathy mingled with a dash of sorrow on the other end. "You never notice, dear. That was always the problem with you."

I noticed, Mother. I noticed a lot of things. But you were never there to talk to about it. "Could we hurry this along, please? Why are you calling? Is there something wrong?"

"Not wrong, exactly." Shawna could envision her mother pouting on the other end. "Why didn't you wake me before you left?"

She'd gone into the tiny bedroom to get her clothes and to take a shower. Sally had slept through it all. She had given the impression she would have slept through a train wreck even if it had occurred in the middle of the apartment.

"You needed your sleep. We were up late last night, remember? And I had to get to work."

It wasn't that Sally wasn't proud of what Shawna had made of herself. It was just that she viewed work, all work, as an evil that was necessary, but which frequently got in the way of having a good time.

"Why don't you take off early and we can go shopping? I hear the mall in South Coast has built up considerably since I lived here last."

Shawna wouldn't know; she hadn't been there. There was never any time. Her mother, she knew, adored shopping. To Shawna it was one of those things that had to be endured every so often if one didn't want to walk around in rags. She took no joy in it.

"I'd love to, Mother, but I have a full schedule this afternoon and then I have to be at the clinic until nine tonight."

She was about to suggest that they have a late dinner together when her mother interrupted with a sigh. "Don't you ever stop working?"

Trust her mother to want to rearrange everything according to her tastes. "I like my work, Mother."

"I think you like hiding behind your work." There was a measure of pity in her voice.

She knew exactly what her mother was referring to, even though they had never discussed it. Her mother, for lack of courage, had never said anything about the accident, not even at the funeral. Because of the pain, Shawna had never managed to bring it up herself.

Which made her talking about it to Murphy all the more difficult to understand.

"I'll see you tonight when I get in, Mother."

Muttering an oath under her breath, she let the telephone receiver drop into the cradle. When she turned around, Shawna stifled a gasp, her hand flying to her chest. Damn him, what was he doing, sneaking around corners?

She glared at Murphy standing in her doorway. "You were supposed to stay put."

He lifted his shoulders innocently, then let them drop. "Your voice carried. You sounded upset. I didn't want my doctor getting upset. Ruins hand-to-eye coordination." His smile slipped away as he crossed to her. "Bad news?"

"No, personal news," she corrected, not knowing why she didn't just tell him to butt out. She glared at the telephone. "That was my mother. She's staying with me for a while."

"So you mentioned." There was a lingering aura of tension around her and an edge in her voice she was still attempting to get under control. "Don't you get along with her?"

He was treading where he didn't belong again. This time she was ready for him. "Don't you know the meaning of the word 'privacy'?"

"I know lots of meanings, but I'm also a lawyer. Very little is private as far as I'm concerned." And he was concerned, he thought. Involved. In a very cursory fashion, he amended quickly, but still involved.

"Well, this is." The No Trespassing sign went up, lit in six-foot klieg lights. "Now, when can I schedule you for surgery?"

She was as persistent as he was, he thought with a smile. They had more in common than she probably thought. "I'll get back to you on that."

The waiting room had been empty when he was finally shown to a room. It was well after twelve. Time for her to be the princess again instead of Cinderella. "Ready for lunch?"

She picked up her purse, but she had no intention of leaving with him. "I thought you were going to take me out only if you were celebrating." She walked into the hall and he turned, ready to follow. "This isn't exactly something a man would celebrate."

"No, but you still have to eat."

"*You* still have to eat. I have patients to visit in the hospital." She moved past him.

Jeanne, Shawna noticed, was at her desk, pretending that she was working, but she knew the woman was absorbing all this like bread soaking up milk. Jeanne was a hopeless romantic who believed that everyone belonged paired off in twos. But she could afford to think that way. Her family was intact.

"I'll be back at two, Jeanne." Shawna glanced at Murphy, then walked past the front desk. "No charge for Mr. Pendleton's visit today." With that, she left.

Shawna stretched, attempting to loosen tightened muscles throughout her body. The last patient for the day had left ten minutes ago. The sound of the outer door opening and closing told her that Jeanne had gone home, as well. Odd that she hadn't stopped in to say goodbye.

No doubt she probably had dairy products on her mind, Shawna thought with a smile, remembering Jeanne's earlier complaint about one of her sons' reports.

It was time for her to get going, as well. Shawna locked her drawer and picked up her purse. Simon McGuire usually left the clinic at six. That gave her approximately an hour to get there before he went home. Traffic permitting, she amended. She knew the doctor would remain if she was late for some reason. McGuire had been the one who had initially recruited her. The clinic was his baby and he was there as often as his schedule permitted. A widowed grandfather, he lost himself in his work.

She knew how that was.

Shawna swallowed a cry as she all but walked straight into Murphy. The man was bent on giving her a heart attack, she thought angrily.

Taking a step back, she tried to compose herself. It was beginning to become a habit around him. "What are you doing here?"

He'd passed Jeanne on his way in and she had told him that Shawna was in her office. He'd heard the woman humming to herself as she left the office. It looked as if he had gotten back just in time. Shawna was obviously on the way out. "I told you I'd get back to you."

He was the most unorthodox man. "Does this mean you've decided when you want to schedule your operation?"

"No, but I did want to get back to you." His eyes swept over her, making her warm, making her feel like something other than his doctor.

He was flirting with her again, treating his situation as if he had all the time in the world. "Murphy, this isn't a game."

He toyed with the tiny dangling pearl at her ear, sending it swaying. But his expression was serious. "I'm not playing games. Games are for children. We're both the type to be up front about things."

"You're right, I'll be up front," she agreed. "Go home."

"Up front," he told her. "Not rude." He took her elbow as she walked out of the office, then waited as she locked up. "I thought we could have dinner together."

She shook her head. Heat-seeking missiles had nothing on this man. "No."

Maybe the idea of having dinner with him was scaring her off. He wanted to spend some time with her. It didn't matter where. "How about coffee?"

It was a short walk to the bank of elevators. Shorter when she hurried. Shawna pressed the Down button. "Only if it's takeout and I can drink it in the car."

The elevator arrived almost instantly and he followed her inside, pressing the button marked *1* before she could. "Whatever you say."

He still didn't get it, she thought. Or didn't want to get it. "No, you don't understand. I have to go to the clinic. It's my shift."

He vaguely remembered her mentioning the clinic. "Oh, the free clinic in L.A."

She nodded. It was after hours and the parking lot was almost deserted. The only cars remaining belonged to diligent office personnel who were still somewhere in the eight-story medical building, working, attempting to catch up in a world that was moving too fast. She hurried over to her car. She recognized his two aisles over. "That's the one."

Murphy felt a nibble of disappointment. "Tonight?"

"Tonight." She unlocked her door before turning around. "So, if you'll excuse me."

He placed his hand over hers. He still wanted to spend some time with her, and although he wouldn't have chosen the clinic as the place to do it, maybe that was for the best. "No."

Shawna's eyebrows drew together into an accusing V. "No?"

"No," he clarified, "I won't excuse you. But I will accompany you."

Maybe the air was a little rarefied up there where he was. "This isn't a joyride."

He grinned, pretending to take her literally. "All right, we can go in separate cars."

Why she remained here arguing with him, instead of getting into her car and driving away, she didn't know. "I have work to do."

He understood that. But there would be moments in between when he could talk to her. Get to know her. "And I'll watch you do it." Needing ammunition, he sweetened the pot a little. "Don't you want some extra time to talk me into the surgery?"

She leaned against her car and studied Murphy. "I have the feeling that no one talks you into anything."

He grinned. She had his number, which was good. He'd meant what he'd said about not playing games. The more they knew about each other, about the way they thought, the better. That way there would be no misunderstanding, no recriminations in the end. "And the reverse is true, too."

Shawna could literally feel time ticking away. She should have already been on the freeway, inching along to Normandy. "Meaning?"

He remained blocking her way. "No one talks me *out* of anything, either."

She was getting edgy. More so because part of her was tempted to let him come along. "This is harassment, you know."

The accusation left him unaffected. His expression softened. "No, it's not. It's friendship."

White flags of surrender began waving in the wind. If she didn't say yes, she could be here all night. If she did manage to drive away now, she knew he'd only follow her. "I suppose I can't stop you."

"Nope." He opened the car door for her. "And unless you want me to get involved in a car chase, you can't elude me, either." He grinned as he read her expression correctly.

He knew she had toyed with the idea. "Call it getting to know my physician." A little of the lightness faded. "I don't go under the knife lightly."

That much she believed. With a sigh Shawna relented. "All right, if you're going to be that adamant about it, get in." She gestured toward the passenger side. "I'll drive you."

He figured she could always bring him back to the lot to pick up his car. "Won you over, did I?"

"No, but as you pointed out, you're just pigheaded enough to follow me, and you shouldn't be driving around at night. Besides, I don't want to be responsible for your car being stripped or stolen. We're not exactly going to Disneyland."

He was accompanying her this time, but all the other times she went alone. He found himself not caring for the idea. "Do you think it's wise for you to go there alone?"

She knew he wasn't thinking about himself. But she wasn't his concern.

"No, not really, but then, it's not wise for the children who live there to be there, either. And if it weren't for the clinic, they might not get even the very basic in medical treatments. I can't not go because of something that *might* happen."

She turned on the engine and pressed down on the accelerator. She had time to make up.

He studied her rigid profile. "You can't cure the world's ills, Shawna."

She knew that. "No, but I can bandage a few of them here and there. If we all did that, eventually there wouldn't be any ills."

She believed that, he thought. He found that rather sweet. A bit unrealistic, but sweet. And, for some reason, damn attractive. "You're a rare lady, Shawna."

"That's what it says in my résumé." She turned to him. There was still time to turn back. "Sure you want to come along?"

There was no way he was getting out of the car now. "I wouldn't miss this for the world."

Chapter Eight

It was a storefront building, like all the others on either side of it. The brick was faded from time and from countless washings to remove the graffiti that had a habit of reappearing like a chronic rash, an outward sign of an inward anger. Short, squat, there was little to distinguish the clinic from its brethren, except for the sign that proclaimed Normandy Street Free Clinic. That, and the patched bay window, which gave Murphy a view of the packed interior. There were more people within the clinic than seemed humanly possible.

The forty-year-old building reeked of poverty, and yet there was a telltale aura of pride about it, as well. And hope. He couldn't quite put his finger on it, but he understood it, understood how necessary it was to have pride, especially when everything else was stripped from you.

Shawna guided her car down a small, tight alley and then shut off the ignition. There was nowhere else for her to leave the vehicle. The first time, she had done it out of frustration, for lack of a parking space. It had turned out to be a safe place. She'd parked it here ever since.

Murphy got out just ahead of her and moved carefully toward the street. There wasn't that much space between the vehicle and the wall.

Dusk was beginning to place a heavy hand on the streets. The air felt stagnant here, as if it were afraid to move for fear of calling attention to itself and begetting harm. There was a sense of apprehension as darkness approached. This was a tough neighborhood, a place where people struggled to survive, to make it through just one more day.

He didn't like thinking of her coming here. It was one thing to know about where she went, another thing entirely to see it. "So, this is the clinic," he murmured as he followed Shawna to the street entrance.

Though Murphy tried his best to hide it, Shawna detected the tinge of disapproval in his voice. She could understand his reaction. The stark contrast between where they had left and where they had arrived, all within just one hour's drive, was a shock. She had experienced it her first time. And, to some extent, she was still affected by it every time she came here. But it just added to her determination to do whatever she could to make a difference.

"Yes." She paused before the entrance. "Before that, it was a storefront church." She recalled the story and held it at a distance. If she allowed things to get to her, she wouldn't be able to function properly. And they needed her here. "The so-called Reverend who ran it was here eight months, they tell me, operating some sort of a con game, until he cheated the wrong person out of fifty dollars."

She glanced down on the sidewalk mechanically. The blood had long since been washed away. "They found him dead in front of his door. His pockets were empty."

She was about to push open the front door when his words stopped her. He knew she wouldn't like hearing this, but he had to at least say it. "I don't like your being here."

Shawna turned very slowly and looked up at him. She had been on her own, one way or another, for most of her life. She had no idea what it felt like to be taken care of, or worried about. Her mother had been too busy and too needy to dispense any nurturing care, and what she'd had with Doug had been more of a partnership than anything else. If anything, she had been the protective one.

This was something she had no idea how to deal with, except to push it away. She felt her independence being, if not threatened, then challenged. "Since when do you think that you have anything at all to say about where I go?"

That was easy enough to answer. "Since last night."

She hadn't thought that he would be the possessive type. In any case, whatever type he was had nothing to do with her. She wanted to make that perfectly clear.

"Don't misconstrue that kiss, Murphy. That just happened."

He saw the warning signs rise in her eyes. Warning signs ten feet in height. "Yes, I know. And I can't wait for it to happen again." The stubborn lines between her eyebrows formed. "Don't tell me you weren't attracted, Shawna."

She thought of denying it, then decided it would be useless. He wasn't a stupid man. Another route suggested itself to her. "Ego in form today?"

"Ego has nothing to do with it. I was just as bowled over as you were." He wanted to caress her face, to see her eyes flutter shut for just a moment. But this was entirely too public a place. "Maybe more. I'd like to follow this path that's opened up in front of us."

Well, she didn't. "There's no path. It was a crack, and it's closed now." Even if she had to cement it shut, she vowed silently.

Her argument left him unconvinced. "Then it needs to be opened again."

"No," she said quietly, "it doesn't."

She took a breath, aware that some of the people within the clinic had turned to look out the large window and watch, even if they couldn't hear what was being said. She recognized several of them. A little girl in patched overalls was smiling at her.

"This isn't going to work out," Shawna said abruptly. "Do you want me to call you a cab so you can go home?"

"Can't get rid of me that easily." Murphy reached around her and pushed open the door. "I'm here for the duration."

"I was afraid of that," Shawna muttered under her breath as she walked into the clinic.

The air conditioner, from a neighborhood appliance store that McGuire had badgered relentlessly into making the donation, was doing its best to cool the room, but it was difficult with the dense press of bodies radiating heat. Air hung like a forgotten ornament on a Christmas tree. There were mismatched chairs lined up with their backs to the bay window that looked out on a street already sinking into mournful shadows. It was enough to make a man claustrophobic.

It was, Murphy thought, a hell of a way to spend the evening.

He was acutely aware of dozens of eyes sizing up and measuring him. No one did it so blatantly as the dark-skinned woman behind the reception desk. She could have been anywhere from thirty to fifty and had hair, he noted, that was not found anywhere in nature. It was a bright orange that, on her, somehow seemed to fit.

"Busy evening, Caro?" Shawna asked needlessly.

Caro laughed shortly. It sounded suspiciously like a snort. "You can say that again." Caro laid down her pen and tuned out the waiting-room noise effectively. She'd been raised one of eleven. Tuning things out was second nature to her. Eyes the color of hot chocolate skimmed over Murphy very carefully. "Bring along your own bodyguard, Doctor?"

Shawna glanced at Murphy, her mind already on that coughing child seated to the left of the door. His mother was holding him protectively against her ample bosom. He was about three, she judged. And so painfully thin. "Unwillingly."

Murphy leaned over the desk toward Caro. Her eyes were quick, sharp. And, he'd wager, missed little. There was nothing he admired more than a sharp mind.

"She's crazy about me," he confided to Caro in a stage whisper.

Caro laughed, making up her mind about Murphy immediately. She liked him. "If she ain't, then she's just plain crazy, sugar." The warm eyes lingered over his face and torso appreciatively. "You get tired of chasing around at her heels—" she jerked a thumb at Shawna, who was already on her way to the back "—you can come chase around mine."

Shawna glanced over her shoulder at Murphy. He was two steps behind her, but not for long. "I do believe you have a taker."

Like the front, the hall was small, crammed, with two rooms pigeonholed on one side and matching rooms on the other. The examining rooms were to the left while the doctor's office was on the right. Next to it was the supply room, where everything from files to morphine to coffee were kept. A minuscule bathroom, hardly deserving of the name, rounded out the area.

Murphy had a feeling that if he took in a deep breath his chest would scrape against either wall. "You certainly make a guy feel wanted."

Shawna turned and brushed up against him. She raised her eyes to his as she felt that flash of electricity again. The one she didn't want.

"That was never my intention, Murphy," she retorted. "You were the one who asked to come along for the ride."

"So I was." Murphy leaned over her, lowering his voice. His breath pushed through the stagnant air, caressing her face as he issued a promise, one that seemed to come almost involuntarily, as much a prophecy to him as to her. "The ride hasn't even begun."

She had an uneasy feeling that he was right. And she didn't want him to be. She wanted no more rides, no more lunges at the brass ring. She'd done that once and had fallen off her horse in the end. She wasn't about to hazard it happening again.

"I was beginning to think you weren't coming." The greeting broke the tense moment into a thousand little pieces.

Shawna turned to see Dr. Simon McGuire standing in the doorway of the small room shared by all the doctors who volunteered at the clinic. She glanced unintentionally at Murphy. "So was I."

McGuire shrugged out of his lab coat. His last patient had just walked into the reception area a moment ago and he felt bone weary. Piercing blue eyes that scrutinized everything in their path were already fastening themselves on Murphy. Odd. Shawna never brought anyone with her, never mentioned any sort of a private life whatsoever. He and the other doctors thought she lived and breathed work and nothing more. In his opinion that seemed such a waste for someone so young and attractive.

He raised a brow, regarding Murphy. "I'm Dr. Simon McGuire. And you are?"

"Murphy Pendleton." Murphy extended his hand to the silver-haired man. "Shawna's work in progress."

McGuire shook the offered hand. Despite his age, there was strength in his grip. He looked like one of those men who, a hundred years ago, would have fit well into the life of a mountain man.

He cocked a shaggy brow in Shawna's direction. "There's a translation to this?"

"He's a patient of mine," Shawna muttered. The look of amusement creasing McGuire's lined face had her hastening to add, "I'm attempting to convince him to have surgery. But he came here of his own volition." She crossed to the small locker and took out the white lab coat that was her badge of authority. Slipping it over her dress, she pulled out her hair from beneath it. "It looks like more than the usual full house out there."

"It is," he acknowledged. It had been like that for the past three hours.

McGuire walked with her to the front, then laid a fatherly hand on her shoulder. "I could stay around for a while, give you a hand. There's nothing pressing waiting for me."

Shawna shook her head firmly. "No, I can handle it from here," she assured him. If given half a chance, the man would sleep here. "You need to go home."

A raspy voice followed her words. "She thinks she's mothering me," he confided to Murphy. He had long since given up his desire to set the world on fire. Now he took the time to notice the small things. The smile of a pretty woman was near the top of his list, right after the cry of a healthy baby. "At my age, I love it."

It was safe to flirt with McGuire. Safe and comfortable. He was old enough to be her father by a wide margin. "You need a wife."

He cocked a wicked brow as he made a final notation in Caro's book. "You volunteering?"

But Shawna shook her head as she picked up the first chart. She was already perusing it. "You're too young for me, Simon."

The man chuckled and nodded sagely. "That's what they all say." He looked from Shawna to Murphy, then smiled to himself. "Good night."

A chorus of voices, some loud, some muffled, followed him out the door.

Shawna announced the name on the chart. A boy about seventeen came forward. "First room on the left," she told him, then looked at Murphy doubtfully. "I don't have time to entertain you." She frowned. This was not his element. "I don't know what you're going to do here."

There had to be something he could do, he thought, looking toward Caro. He could tell by the look on her face that she was thinking the same thing.

"Don't worry about me," Murphy assured the back of Shawna's head, "I'll manage."

"Leave him to me," Caro called after Shawna, though the door to exam room one had already closed.

Caro gave Murphy another long, appraising look. The expression she wore said she was trying to find a slot to put him in other than the one he was apparently suited to. His hands were soft, but his smile genuine. He could be worked with.

She glanced at the tall, haphazard manila stack in the corner. She'd been tossing files there all morning. The ones on the bottom were from yesterday. She hadn't found two minutes to rub together in order to get to them.

"How are you at filing, sugar?"

He glanced at the leaning tower of Pisa. "Haven't done it since my law clerk days."

Caro looked up toward the front entrance as a woman with three children hanging on to her walked in. From the looks of it, all four of them were sharing a bug or something. "Alphabet's still the same."

Murphy had already stripped off his jacket. He hung it on the back of the chair next to Caro's reception desk. He began rolling up his sleeves. "Reassuring."

Caro smiled, looking over her shoulder as she saw Murphy pick up the first armload. "She should have brought you along with her months ago."

He grinned. "Be sure you remember to tell her that."

"I will. File bays are on the other side." She pointed to the makeshift shelves her son had put up for them six months ago.

"Yes, ma'am."

Caro laughed softly to herself as she took down the information the woman on the other side of the desk was giving her.

The next three hours were filled to overflowing with people. Murphy saw an endless parade of patients telling Caro that they had everything from colds to intestinal disorders; one man had a relentless rash that was spreading rather rapidly along his extremities.

Shawna handled it all, dispensing medicine, comforting words and advice. She sent one woman to the emergency room of the nearest hospital. The woman needed to see someone with more knowledge in the area of urinary-tract infections than she possessed.

Murphy observed and was duly impressed. He didn't get a chance to talk to her the way he wanted. The only time he even saw her was whenever she came out to deposit a folder on Caro's scarred desk and pick up another. He'd catch bits and pieces of her dialogue with patients then.

He shook his head, watching her disappear into the back for the twentieth time.

"Keeps busy, doesn't she?" Caro commented for his benefit. She'd had time to pass her own judgments on this man Shawna had brought. She liked him. And she hoped that Shawna had the good sense to like him, as well.

Murphy nodded. That was the last of the files, he thought, settling down into a chair near Caro. He'd been filing since they'd arrived at the clinic. He was tired. He could only imagine what Shawna felt like. "I had no idea how busy."

Caro nodded. There was a special place in her heart for the people who ran this clinic, and she felt very protective of them. She was particularly partial to Shawna.

"She's a whiz, all right. Goes on pure energy." She handed Murphy the folder that Shawna had just brought out. Caro grinned as he groaned, reaching for it. "It's almost as if she's trying to outrun something." Caro realized that perhaps she'd said just a little too much. She lifted thin shoulders, then let them fall. "But, hey, we don't question our good fortune."

She'd used the word *our*. "Are you from around here?"

Caro raised her chin proudly. The neighborhood wasn't much, but it defined who she was.

"Born and bred. Left for a while, got a nursing degree," she confided. That was when she had thought of nothing but escape. It had taken her ten years to realize that you couldn't escape who you were. And you always took a piece of the old neighborhood with you. "Then I thought if anyone who ever made anything of themselves left, who was going to stick around to help?"

She sat down for a moment as she thought back to the day she'd made her decision to return. There were no regrets. "So I came back when they opened this clinic." Her lips curved in a cynical smile. "Pay and hours are lousy, but there are rewards."

As if to emphasize what she meant, Shawna emerged, her arm around the shoulders of a girl hardly out of her teens. The girl was holding a fretful baby in her arms. The baby, Shawna had just diagnosed, was allergic to milk. She'd given the girl a list of things she could substitute. Cans of soybean-based formula were peering out of her oversize diaper bag.

Caro looked pointedly at them, then shifted her eyes toward Murphy. He rose, rolling his sleeves back down along his forearms. "I see what you mean."

Shawna dropped the baby's folder on the desk beside Caro. She felt as if she had been dragged around and used as a human mop. A tired, satisfied human mop.

She looked around at the empty chairs as the young mother left. Darkness was attempting to push its way into the clinic, seeking the light. "Is that it?"

"That's it," Caro confirmed. She pulled out a huge floral purse that she kept tucked under the desk. She sighed, glad to call it a day. And a night. She'd put in a fourteen-hour day today, taking over the shift for the woman who worked before her. The woman had come down with the flu. "Guess I'll go home." She stopped halfway to the door. The brown eyes swept up and down Murphy one last time. "Unless you want me to close up?"

Shawna shook her head as she suddenly thought of her mother. Sally was undoubtedly upset about being abandoned this way, and Shawna was far too tired to face going home for a lengthy lecture about how she was using up her life without ever having lived it. The longer she could put it off, the better. "No, I'll take care of it, Caro. You just go home to Jamal."

"Have it your way. Don't say I didn't offer." She turned her attention to Murphy and slid a thin hand along his arm by way of parting. "I'm going home to my own sugar now." She looked at Shawna. She knew what the woman was capable of. "Don't stay too long, you hear?" she warned. "You close up as soon as I go."

Shawna hardly noticed Murphy disappearing to the rear of the clinic as she commented on Caro's warning. "I'm so tired I'm liable to misdiagnose anything that comes in."

"You work too hard, lady."

"Go home."

"Don't have to tell me twice. I'm not the stubborn one." Caro waved as she slipped out the door, closing it behind her.

Shawna turned in time to see Murphy coming toward her with a mug of coffee. She silently blessed him. The only way she was going to make it to her car was if there was caffeine renewing her system. How could a twenty-four-hour day seem as if it had forty-eight hours in it?

She accepted the mug with gratitude as he slipped it into her hands. "So, what did you do?" She took a long, fortifying sip before continuing, "While I cleaned and sutured and medicated?"

"I filed." He gestured to the empty corner.

She vaguely recalled that there had been a tower of files there when she'd entered. And that there had been a collection on either side of Caro's desk. They were all gone.

"You really did that?"

He didn't know why she looked so skeptical about it. "Sure, why not?"

She wrapped both hands around the mug. Though it was still hot in the clinic, there was something comforting about the warmth coming from the mug. Almost as comforting as the warmth in Murphy's eyes.

"Filing isn't beneath you?" There was a hint of amusement in her voice.

He leaned a hip against the desk, looking at her. Even exhausted, there was a radiance about her. How could he have gone through high school and not noticed her, he wondered. "It wasn't as if it was latrine duty. And work that has to be done is not something that's beneath anyone." He waited until she lowered her mug again. "Tell me something."

If she hadn't been so tired, her guard would have gone up. As it was, all she could do was qualify her ability. "If I can."

He crossed his arms before him as he continued studying her. This was an unorthodox way to spend an evening with someone you were interested in, but it had its merits. At least he had gotten to see the real Shawna in action.

"How does an eye specialist wind up volunteering at a free clinic?"

"It needed doing," she said, echoing his earlier sentiment. "Besides, that silver-haired fox you met earlier this evening can be very persuasive. And he said he needed someone to pitch in." It hadn't been a hard sell, really. She had been looking for something just like this to take up her free time. If it hadn't been at this clinic, it would have been at another one. "I'm a doctor first, a specialist second. I know how to diagnose a cold from appendicitis. Besides, since I've come here, I've been boning up.''

''I didn't mean—''

Murphy never got a chance to finish his statement.

When he heard the door behind him open, he realized his error. They should have locked up as soon as Caro left. Now they would have to remain here awhile longer.

With a sigh he turned, and then instinctively froze.

Two men entered. Both were nondescript, of medium height and wearing worn army fatigue jackets that appeared to have come to them secondhand.

Murphy felt every muscle in his body tense. There was an aura about them, the kind he was willing to bet wolves had when they stalked a prey. They weren't here looking for anything that Shawna would willingly dispense.

Murphy moved closer, stepping forward to shield her.

If she was nervous, she had the good sense not to show it.

''I'm Dr. Saunders.'' She looked from one man to the other. The one closer to her had pupils that were larger than they should have been in this light. ''What can I do to help you? We were about to close up.''

The man gestured broadly. His gait was a little unsteady as he took a step toward her.

''You can close if you want to, pretty lady.'' He looked back at his friend for confirmation and then smiled almost foolishly. ''All we want is for you to open the medical cabinet in the back.''

She had known as soon as they entered, although she'd hoped otherwise. They wanted drugs. She concentrated on remaining calm. There was nothing to be gained by panic. ''Nothing but cotton balls, antiseptic and bandages back there,'' she informed him coolly.

The foolish grin faded into something deadly. It made her blood run cold. From the depths of the oversize pockets the first man pulled out a pistol. By street standards it was almost primitive.

But it could blow a hole in her very easily.

Swallowing a curse, Murphy moved in front of Shawna.

The man with the weapon swore viciously. ''Stay out of this,'' he warned Murphy. He jerked his hand toward

Shawna. "Don't lie to me, Doc. Everybody knows you've got some stuff back there." His eyes, wild a moment before, almost shone as he said wistfully, "Stuff to take the edge off the pain."

Was he hurt? She scrutinized him quickly. He hadn't favored anything when he entered. Maybe she could divert him. "What hurts?"

His lips curled away from his teeth. On an animal it would have been a snarl.

"Life, Doc, life. Now get back there and open it." He waved her back. When Murphy moved toward him, the barrel of the gun swung in his direction.

Shawna swallowed a sound born out of fear. Why had she let him come along? "Stay out of this, Murphy."

"Listen to her, jerk. Zach and me are real edgy right now. We get that way without our medicine." He laughed at his own joke, his hand tightening on the gun. Murphy noticed that it was shaking. "Make myself clear?"

Murphy never took his eyes off the man's face. "Very."

"Smart." His head bobbed up and down like a Ping-Pong ball caught in a riptide. "Good. Nobody gets hurt and everyone's happy." It was as if he was saying the words to himself. He roused, blinking his eyes, trying to focus. "Move it, Doc. I don't want to hurt you."

But he would. In an instant. Murphy doubted if the man knew what he was doing. Or cared. "Do as he says, Shawna," Murphy ordered gruffly.

It went against everything she believed in, but there was no arguing with the point of a gun. And she couldn't put Murphy at risk. "All right." Very carefully she turned around, knowing a sudden move might make the man shoot.

Murphy saw the way the gunman's friend was looking at Shawna—as if she were a stick of candy he wanted to unwrap and devour. Murphy didn't believe that they would leave quietly once they got what they wanted. There was too much at stake for him to place his faith in that.

"Move it," the gunman ordered. He was scratching his arm, trying hard to aim the gun.

He was having withdrawals, Shawna thought.

"Sure, anything you say," Murphy agreed, his voice low, soothing. He half turned his body, appearing to follow Shawna into the back. He waited until she was a step farther away and his body was between her and the gunman.

With a cry meant to throw them off, Murphy swung around. One fist went to the gunman's throat while Murphy jerked his hand upward with the other. The gun went off, the bullet lodging itself in the ceiling. Murphy tried to shake the weapon from the man's hand.

In an instant both men were on Murphy, swearing at him and punching wildly.

Shawna grabbed the first thing she could, Caro's portable radio and hit the man on top of Murphy with it. The radio smashed. With a scream the man turned, dazed, and lunged for Shawna.

Murphy saw it out of the corner of his eye. Rage filled him but there wasn't anything he could do to help her. The man who had pointed the gun was swinging at him viciously. Murphy ducked and then swung hard, connecting with the man's nose.

Blood spurted, accompanied by a guttural scream. The sickening crunch told Murphy he'd broken the man's nose. Murphy was frantic to get to the man who was grappling with Shawna.

Adrenaline pumped through his body, giving him strength that he would never have thought he had. Fists flying, Murphy fought the man to the wall. Connecting with his chin, Murphy sent the gunman sinking to the ground like a puppet whose strings had been cut. Free, Murphy almost flew across the room to the other man.

She couldn't pry him loose. He had his hands around her throat and was squeezing it as if he didn't know that he was killing her. As if it were only a game to him, a way of getting even because she had hit him. The room began to go black.

Murphy grabbed the assailant by the shoulder, trying to pull him off Shawna. The man held on as if this was his only purpose in life.

Locking his hands together, Murphy swung hard against the man's head, knocking him over to the side. The assailant's hands loosened from around Shawna's throat.

Murphy grabbed her, holding Shawna to him as she gasped. "It's all right," he soothed. "It's all right."

But it wasn't. He heard movement behind him and knew the first man had gotten up.

Suddenly the outer door crashed open against the opposite wall. The biggest man Murphy had ever seen walked in. There was anger in his eyes and he had the unmistakable smell of death about him.

Murphy held Shawna against him, his mind racing for a way out. This had to be the ringleader, the man in charge. Murphy could tell by the way he moved, by the icy way he regarded the two men in the clinic.

And the way they both froze when he entered.

For a long moment there was only the sound of Shawna trying to pull air into her lungs.

Finally he spoke. The man had a voice like gravel. "Get out of here," he growled at the two men. "Now."

The gunman held his nose. Blood seeped through his hand. "But he—"

"Now." The dark eyes became slits and all the more frightening. "Don't make me say it again."

There was no need. The two men scurried off like mice fleeing from an oncoming flood, squeezing past the big man to get out the door.

He didn't move out of the way.

Within a moment they were gone. The silence in their wake was overwhelming.

Murphy's eyes locked with his, searching for a sign that they hadn't just gone from the precipice into the mouth of the volcano.

Without a word he strode into the clinic. The man was so big around the middle that he wore suspenders because it didn't seem possible that a belt could span that girth. His chest was even bigger. Standing before them, he extended his hand toward Shawna. Her eyes on his, she took it and allowed him to help her to her feet.

"You all right?"

"Yes," she breathed. She felt Murphy's hands tighten on her arm. It helped.

The man nodded.

"I don't know you, do I?" she asked. It was a rhetorical question. She would have remembered someone like him in the clinic. "Who are you?"

"People call me a lot of things." His eyes were unfathomable. Murphy guessed that he'd seen more than most people would want to ask about. "I answer to Mount."

"Short for Mountain," Murphy guessed.

The flash of white teeth was instantaneous. And fleeting. "Yeah." His eyes shifted to Shawna. "They won't bother you anymore. You've got my word."

She knew it was a promise. "Thank you."

Murphy wasn't satisfied. He regarded the tall man. This was not your average, garden-variety Samaritan. "Why did you come and help us?"

"Not you," he said to Murphy. He pointed a thick finger at Shawna. "Her. You patched up my little sister the other night." He nodded, as if conferring with himself. "You're okay. We could use your kind around."

Shawna passed a hand over her throat. Murphy was at her back and she found that infinitely comforting at the moment. "I don't know how to thank you."

There was no discomfort at the comment and hardly an acknowledgment.

"You already did. By coming here." Mount was already easing out the front door. "I'll be around." His eyes held hers one last time. "Don't let them scare you off."

She shook her head. "I won't."

He smiled then. A small, tight smile that softened his hard features that the street had hammered in from an early age. Then it vanished, leaving behind no trace.

"Didn't think so."

He walked out without bothering to close the door. The night swallowed him up before he had taken half a dozen steps.

Chapter Nine

Moving the dead bolt into position, Murphy turned around and crossed to Shawna. She looked whiter than the lab coat she was wearing.

When he placed his hand on her shoulder, she sagged against him. He was afraid that she was going to faint. Holding her to him, he looked at her face.

No, she wasn't going to faint. She was far too strong for that. He could see it in her eyes. "Do you want me to call the police?"

Shawna shook her head, unable to speak for a minute. The full impact of what might have been had hit her and she was trying to push it away as quickly as she could. "No. It wouldn't do any good and nothing was stolen."

There were a great many more violent crimes in the area. The police had their hands full. Besides, there had to be a better way to handle this.

He studied her face, trying to second-guess her. "You don't want the publicity."

He was blunt, but he had also gotten to the heart of it. "That's right. I want this to go on being a little clinic that people feel safe coming to. And once you know something bad happened in a place, it's never the same again."

She had a point. And though he didn't like her being here more than ever, it was probably less dangerous for her now than before. "I see what you're getting at. And I suppose you do have yourself a rather large guardian angel now."

Mount hardly looked as if he fit the part of an avenging angel. But there was no doubting the fact that the big man had appointed himself the clinic's protector. More important, that he had appointed himself *her* protector. That went a long way in reassuring Murphy.

She nodded. "I think word'll spread about Mount. Nobody's going to try to break in or bother us with him to worry about." It sounded good. Shawna looked down at her hands. "So why am I shaking like this?"

Murphy moved behind her and slowly slipped his arms around hers, embracing her. Offering comfort and warmth. The sexual pull was only a by-product.

But it was there.

For both of them.

"Because you're human." His breath fluttered along her temple. It soothed and aroused her. "I was really beginning to wonder about that earlier. Even that pink rabbit with the drum needs batteries once in a while."

She turned slowly, her body brushing against his. She felt so many things right now it was confusing. But predominately, she felt grateful that he was here with her. "Never saw anyone change them."

Murphy winked. "They do it during the programs so that he can keep running during the commercials."

He said it so seriously she couldn't help laughing. "Oh." It felt good to laugh, good to release the tension that had her in a vise grip. The laugh turned into a sob. What if he had been hurt? She'd never have forgiven herself for bringing him along.

Murphy's heart wrenched within his chest. He wouldn't allow himself to dwell on what might have happened to her. Gently he stroked her hair, holding her to him. "Yeah, I know. I know."

GET 4 BOOKS
A FLUFFY DUCK
AND A MYSTERY GIFT

Return this card, and we'll send you 4 specially selected Silhouette Special Editions absolutely FREE! We'll even pay the postage and packing for you!

We're making this offer to introduce you to the benefits of Reader Service: FREE home delivery of brand-new romances at least a month before they're available in the shops, FREE gifts and a monthly Newsletter packed with information.

Accepting these FREE books places you under no obligation to buy, you may cancel at any time simply by writing to us — even after receiving just your free shipment.

← TEAR OFF AND POST THIS CARD TODAY ←

Yes, please send me 4 free Silhouette Special Editions, a fluffy duck and a mystery gift. I understand that unless you hear from me, I will receive 6 superb new titles every month for just £2.20* each postage and packing free. I am under no obligation to purchase any books and I may cancel or suspend my subscription at any time, but the free books and gifts will be mine to keep in any case.

(I am over 18 years of age).

6S5SE

Ms/Mrs/Miss/Mr _____

Address _____

_____

_____ Postcode _____

*Prices subject to change without notice.

Get 4 books a fluffy duck and mystery gift FREE!

SEE OVER FOR DETAILS

And somehow, she knew he did. Somehow, he was privy to all the emotions that were ricocheting through her. Feeling foolish, Shawna scrubbed her face with her hands to erase the tearstains. She took a deep, cleansing breath and released it before she looked at him.

He had the beginnings of a bruise just below his right eye. A bruise and a superficial cut. The latter matched the one over his temple. It took very little imagination to think of what other blows he must have taken during the fight. "Are you all right?"

He tightened his arms around her and grinned. "Right about now, I'd say I was great."

This wasn't the time for his humor. On closer examination, it looked like a nasty bruise. "I'm serious."

The laughter receded just a little from his eyes. "So am I."

And in a way, that scared him, he thought. She felt so right just where she was. Too right. And he knew where that could lead—to mistakes being made.

Why shouldn't she feel right? She was beautiful, and he was a man. There wasn't anything more to it than that, he silently insisted.

Impatience bubbled in Shawna. Didn't he realize the kind of danger he was in, walking around with that blood clot? "He could have hit you in the head."

Murphy ran his fingertips lightly along the tender area beneath his eye. He was probably going to have a black eye tomorrow. Thank God he didn't have to be in court to plead a case. "He did."

"I meant—" There was no sense in continuing, not until she could talk him into having the surgery. She blew out a surrendering sigh. "Sit down—let me tend to that." She wanted to clean the cut before it became infected.

Murphy shrugged, unwilling to be fussed over. "It'll be all right."

The hell it would. She could put up with just so much obstinacy. She pointed to Caro's chair. "Sit."

"Yes, ma'am."

Shawna waited until Murphy planted his rear on the chair, then hurried to the back to get what she needed to clean the wound.

Murphy raised his voice. "Ever think about training animals as a sideline?"

Shawna emerged from the back, a tube of antiseptic in one hand, applicator and bandage in the other. She set everything down on the reception desk. Taking the tip of his chin in her hand, she tilted his head back toward the light for a better view.

It probably looked worse than it was, she judged. And it would look even worse tomorrow. "Are you equating yourself to an animal?"

He tried not to wince as she applied some sort of ointment to the cut. "Maybe. What kind would I be?" He tried to focus on her and found that she was just a little murky. He refused to let that worry him. It would pass. "Panther?"

She stopped and looked down into his face. "Pussycat."

"Ouch." The response was to her term, not her ministering. He sat perfectly still as she cleaned away the residue. "At least say ocelot." He paused, but she didn't take up his suggestion as she tossed aside the cotton swab and covered the bruise with a bandage. "For a pussycat, I think I defended us pretty well."

"Yes." Her eyes met his. "Yes, you did." She recapped the tube of ointment and twisted it closed. "And if it hadn't been for you, that man would have choked me to death."

He didn't like seeing that wisp of fear dancing through her. She shouldn't have to deal with something like that. "All in a day's work as a superhero." He purposely teased the hoop at her ear, sending it swaying.

"From pussycat to superhero. Some leap."

He raised one hand innocently. The other he rested not so innocently on the swell of her hip, holding her in place. "Tall buildings in a single bound, that's me."

She started to laugh at the absurdity of the conversation. He knew how to make her feel better. "Murphy?"

"Yes?"

"Shut up."

Catching her completely off guard, Murphy pulled her unceremoniously onto his lap. "Make me."

Shawna twined her arms and rested them around his neck. It felt as if she belonged right here. If she was honest with herself, she knew there wasn't anywhere that she would have rather been at this moment.

That was just the trouble.

She knew she was being too vulnerable again. But just for a moment, if she kept a tight rein on her emotions, she could enjoy this.

Just for a moment.

Leaning her face down to his, Shawna brushed her lips across his. It was over before it began.

Murphy had other ideas.

"Good." He nodded his head as if he were judging a sample of pie in a competition at a county fair. "Good start." A smile coaxed its way from his lips to hers. "Now do it again. With feeling."

Before she could protest, he cupped the back of her head with his hand and leaned forward, kissing her. Really kissing her. All the stops had been pulled out. He'd almost lost her and the emotion that thought generated overwhelmed them both. If the nagging thought whispered along the corners of his mind that this was getting out of hand, that this had the potential of being far more serious than he wanted it to be, he ignored it.

The tidal wave came for her immediately, without warning, without a single alarm going off. Without allowing her to swim for shore. Shawna was swept completely away, drowning in him, in the swirling waters that surrounded her and pulled her under.

Her arms tightened around his neck, encircling him without her conscious consent.

All she could think of was him. Her mouth slanted over and over again, meeting every onslaught. Losing the battle for her soul.

She tasted of fear, of excitement, and everything he had ever dreamed of feasting on. She was like a trip into virtual reality after a lifetime of looking at two-dimensional black-and-white drawings.

Hold it.

The warning throbbed in his head, admonishing him to back off and reassess the situation. He was getting in over his head. Things were happening more swiftly than they ever had before. Relationships had a natural progression for him and this was an entirely unnatural state.

Too fast, too fast.

Yet he couldn't pull himself free of the whirlpool he was in, couldn't summon the strength to do it.

She didn't want to stop but knew she had to. She wanted to make love with him too much not to give in if they didn't leave now. Immediately.

Shawna jerked her head away, her breath ragged. Unable to steady it, she leaned her forehead against his, hoping he wouldn't notice how rattled she was. Hoping if he did, that he'd think it was due to the assault and not him.

"It's getting late—we'd better go," she murmured.

Her breath, sweet and enticing, wafted along his face. Everything within him tightened like a coil, ready to spring.

"You're absolutely right." He left his hands resting comfortably on her hips. With the slightest bit of encouragement he'd willingly go on to explore new terrain, despite all the alarms going off in his head. "So why don't I feel like getting up?"

One of them had to make the first move, before there was no turning back. "Because you're lazy." She allowed herself one quick caress along his cheek before she rose.

He'd hardly noticed her weight when she was on his lap. So how was it possible that the lack of it could create such a sense of loss?

He jerked a thumb toward the rear of the clinic. Survival, his own, lay in playing the part of a Casanova. "Sure I couldn't interest you in taking me into one of the back rooms for a thorough exam?"

She was becoming accustomed to the smiles he pulled from her, like a magician lifting an endless supply of rabbits from his hat. Even in the aftermath of the attempted robbery, he made her feel good.

"I don't think that's necessary." Ducking into the office, she took off her lab coat. "Besides, I'm a doctor. I don't *play* doctor.'' She picked up her purse and slung it over her shoulder.

"Too bad.'' Murphy laced his fingers through hers and began to lead her to the front door. "C'mon, let me drive you home.''

"We came in *my* car,'' she reminded him.

He flipped the lock after taking a cursory look outside through the door. The street was empty. "I can still drive.''

She was going to argue that he wasn't in any condition to drive, but maybe he was. Maybe he was in better condition than she was, at least emotionally.

"All right.''

Murphy got in behind the wheel, feeling in control again. For the time being.

Murphy slowly brought Shawna's car to a stop beside his own in the deserted parking lot. The eight-story edifice at the far end was completely dark, a testimony to the fact that everyone in the world with half a brain had gone home for the night.

For the last few miles he had been aware of a dull buzz, accompanied by an even duller ache in his head. It had made him just the slightest bit nervous. But Shawna had drifted to sleep the first mile into the trip home and he didn't want to wake her just to complain about it. Knowing her, she wouldn't have reassured him, anyway. More likely than not, she would have insisted on another one of those iron lung tests. He wasn't in the mood to lie still in a silver tube. Not unless she was lying there next to him.

He had his doubts about how still he'd remain.

The symptoms were probably just a leftover calling card from the altercation in the clinic. He'd be fine in the morning. Better than ever.

Murphy pulled up the hand brake and turned off the engine. He was tempted to just sit here and watch her sleep, but he knew she would be better off in bed. His, he wished. But he knew hers would be the bed of choice. And a solitaire choice at that. Maybe that was for the best.

Very slowly he brushed a kiss along her brow. She stirred and said something he couldn't quite make out.

He kissed her again. This time her eyes flew open in surprise. He leaned back. "We're here."

"Here?" Shawna bolted upright, like a jack-in-the-box with a delayed release. She looked around, slightly bewildered by her surroundings. The last thing she remembered was pulling out onto the street by the clinic.

"The parking lot by your office. We left my car here, remember?" He gestured to it on her right. She looked too tired to drive. "I could take you home."

She shook off the last layers of sleep from her brain as she dragged a hand through her hair. "No."

"You haven't heard which home yet."

Why did she find the fact that he never stopped pitching at her endearing? It was supposed to be irritating, the way it had been before.

"Mine," she told him. With effort, she opened the door and got out. The cool breeze helped wake her up. "I can drive myself home. It's only a few blocks from here."

Getting out, he came around to stand beside her. "I could follow you and let myself be invited in for a nightcap." He stood over her for a moment, just a man and a woman in a deserted parking lot. For lack of a desert island, it would have to do. "You know, the damsel in distress thanking her knight."

She knew where he wanted it to lead. Where she wanted it to lead. And where she wasn't ready to let it lead. "I'll give you a rain check."

He spread his hands wide before him. "Knights rust in the rain."

"I'll keep a can of oil handy." She rounded the hood, then stopped at the driver's side. She bit her lip uncertainly as she looked at his car, thinking of the potential time bomb he insisted on walking around with. "Are you sure you're all right?"

"Other than a deflated ego." He gave a perfunctory nod, then stopped midway. The sensation of pins and needles being jabbed around the region of his eye wouldn't abate. "I'm fine."

Something in his expression alerted her. "You're lying."

"Lawyers never lie. They just find different ways to approach the truth." He sighed, unwilling to call an end to the night. "Certainly can't say that you're a dull date."

Amusement quirked her mouth before she could stifle it. "Was that what this was? A date?"

"Yeah." The look that washed over her was warm, compelling. It reeled her in as surely as if she were a nickel goldfish on the end of a line. "And I'd like to say painless, but..." He let the word slip into the darkness as he drew closer to her. "You're going to have bruises of your own tomorrow."

He touched her throat lightly and silently cursed her attacker. He'd never wanted to kill anyone before. Had he had half the chance, he wasn't able to say what the outcome would have been.

She shrugged a little too carelessly. The bruises on her throat were the least of it. "I have this new scarf I've been meaning to wear."

He had an early meeting to get to tomorrow. Murphy moved to his car and unlocked the door. He looked over his shoulder at her before getting in. "Slip into a hot tub tonight and think of me."

The problem was, she knew she would. "Go home, Murphy, and get some rest."

"You should talk." He was almost inside the car when he remembered. "See you Saturday at eleven?"

"Saturday?" she echoed. Had she told him that she would see him in her office on a weekend?

She'd forgotten. Murphy was amazed. There was no space for anything in that woman's head but work. "Harmony's birthday party," he prompted. Even in the moonlight he could see the protests multiplying in her mind. "After tonight, meeting my relatives should be a snap."

Unconsciously she ran her hand along her throat. It felt raw. "I guess I owe you something."

That wasn't why he wanted her to come. "Not me— yourself, Shawna. You owe yourself something."

He came to her side and kissed her lightly. Then he got into his car before he was tempted to deepen the kiss, to show her the error of her ways. He might ache from the struggle at the clinic, but that wasn't the most persistent ache that was battering his body.

Murphy waited until Shawna pulled out of the parking lot before he started his own car. And began to wonder all over again where this was leading. He hadn't the faintest clue. All he knew was that he was bound to follow the path.

He couldn't help himself. He didn't like it, but it didn't change what was.

Shaking his head, he pulled out of the lot.

She didn't know about this.

Shawna looked at her reflection in the closet mirror. She just didn't know.

It was one thing to have Murphy dog her tracks. To have him pop up unannounced and unappointmented at her office and follow her to the clinic. She had no control over his behavior. It was another thing entirely to dress up with the intention of going out with him. Anywhere. It changed the game plan.

And the game was going over the falls in a barrel.

She wasn't cut out for this.

She hadn't had even so much as one date in high school. No one had asked her. In college, she and Doug had met in the first class she had ever walked into. They hadn't dated as much as just been around each other. Their relationship had begun with their studying together. Only later did it work its way up into something that had nothing to do with their grades or their future careers.

And it all seemed light-years away now. Able to perform complex eye surgeries with enviable ease, Shawna hadn't the slightest idea how to behave on a so-called date. Nerves threatened to swallow her whole. She could very easily get to hate this, she thought as she slipped on her shoes.

"You look lovely."

Startled, Shawna looked up and saw her mother's reflection in the mirror. She was standing in the doorway of the bedroom, looking at her.

Sally crossed to Shawna in small, graceful steps, as if she were playing to some invisible audience. "What a lovely girl you are."

The label hardly seemed to fit. In all likelihood her mother had forgotten how old she was. Birthdays, both her own and her mother's, were forgotten with regularity when she was growing up.

Shawna turned to face her. "I'm thirty."

"I'm older," Sally responded whimsically. "You're a girl." The discussion ended there. Sally ran her hand lightly along her daughter's hair. Shawna sensed ambivalent feelings in the way her mother looked at her. "Why didn't you ever dress up like this when you were in high school?"

It was an old song, with an old refrain to match. "I was too busy studying."

That made no sense to Sally. She had always preferred the company of people to that of books. She always needed to see herself admired in someone else's eyes. With a sigh, Sally supposed Shawna was luckier that way. She didn't seem to need that sort of thing.

"You could have found a whole new way to study anatomy."

Shawna raised a brow. One of them playing house while she was growing up had been enough. Her mother had had four husbands and Shawna had lost count of the number of boyfriends who had been potential husbands until they fell into her mother's disfavor. "Mother."

Sally frowned. "Oh, don't tell me that you're still a prude."

Shawna took exception to the term. She'd never been a prude. She just didn't believe that a woman always had to have a man at her side to be complete. There had been a great many men in her mother's life and she had never seemed complete.

"No, but—"

"Good." Sally moved around the room like a butterfly looking for somewhere to light. "You had me worried for a minute." Her eyes shifted toward her daughter. There were lost opportunities here, hers and Shawna's. "I had hopes that you'd open up a little. You can't live if you don't."

Shawna didn't want to get into this now. She was having difficulty taming the upheavals in her stomach. Why had she agreed to this party? She didn't know anyone who was going to be there, not really.

"I'm doing fine, Mother." The words were ground out between teeth that hardly moved.

"Are you?" Sally hesitated before plunging onward. "Look, I know I wasn't exactly like Carol Brady when you were growing up..."

The reference to the fictional perfect mother of six made Shawna smile despite the jumbo jets waiting for clearance in her abdomen. Her mother couldn't raise one child—what in the world would she have done with six? "More like Auntie Mame." Her tone was devoid of censure. Her mother was what she was.

Sally's eyes darted to look at Shawna's face. There was a hopeful look in her own. She had done a great many things wrong, probably more than she was aware of, she estimated. "It was fun, wasn't it, honey? A little?"

"A little," Shawna agreed.

What was the point in saying otherwise? Nothing would be changed, and she didn't want to cause her mother any grief or remorse. She was confident that somewhere, deep down, the woman was aware of her own shortcomings.

With absolution in hand, Sally brightened visibly. She placed her arm around her daughter's shoulders, one sorority sister to another.

"Anyway, I might not have the right to tell you what to do now—to *suggest* what you do now," she amended quickly when she saw a glint enter Shawna's eyes. If nothing else, Sally was versed in the art of survival and saying the right things. "But if someone's interested in you, don't turn your back on that."

"You don't even know him," Shawna observed.

The smile on Sally's face bloomed and spread like a sped-up video of a budding morning glory. "That's easily fixed. He's coming to pick you up, isn't he?"

Alarms went off in Shawna's head. "Leave him alone, Mother."

"Protective." Sally nodded her head, pleased. Shawna had no idea what her mother was going on about. "Good sign. You always were a good protector, honey. There were times I thought of you as the mother and me as the kid, even when you were small.''

''That makes two of us,'' Shawna murmured under her breath as she went to answer the doorbell, which had mercifully chosen this moment to peal.

It was the first time she'd been relieved to see Murphy standing in a doorway. But the relief faded, absorbed like a spill by a paper towel as her nerves reemerged. She could almost feel his eyes slide over her.

She shrugged self-consciously. ''I didn't know what to wear.''

It was his opinion that she probably would have looked good in anything. As long as he hung on to the fact that this was just physical between them, he'd be all right. It was admitting anything else that would undermine him.

''Cellophane comes to mind, but there will be children there.'' He brushed a kiss quickly over her lips before she had a chance to protest his comment or his action. ''Anything you're comfortable in would be my second recommendation.'' She was wearing a light pink dress that fluttered about her body like a spring breeze when she moved. The halter top made him want to slide his hand along her bare back. ''Like that.''

She'd changed three times. Nothing felt right. Or looked it. ''I'm comfortable in my lab coat.''

''Given the right accessories that would work.'' He didn't mention that the accessories he had in mind ran into sheer black lace. ''This isn't going to be easy, is it?'' He laughed at the scowl on her face.

He stopped when he saw the woman on the other side of the small living room. There was more than a passing resemblance. Given a guess, he would have said that she was Shawna's older sister, except that he knew Shawna was an only child.

Murphy felt Shawna tense slightly at his side. He laced his hand through Shawna's, then nodded toward the other woman. ''Mrs. Rowen?''

When her daughter finally picked them, she really picked them. Sally's smile was wide and appreciative. If he hadn't belonged to Shawna, she would have been tempted to flirt with him herself.

"Sally," she corrected as she floated across the small space to stand next to him. She extended her hand to Murphy, employing the same mannerisms a queen might when she offered her ring to be kissed.

Mother always knew how to make an entrance, Shawna thought. Even in a tiny apartment like this one. She saw the light of approval in her mother's eyes and for a moment wondered if she would attempt to make a play for Murphy. Murphy Pendleton was just the type of man Sally Rowen gravitated to. Young, virile and exciting.

Her other hand now wrapped around Murphy's, Sally looked at her daughter. "Shawna, you never said he was this gorgeous."

"What did she say about me?" Murphy asked, amused. Shawna's makeup didn't hide the flush of pink that rose to her cheeks.

Sally shook her head. "Nothing."

He grinned as he casually broke the connection between them. Murphy hooked his arm through Shawna's. "That's what I thought."

Sally noticed the faint trace of a bruise beneath his eye. A brute. How wonderful. "Did you get into a fight?"

Shawna shot Murphy a warning glance. She'd said nothing to her mother about the incident at the clinic. There was no point in worrying the woman or in opening herself up to lectures. "He raced into a burning building to save a little girl."

Sally clapped her hands together, delighted. "A hero."

"Not exactly," Murphy interjected, then turned and looked at Shawna. "Why don't you take a few lessons from your mother?" he asked teasingly.

Sally needed no more to set her on course. "I'm afraid she's hopeless when it comes to simple appreciation. Lord knows I've tried." She gestured at Shawna, talking as if she wasn't even in the room. "I've never seen her this dressed up before." Like a tennis ball that had been lobbed back across the net, Sally turned her attention to Murphy. "You seem to have more of an influence on her than I do. Do you think you could—''

Murphy had a feeling that the woman could probably talk nonstop all day and all night if she was allowed to. He had no intention of allowing her to. ''I'm supposed to be in charge of the pony, so we'd better go.''

Sally stared and wondered what he was up to. It sounded interesting. ''Pony?''

He was already steering Shawna out the door. ''It's a long story,'' he told Sally over his shoulder. ''Nice meeting you, Mrs. Rowen.''

''Sally,'' she called after them. ''Mrs. Rowen makes me feel too old.''

''We could bring her along,'' Murphy offered, amusement playing along his lips as he closed the door behind them.

Shawna shook her head. ''*You* could bring her along.''

He grinned. ''Need a respite?''

She felt a little overwhelmed by it all. ''What do you think?''

He brought her to his car. ''I think it's nice to be the cavalry once in a while. One respite coming up.''

She had her doubts about that, she thought as she got into his car. She sincerely had her doubts about that.

Chapter Ten

Murphy was aware of the tension sharing the car with them as soon as he got behind the steering wheel. He wondered if it was the party she was going to or the woman she had left behind that was responsible for the rigid set of her shoulders.

He took a stab at exploring the latter. "I like your mother."

Her mother had all but handed Shawna to Murphy on a silver platter, as if she were an hors d'oeuvre that had just been whipped up in the kitchen. Embarrassment and annoyance were vying for the center stage within her.

"Most men do." Shawna stopped, then looked at Murphy. "Did that sound a little bitter?"

"Maybe a touch."

She saw the smile that lightly curved his mouth. Was he amused by it? Maybe he had a right to be. To him it seemed like a typical mother-daughter tug-of-war. How could he know that there was so much more to it?

"I guess it was." She didn't want him getting the wrong impression. Shawna looked through the car window. They were headed toward a somewhat more rural section of town. The peaceful scenery calmed her.

"I didn't mind her getting attention when I was growing up. I just minded it cutting into our time. Our time." She repeated the phrase with a deprecating laugh. It sounded foreign to her ear. Foreign to her life. Sally Rowen had always been too preoccupied with the next date, the next man, to make time for her daughter. "As if we had any." She sighed. Shawna was long past recriminations. But the hurt had a way of lingering. "She was always going out, or getting ready to go out. Between that and her job, I hardly saw her."

The road from Bedford to Kelly's home was a long, winding one, with trees on either side of the narrow, ribbonlike path. Though he was more than familiar with the way, Murphy still had to remain alert in order not to miss the turnoff that led to her neighborhood.

But the wistful note in Shawna's voice was interfering with his concentration. His life had been a complete contrast to hers. Growing up, he'd never known what it was like not to trip over someone at home. It had been a full house, and his family had always been there for him.

"Sounds lonely." He glanced at her, maintaining one eye on the road. "What about your father?"

Shawna lifted a shoulder and let it fall. "I have no idea who he is." Her voice was distant, flat, as if she were deliberately keeping her emotions out of it. "She never mentioned him."

"Didn't you ever ask?" He knew he would have.

"Once."

If she let herself, Shawna could vividly recall the scene. It had been her tenth birthday, and her mother was going out. In typical careless fashion, she'd completely forgotten what day it was. Hurt, Shawna had lashed out the only way she knew how. She'd demanded to know who her father was, confident in her ignorance that *he* would remember what day it was. She'd never received an answer.

"My mother became very quiet, very pale. She looked as if I'd just run a jagged glass bottle over a gaping wound."

It had shaken her into silence. "So I never brought him up again."

It seemed inconceivable that curiosity hadn't motivated her when she had become a grown woman. "But you wondered, didn't you?"

She shrugged again as she saw the path ahead of them widen. Large, single-story houses began appearing in the distance. "What good would it do? He'd left a long time ago and I managed."

He thought she'd phrased it rather oddly. "You mean you both managed."

She had no idea why she was telling him all this, only that somehow, once again, he was drawing things out of her, things that hurt like nettles being pulled across the tender flesh of her palm.

"From a very early age I discovered that my mother needed a mother." Shawna watched as the sun hopscotched through openings in the nearby trees, shining intensely whenever it was able. It made her think of her mother, bright, sunny at the least hint of affection being bestowed on her. "She was an orphan. Maybe that was what created her endless quest for love."

As she spoke, Murphy caught glimpses of the little girl Shawna had been. Hurt, lonely. He placed a hand over hers, offering mute comfort. "Seems to me she was looking in all the wrong places."

She knew what he was telling her. He understood. "You don't expect it to be in your own backyard."

The house just up ahead was a wide, sprawling single-story ranch house with a rustic-looking rail fence framing the front lawn. Kelly and Thomas had moved here from Thomas's house shortly after Harmony's birth, wanting something that was neither "his" nor "hers," but theirs.

Murphy pulled up along the curb, squeezing into one of the last remaining spots. There were cars all along both sides of the road. "That's where some people are mistaken."

She gathered her purse to her, ready to get out. This, too, she understood. "You're getting serious again."

"And you're evading again." He placed a hand on her arm. Now that they were here, he was in no hurry to join the party. He wanted her to himself for a little while.

The look in his eyes was easy to read. She knew what he was thinking—exactly what she had been thinking. What she couldn't, under any circumstances, let happen. Having her heart torn out of her chest once was all a person should be required to allow.

Shawna withdrew her hand from beneath his. "I don't want this, Murphy. I don't want any entanglements, any promises."

They were going to come together, to make love passionately. It was just a matter of time. He knew that and so did she.

"Then we won't make any promises, except that there'll *be* no promises." Humor lifted the corners of his mouth as his eyes coaxed her to relent. "Fair enough?"

He put out his hand, waiting for her to take it, to accept the terms he was offering. No strings, no attachments. It was what they both wanted. Being mature adults, it was something they could both live with, as well.

After a beat, Shawna took his hand. He could see by the look in her eyes that she was afraid that taking it meant tacitly giving her consent to whatever it was that followed.

"I'd be very careful what I was agreeing to if I were you," she heard a male voice say.

Shawna turned to see Thomas bending over, peering into the car window.

"He's a slippery one," Thomas told her. He opened the passenger door and stepped aside. When she got out of the car, he offered her his hand. "Hi." He smiled at her warmly. "I'm Thomas Sheridan, in case you don't remember."

Murphy was quick to place a proprietary arm around Shawna. "She remembers. She's got a great memory."

Thomas did nothing to hide his amusement. Whether he knew it or not, Murphy was very interested in this woman. He and Murphy exchanged looks and Murphy gave an involuntary shrug, reinforcing his rakish smile.

"Then I'd be embarrassed if I were you." Thomas turned toward Shawna. "Fortunately, I'm not him." Expertly he extricated her from beneath Murphy's arm. "C'mon, let me introduce you around."

Murphy maneuvered to Shawna's other side. "Thomas has gotten a lot pushier since high school."

"That's charm," Thomas corrected.

His eyes shifted from his best friend to Shawna. If he wasn't mistaken, he saw a little of himself within her, the way he'd been too many years ago to count. That first time, Murphy had brought him home because Thomas, new to the school, had taken Murphy's part against a bully in the school yard. Thomas had been seven, living his life as an outsider. It took the Pendletons and their warmth to make him feel alive. She could use a little of that, he mused, looking at Shawna.

"Murphy," he confided in a stage whisper, "wouldn't know charm if it raised its head and bit him."

"If it bit me, it wouldn't be charm, now, would it?" Murphy turned his back on Thomas, his attention solely on Shawna. "He's got a lot to learn about charm."

"Those of us with a genuine supply of charm," Thomas countered, tongue in cheek, "don't need to learn anything about it."

Caught between the two men and this so-called argument, put on solely for her benefit, Shawna laughed, entertained. "This I remember."

Murphy looked at her, his brows drawn together into a single line. "'This'?"

She nodded. "You two were always being competitive in high school." She had watched and secretly envied them their friendship then.

"Competitive?" Thomas echoed. He made the most of the three-inch difference in height as he looked down his nose at Murphy. "Why would I compete against him? It wouldn't be a fair match."

"My sentiments exactly," Murphy told Thomas. Then his eyes shifted to Shawna. Pleasure filled him. She looked relaxed at last. "I never challenge an unarmed man."

Murphy pushed open the unlocked door. A wall of noise and mingling voices greeted them. Shawna looked around the sun-splashed living room with its wide, comfortable pieces of furniture. There were too many people here, she thought.

Murphy sensed her unease immediately. He leaned his head in toward hers. "They're just people, Shawna," he whispered. He straightened, his voice rising to a conversation level as he continued. "They get dressed like everyone else. Except maybe for Thomas." He looked over his shoulder as his brother-in-law joined them. "We haven't figured out just what he is yet."

"Proud," Kelly told her brother, coming to her husband's defense. She slipped her arm through Thomas's. The flash of intimacy between them stirred a sense of longing within Shawna that she quickly dismissed as foolish. But it lingered just on the fringes. "Very, very proud."

Murphy raised an eyebrow. "Yeah, like everybody's kid doesn't have a first birthday."

"Harmony's special," Kelly said defensively, though a smile played on her lips.

Harmony was *very* special. To the whole family. Her golden-haired daughter was the child Kelly had been afraid she would never have.

"Did you ever notice how cynical he's been getting? That's what comes of leading the life of a confirmed bachelor." Kelly had aimed the remark at Thomas and Shawna. She stopped abruptly, realizing her mistake. Her eyes instantly filled with an unspoken apology. Murphy merely waved the matter away.

But not before Shawna saw it.

She wondered what was being silently communicated between brother and sister, because something obviously was.

Shawna looked at the group around them. From her vantage point she could see more people in the kitchen and the family room. The window on the side looked out on the backyard, where there were even more people. Murphy had said that it was going to be a family party. This was the largest family she'd ever seen outside of the Kennedys'.

She turned to Kelly. "Is everyone here related to each other?"

Kelly nodded. "One way or another." She separated Shawna from her brother. The woman needed a breather, she suspected, another woman to turn to. "Some we've adopted. Come." She nodded toward another room. "I'd like to introduce you to my pride and joy."

Thomas slipped his arm around Kelly's waist. It had taken him a long time to realize that he was in love with her. There was a lot of time to make up for. "She's already met me."

Kelly disengaged herself. "Boy, one baby and they think they invented the process," she confided to Shawna with a wink. "I was talking about Harmony," she told Thomas.

Kelly threaded her arm through Shawna's as if they were lifelong friends and then led her away. Kelly had never had trouble making friends. She had a manner that made *everyone* feel as if they were her friend. With the eye of a veteran hostess, she looked around the room. Everything was going smoothly.

"Thanks for coming."

Shawna laughed, thinking of the way Murphy had maneuvered her into this.

"I didn't seem to have a choice." She stopped abruptly, feeling the flush creep along her neck. *Boy, take the woman out of the operating room...* "Not that—" She sighed. Kelly, she knew instinctively, would be the type to appreciate honesty. "Sorry, I get a little tongue-tied in crowds."

Compassion flooded through Kelly. She had never had a problem around people. The more, the better. But she could still sympathize. "Is that why you never spoke very much?"

Shawna looked at her, confused.

"In high school," Kelly clarified. "You were two grades ahead of me, but we had the same lunch period. You used to sit at that lunch table in the corner, all by yourself, studying. I thought you were probably the most intelligent person I'd ever seen."

Shawna laughed softly. The truth was that she had been shy. Painfully shy. "Books were a buffer. They didn't make me feel awkward or inadequate."

"Inadequate?" From what she remembered, Shawna, with her perfect grade average, had been more than adequate.

Shawna nodded. It was almost painful to remember the way she'd been. She'd progressed light-years from then, but there was a part of her that still felt like that sixteen-year-old girl.

"I had braces, glasses, and I was always the new kid in school." Kelly urged a soft drink on her. Shawna accepted the can gratefully. "By the time I went to Bedford High, I'd been to eight different schools. Two in one year once."

That had been a particularly rough year, she recalled. Her mother had divorced Jack and tried to put as much distance between herself and her ex as she could. The country was pockmarked with men Sally had left behind for one reason or another.

Kelly had never had to make those kinds of adjustments. She was living exactly ten miles away from the house she'd grown up in.

She smiled at Shawna sympathetically. "Was your father in the service?"

There was no point in saying anything about her nonexistent father, or the fact that she suspected that she was probably illegitimate.

She merely shook her head. "My mother liked to travel. I think she was looking for the end of the rainbow," she added lightly. "It was always over the next hill." She looked down at the soft-drink can in her hand. "There were a lot of schools on those hills."

It was an experience that could easily have driven a person into herself, Kelly judged. She'd seen the discomfort in Shawna's eyes when she looked at the sea of faces.

"Well, this crowd is harmless. I know you'll have a nice time." The way she said it left little room for doubt on either on their parts. She placed a sisterly hand on Shawna's arm and waited until the latter had lifted her eyes to hers. "Like I said, I'm very glad you could make it."

She had eyes like Murphy's, Shawna thought. Like warm turquoise stones bathed in the sun. "Why?" Why should it make a difference to Kelly if she came or not? They really didn't know each other.

"Because you're the first person Murphy's brought around in a long time whose intelligence exceeds her dress size."

The description brought a smile to Shawna's face. "Maybe he's just looking for a change of pace."

If he was, Kelly took it as a hopeful sign. "I hope so. After Janice..."

Damn, she'd done it again. What was it about this afternoon that had her sampling shoe leather like this?

"Janice?" Why had Kelly stopped talking so abruptly? Shawna had a feeling that this was in some way connected to Kelly's earlier mistake around Murphy.

Kelly pressed her lips together, as if that could somehow keep her from putting her foot in her mouth again. She didn't know what was the matter with her. She hadn't mentioned Janice at all since the woman had left Murphy at the altar. Murphy had never wanted to discuss the incident. Now it had slipped out twice in the space of ten minutes.

"That's something Murphy's going to have to tell you about on his own." And she sincerely hoped that he would. It would mean that Murphy had found someone he wanted to get serious about. It was high time he did. High time he stopped eluding a shadow.

She flashed an apologetic smile at Shawna. "My mouth tends to move a little too fast at times. It takes my brain a minute to catch up."

"Sometimes two minutes," Murphy put in, coming up behind them. "You've had her long enough Kelly, and you still haven't brought her to see Harmony." He looked around. The room was thick with people, but one was conspicuously missing. "Where is the birthday girl?"

"Down for her nap." Kelly had put her sleepy daughter in her crib just before Murphy had arrived with Shawna.

"She has that laid-back Pendleton attitude," Murphy confided teasingly to Shawna. Kelly was about to lead them to Harmony's room, but Murphy caught her arm. "Let me show her off," he said when she raised a quizzical brow. "You always get to have all the fun."

Leave it to a bachelor to forget about all the work that went into raising a child. "I also change the diapers and got up for middle-of-the-night feedings."

Murphy tugged on a lock of her hair. "Like I said, brat, all the fun."

Without waiting for Kelly to respond, the way he knew she was quite capable of doing at length, he took Shawna's hand and led the way to the rear of the house. He nodded at several people as he passed, but though a couple stopped, ready to talk, Murphy continued moving.

"This is like a subway at rush hour," Shawna commented, following.

"Been to New York?" He threw the question over his shoulder.

"Among other places."

She hadn't been a willing traveler, he decided.

He eased Harmony's door open and then slipped in softly, closing the door behind them. It was like entering another world.

The room looked as if it had been plucked out of a storybook. There were floor-to-ceiling murals on two of the walls, depicting sweet-faced children playing with furry kittens and plump puppies. The only sound that was heard was the soft, steady breathing of the child who lay sleeping in the crib.

Murphy saw the way Shawna was looking at the walls, like a person who had unintentionally slipped into Wonderland. "My sister Kimberly paints," he said in a whisper so low she almost didn't hear him. "This was her contribution to the room."

His smile deepened as it softened. He was looking at the small occupant in the crib. "And there she is, the birthday princess herself."

They drew closer, like hushed worshipers to a cathedral railing. Shawna looked down at the little girl. She was sleeping on her tummy, her knees drawn up under her. She had a cherubic face, partially hidden by the ruffles of her pink-and-white dress, which had flipped upward.

The sweetness that seemed to radiate from her was almost unbearable.

It came to her without her summoning it. She remembered standing over another crib, in another room. Her son's crib. She'd stood there for hours, in awe of the miracle of birth, the miracle of having a child of her own. Shawna backed away, feeling the tears gather in her eyes.

Murphy turned. Surprise melted into concern. "Hey, what's the matter?" Without thought he took her into his arms.

Shawna tried to pull away, but his arms tightened around her. She shook her head, feeling foolish. "It's nothing, really."

He knew Shawna wasn't the type to weep over sentimental scenes for their own sake. "You don't cry over nothing."

She blew out a long breath, attempting to regain control. She was behaving like an idiot. It was just that being here, in the heart of this family scene, had stripped her of her protective layer. "I was just remembering..."

He understood without having her say any more. "Let it go, Shawna."

She looked up at Murphy in surprise. How could he ask her to do that? "He was my son."

"You can't bring him back by grieving. By feeling guilty." He didn't want her ruining the rest of her life by torturing herself like this. "Don't stain his memory with bad emotions. He doesn't deserve it."

He was making sense, even if she knew she was a long way from accepting his advice. "How did you get to be such a philosopher?"

He laughed softly. "I come from a large family. You tend to pick up a few things." His smile faded into seriousness. "I didn't bring you here to make you sad, Shawna. I brought you here so that you could see me in a family setting. So that you could feel more at ease with me."

An ulterior motive, she thought with a sad smile. He was attempting to tease her out of this oppressive feeling that threatened to overtake her. She worked with him. "So you could seduce me later?"

His smile was gentle, kind and understanding. Though he hadn't shared her experience, he knew what it felt like to have your heart wrenched out.

"Later will take care of itself, but I have to admit, that's not a bad suggestion." He kissed her forehead. He wasn't quite prepared for the warmth that flooded through him when she leaned into him, as if she were taking refuge there for a moment from everything that troubled her. "Feeling better?"

"Yes." She looked up at him and let herself remain in his embrace for a moment longer. What would it hurt? "You do have a way of making me feel better."

He caressed her face, sorely tempted to forget the party, to forget everything and find a haven for himself and this woman who had captured his fancy in such a viselike grip. But they couldn't just slip away, as much as he wanted to.

He crossed to the door, his hand in hers. "Heady stuff, coming from you."

"Speaking of heady." She moved closer to him as they left the room. "Have you given any more thought to—"

He knew what was coming from the tone of her voice and headed it off at the pass. "Lots of thought." He moved ahead of her, still holding her hand. "I want you to meet a few people."

She wasn't about to stay behind like a pull toy. Wiggling through an opening, she wedged herself in beside him. "You're being evasive."

"You betcha."

This wasn't the time to talk about it. He still hadn't found a niche for this new fact of life. He needed time to assimilate it. To accept that things could go wrong with him no matter how in control he thought he was.

"Murphy." Shawna tugged on his arm, forcing him around to look at her. "I don't want anything happening to you."

He raised a brow, surprised at the fierceness in her voice. It attracted him and made him want to flee at the same time. "Why, Shawna?"

The words had just tumbled out. She hadn't meant to say that. Shawna bit her lip. "That's simple. You're my patient and I don't want something bad happening to a patient of mine...."

He wasn't buying it and she knew it. "Is that the only reason?"

Flustered, she hesitated. But she wasn't one to run. She lifted her chin as she looked back at him. "Don't cross-examine me, Counselor."

The smile that slipped over his lips was definitely sensual. "I could think of a lot of things I'd like to do with you, Shawna. Cross-examination is way down on the list."

Shawna gestured at the crowd with her free hand. "You were saying something about introducing me to people?"

He laughed. "You know, you would have made a good lawyer yourself."

"Thank you." Her hand in his, she followed him outside to the backyard. "I'll take that as a compliment."

"Some people," he commented, "would have taken that as an insult."

Outside, there was a gaggle of children all grouped around a docile-looking pony. A very harried-looking man was holding on to its reins.

One hand on her shoulder, Murphy pointed toward the center. "The ones in the middle are Kimberly's kids." His affection was easy to detect. She liked that about him. "They're the ones making the most noise."

No sooner had he pointed the two of them out than Casey and Cathy ran over to him.

"You can do it, can't you, Uncle Murphy?" Casey insisted.

Suspicion nudged at him. "Do what?"

"You can 'semble the bike for Harmony," Cathy piped in.

"Assemble," Murphy corrected. He glanced toward Thomas, who was approaching with screwdriver in hand. "And isn't Harmony a little young for a bike?"

"She'll grow into it," Thomas said. Casey and Cathy had each taken a hand and were pulling Murphy over toward a pile of wheels, handlebars and gears spread out on the lawn. Thomas surrendered the screwdriver. "Be my guest."

Murphy sighed and got down on his knees. A ring of children closed in, all offering advice. Simultaneously.

Shawna laughed as she stood back and watched. He looked good that way, she thought, surrounded by children.

* * *

"They liked you." Murphy glanced at Shawna. Wisps of moonlight were probing the interior of the car as he drove away from Kelly's house and the party.

She looked very sexy by moonlight, he mused.

Shawna leaned back in the bucket seat, a hazy feeling of contentment enveloping her. "I liked them."

She smiled. Everyone had gone out of their way to make her feel at home. But it wasn't the artificial kind of welcome where conversations dried up after a few perfunctory words. On the contrary, conversations had swelled. One thing had led into another in a fascinating weave. Murphy had to practically drag her away.

It felt good.

She smiled as she turned her head to look at him. She couldn't quite remember ever feeling like this before. This contented, this good. "I had a great time, Murphy. Thanks for making me come."

He allowed himself one look in her direction before gluing his eyes back on the road. It was dark, and that made the trip twice as much of an adventure. Twice as unpredictable. There were nights when he came to visit that he half expected to see the Tin Man leading the Cowardly Lion and the Scarecrow toward Oz.

"How great?"

She sighed, stretching. "Very great."

He chose his words carefully. "Great enough not to call it an evening?"

She eyed him with humor. "What do you have in mind?"

"That nightcap that I suggested the other night. The one you gave me a rain check for. How about now?"

She had to admit that she didn't want the evening to be over. Any of it. But Sally would pounce on him as soon as they walked through the door. She shook her head, genuine regret in her eyes. "My mother's home."

He nodded, turning the wheel sharply to the left as the path went that way. "Which is why we're going to my place."

Tiny alarms went off, but they all rang without enthusiasm. She hesitated. "I don't—"

"A drink, Shawna. Just a drink." He slid one hand along her bare arm and felt her shiver slightly. It generated something in kind within him. "And maybe a little more conversation on the side. I like talking to you," he told her honestly. There wasn't game playing with her. After a sea of women who were interested in inconsequential things, she made a wonderful change. "Kelly said I never go out with women I can talk to. I think she might be onto something."

They drove onto the main road. Streetlights came into view and a traffic signal loomed in the distance. Shawna plunged ahead.

"She mentioned someone named Janice." She noticed that Murphy's hand stiffened ever so slightly on the wheel. She'd struck a nerve, she thought.

"Did she? What did she say about her?" It wasn't like Kelly to bring that up.

"That you would have to tell me."

Trust Kell to set the stage, he thought. "She'd make a good mystery writer, my sister. She dangles clues in front of people and makes them wonder."

And she had, Shawna thought. Kelly had stirred her curiosity quite a bit. "I'm not people, I'm your doctor," she reminded him. "Besides, you delved into my life. Turnabout is fair play."

She had a point, but he really didn't want to talk about it. "Nothing important, really." He shrugged, wishing the topic had never been raised. "We were going to get married."

She stared at him. "And you don't think that's important?" Just when she was giving him points for sensitivity! "What happened? Cold feet?"

He set his mouth grimly, refusing to let the memory play across his mind. "Yes."

Shawna pretended that it didn't bother her, but the damn thing was, it did. "How did she take it?"

The laugh had no feeling behind it, no depth. Like painted scenery on a movie set. "The way anyone with a pair of cold feet would take it. She slipped them into a pair of boots. He took size ten, I'm told."

He was getting her confused. Shawna turned in her seat in order to look at him better. "Is this some kind of lawyer jargon I'm going to figure out later?"

Murphy debated rushing through the yellow light, and decided against it. He eased onto the brake.

"Nothing to figure out. Janice called it off—rather dramatically, I might add—and ran off with a guy who was on his way to Montana to start a ranch." It didn't hurt anymore, not really. But it still annoyed him. She should have had the decency to tell him, not leave him standing in front of all those people. The fact that he had once loved her and planned to grow old with her was something he pushed into the recesses of his mind.

Shawna was still trying to get it straight. "*She* had the cold feet?"

"Yes."

She was almost afraid to ask the next question. "What do you mean by dramatically?"

He tried to laugh it off. He certainly hadn't meant the explanation to go to these lengths. "She did it during the strains of 'Here Comes the Bride.' By proxy. Her sister told me," he clarified.

Shawna couldn't believe that anyone would be so cruel. "She left you at the altar?"

"No," he corrected, "she left that morning. I was the only one at the altar." And feeling like a damn fool, the focal point of collective pity.

"Oh, Murphy." She reached to touch his arm. "I'm so—"

He held up a warning hand. He didn't want to hear the word *sorry*. The last thing in the world he wanted was her pity. "Yeah, well, it's in the past, and it taught me a lesson."

He turned his car toward his own development.

"That being?"

"That some people have marriage in their future, and some don't."

"And you belong to the latter group." She could tell by his tone that he thought he did.

Murphy nodded. "Which makes it good for you. No ties. You have nothing to be afraid of with me."

I wouldn't exactly say that, she thought.

Chapter Eleven

Shawna knew as soon as she set one foot over the doorway into Murphy's house. Knew that she was giving her consent without saying a single word. Knew, without conscious thought or agreement, where the evening was going.

If she pretended to herself that she didn't, it was only to protect her emotions. To place them in bubble wrap and keep them safe, out of harm's way. For there was great harm in caring.

Still, she couldn't get the nervous flutter that persisted in swooping over her, full-blown and unannounced, under control. Taking a deep breath, she looked around at the spacious living room with its vaulted, wood-beam ceiling. There was a navy blue leather sofa in the center. Across from it, sharing a wide, ash-wood coffee table, were a matching chair and ottoman.

He liked his comfort, she thought.

The rest of the house undoubtedly matched this sense of openness. "This certainly is a lot of room for just one man." Her voice sounded a bit hollow, as if she was throwing it from the bottom of a well. Shawna realized that she was holding her purse tightly against her side like a security blanket and forced her arm to relax.

It didn't help.

Murphy turned. She hadn't followed him into the room. She was still standing with her back practically pressed against the front door, like a woman bravely facing a firing squad.

"It looks even bigger once you step away from the doorway."

He crossed to her and took her hand in his. Her fingers were cold. She was afraid of him. The thought disturbed Murphy as he led her into the room.

"This isn't a den of iniquity, Shawna." His mouth quirked slightly. "No chains or leather applied to strange places. The only leather in the house is right here." He patted the sofa as he sat down, his other hand still linked to hers. "You don't have to be afraid."

Shawna had no choice but to sit beside him. "I'm not afraid." Defensiveness throbbed in every syllable. Murphy said nothing as he continued looking at her. She shrugged, relenting. "All right, maybe just a little."

He knew it cost her to admit that. He understood what control meant to her. Because it meant the same to him. Murphy enveloped her hand in both of his, the very gesture coaxing her to relax.

"Don't be, not with me." He looked into her eyes and saw desire peering through the uncertainty. He didn't believe in convincing people. People did what they wanted to. But he wanted her here tonight. More than anything, he wanted her. And as long as she resisted entanglement, he was safe. He could allow his attraction to flow a little longer, go a little deeper. There'd be no harm done. She was a soul mate. She understood what emotional pain was and why distances had to be maintained.

The pull was overwhelming. "There's something here between us, Shawna, something very real. Something that bears exploring."

Shawna didn't want to explore anything. She didn't want to discover that there might be more to this than just physical attraction. If it was physical, it didn't have to involve her heart. "Parlor tricks lose their magic when explained."

Why did he find her comment so disturbing? It only echoed what he felt. "Is that what you think it is, a parlor trick? Something done with mirrors? Illusion?"

Was that pain in his voice? Shawna didn't want to hurt him, but she didn't want to be hurt, either. She couldn't let him breach that space that separated her from the rest of the world.

Shawna lifted a shoulder and let it drop, feeling helpless and confused. And hating it. "I don't know what it is."

Softly he brushed aside the hair that fell into her eyes. Something flickered there for a moment and then faded. She was feeling this, just as he was.

"We'll never know until we find out, will we?" Maybe her reluctance was because she thought he was being insincere. A smile curved his mouth. "I'm not going to pretend that there haven't been other women."

"A whole army by last count." She thought back to high school. There had always seemed to be girls around Murphy. Or wanting to be around Murphy. She'd been guilty of that herself, except that she had known better than to try to compete with cheerleaders whose breasts were perpetually nubile and whose lips were eternally moistened.

He laughed and shook his head. "Not quite. My reputation back then got a little out of hand. It was a lot larger than was actually warranted." He looked unabashed at his admission. "I let it stand because I was young and foolish. I have to admit that it did wonders for my male ego."

"And now?"

He slipped his hand to the back of her neck, his thumb slowly rubbing along her cheek. He succeeded in arousing both of them.

"And now I'm not quite so young, not quite so foolish. That kind of reputation doesn't flatter me anymore." He dropped his hand. "We've both been hurt, one way or another. And neither of us wants to be hurt again. That's our cornerstone." He drew closer to her, having no choice in the matter. It was as if she were some irresistible force, pulling him toward her. "The rest of it we'll take one step at a time."

She was struggling not to let herself be swallowed up in the storm he was creating around her. "That sounds like a business negotiation."

A sensuous smile met her comment. "Only if you mean business." Slowly his hands played along the planes of her face, just lightly skimming it. Shawna felt the muscles in her stomach tightening, like wet leather left lying out in the sun. "I know I do," he whispered.

His breath was warm as it brushed her face. Barely touching her, his lips followed the trail his fingertips had forged.

She could hardly stand it. Shawna felt her heart hammering as the sigh escaped from her. She wanted to still his hands, to pull away from that deep, sensual kiss. But it was too late for that. Too late for sense and sensible thoughts. All her thoughts were of him. And of the needs that were begging for release.

Her lips brushed against his as she turned her head. The battle was lost without a single shot being fired.

Murphy's arms tightened around her, pulling her to him. With infinite gentleness he spread his fingers, gliding along the bare expanse of her back. Every movement hummed of intimacy.

It had been so long, so very long since she'd let a man touch her like this, so long since she had loosened the deathlike grip she had on her feelings. Now, even if she wanted to hold them in a state of abeyance, they seeped through her grasp, melting like an ice cube and dripping through the spaces between her fingers.

Her breathing grew ragged. His lips were pressed to her throat, creating such havoc that Shawna could barely remember where she was. Or who she was supposed to be.

"Murphy." It took effort just to form his name when her mind was spinning like a child's top. Like a planet about to collide with a meteor.

"Shh." The sound feathered across her mouth. She could almost taste him, and yearning sprang into her veins. "It's all right." Murphy raised his head to look at her. The fear in her eyes was fading to a pinpoint. But it still hadn't left completely. "I promise I'll be gentle, though you make me want to behave like a plundering Viking."

Picturing Murphy as a Viking had her mouth curving in a smile. "You haven't the coloring for it."

"No, but I do have the stamina." He liked seeing her smile. It coaxed out a joyousness within him he would have been hard-pressed to describe. But it existed nonetheless. "And the inclination." Which, he promised himself, would have to remain under wraps. He didn't want to frighten her away with the intensity of what he was feeling at this moment.

It damn near frightened him away.

Murphy rose, drawing her up with him. As he did, he slipped his arms around her. Her body was flush against his, filling in all the crevices that were left as an open invitation.

Pleasure washed over him and he smiled down into her face. "I always knew it."

When she breathed, she could feel her breasts moving against his chest. It was hopelessly erotic and hopelessly exciting. "Knew what?"

His arms tightened around her. She felt his body hardening with desire and could feel her own humming with anticipation.

"That you'd fit."

"How far back does 'always' go?" She half expected him to say something about "forever," or since he first saw her in high school. She didn't want him mouthing lines that belonged to an ordinary Casanova. She wanted him to be special. Because what she was feeling right now was so special. So unique.

He nuzzled her neck. "That's easy. Since I first opened my eyes in the emergency room and saw three of you hovering over me." Desire throbbed, demanding tribute. He felt like making love to her right here, in the living room, on the gleaming hardwood floor. But she deserved better than that. Much better.

The emergency room. His injury. Doubt began to raise its head again. "I—"

He could almost see her thoughts forming. Murphy laid a finger lightly to her lips.

"No, no shoptalk, Doctor. Not tonight." He melted away any words in her mind with just a look. "No talking at all."

The rest of tonight, he thought, was meant for loving. And for crossing into new frontiers. Because as much as he might deny it, she did mean something more to him than the others had. Having her here tonight wasn't just for an evening, meant to entertain them both. There was a whole new set of parameters involved.

Now wasn't the time to explore them, but he knew that he would, eventually. And might be surprised at what he found.

Murphy felt Shawna tremble against him as he brought his mouth down to hers. He was startled by what he discovered in her kiss. It was almost savage in its neediness. The groan that vibrated between them could have come from either of them. Murphy had no idea where its origin lay. He didn't care. All he knew was that, for now, she belonged to him.

Just as much as he belonged to her.

Murphy swept her up into his arms. Shawna felt excitement racing up and down her body, like lightning along a metal rod. It felt delicious, almost decadent, to be carried off like this. What she didn't feel, she realized, was helpless. Instead, she felt safe, cherished.

And perhaps even, just for the moment, loved.

It would be foolish to build dreams on transparent foundations. But for now, she could pretend. There was no harm in that. As long as she remembered that it was just pretend, nothing more.

It felt as if she was standing on top of a high peak, overlooking a valley that was filled with such wondrous colors it nearly blinded her.

Encircling his neck as she nestled against his chest, Shawna sighed. "I can walk." There was absolutely no feeling behind her softly voiced protest. She was reluctant to leave this haven he'd created for her.

"I'm sure you can do a lot of things." Murphy kissed her again, nipping her lower lip. She tasted of desire and ecstasy. "But indulge me a little. I like holding you like this."

Teasing her mouth, he walked toward the stairs. She was hardly aware of her surroundings, of where they were going. All she was aware of was the comforting beat of his heart against her chest.

And the anticipation that was vibrating through her like the wings of a hummingbird.

When she opened her eyes they were in his bedroom. She could detect the faint scent of his cologne here as she looked around. The drapes were drawn, shutting out the world. Muted browns and grays were spread throughout the room. On the king-size bed there was a turquoise comforter that paled before the intense color of his eyes.

His eyes. They held her prisoner as firmly as if she had been shackled to him.

More.

He thought of setting her down on his bed, a prize to be examined and worshiped, but instinctively knew she would feel better if they worked up to that slowly. Murphy set her down on the floor, releasing his hold on her by small degrees.

When her feet touched the rug, Shawna discovered that her knees were no longer fully functional. Her arms remained around his neck until she regained her sea legs.

"What's next, Counselor?" The words came out in a breathy rush. He had splayed his fingers along her rib cage. She could feel the heat from his palms as he cupped her breasts. Desire soared through her instantaneously.

"We switch roles." There was just a hint of mischief in his eyes. "You cross-examine me," he explained when she looked at him quizzically. "And I play doctor." Then, to seal the bargain, he pressed a warm kiss to the pulse in her throat.

Her head dropped back as every fiber in her being absorbed the kiss, hugging it to her soul.

"Where does it hurt?" he murmured.

If she were a string on a harp, she would have been vibrating madly. She ached for him. It had no center, no beginning, no end. It just was. "Everywhere."

Murphy smiled. It encompassed his entire face. "Then we're just going to have to examine you everywhere."

Shawna caught her breath as she felt his hands undo the single tie that held her dress anchored at her side. The pale pink material immediately loosened from her body, like a sigh that was leaving it.

"Is that necessary, Doctor?" she quipped, though how she managed to form the words was beyond her. Her mouth was drier than dust.

"I believe in being thorough."

That she could readily believe. He had thoroughly undone her and he had only begun.

She was silent, her eyes wide. Her sharp intake of breath as he slowly slid the halter from about her neck echoed in his chest. "No more questions, Counselor?" he urged.

She moved her head slowly from side to side, her eyes never leaving his. "The defense rests."

"Not for long," he promised.

Murphy let the dress fall from his fingers. He only had eyes for her. She was standing before him, Venus rising from the sea, standing in silver-strapped high heels instead of on a seashell. There was just the barest bit of silk covering her. And it would be gone soon. He fervently hoped he wouldn't tear it off her.

The way he wanted to.

"You are magnificent."

Shawna tried not to think about the fact that he had probably said those very same words to at least a dozen other women before.

Tonight, those words belonged to her. Tonight, she wasn't Shawna Saunders, she was someone she had once fantasized about. A woman Murphy made love with.

Summoning all her strength, Shawna took a step back, just out of his reach. His eyes were smoky and he looked confused. Dazed.

Good. At least she wasn't alone in this. She needed to know that she was having an effect on him, that he felt at least partially as unsettled as she did right now.

A spark of triumph shot through her.

When he reached for her, she shook her head, a completely foreign, playful look slipping over her face.

He misunderstood. Was she having second thoughts? "The jury can't adjourn to deliberate the verdict yet," he told her, his voice thick with wanting as he reached for her.

Her smile grew. "I told you earlier today that turnabout was fair play, remember?"

His brows drew together, but he couldn't clear his mind. She was in every corner of it. And only her.

"Vaguely. A hundred years ago." He took a second to pull himself together. The last thing in the world he wanted was for her to think of him as some out-of-control animal. But with her standing before him like that, her body bathed in the dim lamplight, it was hard not to give in to the passion that was beating within him. "What did you have in mind?"

Moving forward, she slipped her fingers gingerly beneath the first button of his shirt. His skin was hot, singeing her. "I was thinking I shouldn't be standing here, nude, while you look as if you're about to go out to dinner."

"Dinner is the furthest thing from my mind." He moved closer, fitting his hands lightly on the swell of her hips. "And you're not nude." His eyes swept possessively over her body. "Not yet."

She swallowed, fighting to keep her voice steady. Her pulse was a lost cause. "You have to catch up."

Murphy raised his hands in complete surrender. "Make me."

Her eyes on his, Shawna began to work on freeing the second button, and the third, until his shirt hung open on his chest. The shiver that overtook her was more from wanting than from the cold. Impatience beat a heavy tattoo through her. She wanted it all now. She wanted him to make love with her the way she knew he could. With tenderness and with a mind-blotting passion that would send her reeling.

She moved her hands to his shoulders, sliding along the smooth material. "You're high maintenance, do you know that?"

"No, I'm not." He shrugged out of his shirt, savoring the feel of her long fingers along his skin as she slid the sleeves from his arms. "I even left my armor in the closet for you."

She felt her smile budding from the depths of her very core as she recalled his knight-in-shining-armor allusion the night those men had broken into the clinic.

With a quick tug she unhooked his belt. "I guess I should be grateful for small things."

He watched her hands as they moved competently over him. "Small? Weigh your words carefully, Doctor. My ego bruises easily, remember?"

Shawna opened the button at the top of his trousers, then stopped.

Murphy placed his hands over hers, guiding her back. "Oh, no, you've come too far along to stop now, Shawna." His stomach tightened like a newly wound spring as he felt her slide the zipper down. "Tell you what." He feathered a kiss along her temple that had her senses spinning. "I won't make you give me a sponge bath."

Her heart rate increased as she slipped her hands between his briefs and his skin. "Nurses do that."

Very slowly he outlined her ear with the tip of his tongue. And smiled when she quivered. "How do you feel about expanding your horizons?"

Like a person seeking warmth from the cold, she pressed closer to him. All the while, her hands worked the material down his hips. "Wonderful."

He laughed and she felt the sound rumble in his chest, touching her. "That's my girl."

She stopped and looked at him, her heart thudding against her rib cage so hard she was certain it would leave a permanent dent.

His girl. His.

The sound surrounded her, infiltrating her senses until she was almost dizzy. It was silly to react this way about a line he probably didn't even know he'd said a second after it was out of his mouth. But no one had ever said anything like that to her before. No one had ever wanted her that way before.

His.

Murphy realized his error immediately. She probably thought he was attempting to back her into some sort of commitment, after he'd promised he wouldn't. He was getting himself tangled in the strings he'd said wouldn't exist. "Just a figure of speech, Shawna."

"I know that." Her voice was low, like brandy being poured into a snifter. It was too low for him to detect the sadness in it.

He stepped out of his trousers, kicking them aside. They gathered about the pool of her discarded pink dress. She was still wearing that small piece of silk that he found hopelessly enticing. Murphy hooked his thumbs on either side of her hips and slowly drew it down.

"No more barriers, Shawna," he whispered. The words tasted tempting against her mouth.

Her eyes half-shut, she lifted her head. "No, all the clothes are gone." She wished that the other barriers were as easily shed.

And then there was no space to wish anything at all. No space to think.

It was all flash and fire from then on. Like a discarded Christmas tree, left out in the field with a match put to it. One moment it was there, dried up and faded, the next moment flames were consuming it with a breathtaking voracity. And then it was gone.

Just as she was.

His hands, worshipful and gentle, stroked her until she ached. It was as if they had always been lovers. He seemed to know all the right places to touch, all the things that would set her off.

And yet, all this was so new to her, so overwhelmingly wonderful.

Shawna felt like a virgin being taken for the first time, but with none of the accompanying awkwardness. None of the shyness.

She didn't feel shy at all. She felt deliriously wanton, deliciously wicked. Murphy was making things happen to her that she had never read about in textbooks, that had never been hinted at in any clinical anatomy lesson.

She had nothing to go by, no road maps to follow. The memories she had to draw on did not begin to touch upon this. She'd sipped club soda and this was champagne.

Shawna gasped as Murphy, with just a few strokes of his hand, took her over the first crest, bringing her over it before she'd even realized that she was approaching it. Flares exploded within her and her eyes flew open in dazed wonder.

Shawna hurried to keep up.

He knew then what he had only suspected before. That he would never find anyone who matched him so perfectly as she did. With only instinct to guide her, she seemed to second-guess him to every turn. She wanted everything that he wanted, needed it the moment that he did. Offered it the moment that he sought it, as instinctively, as willingly, as if she could read his mind.

As if she could read his heart.

How could an innocent know so much? And she was an innocent. She might have been married before, but it was evident that no one had loved her the way she'd deserved to be loved. The surprise was there in her face, at her own responses and at his.

Murphy held himself in check as best he could, determined to show her this brave new world she hadn't even known existed until now. Needs and desires beat impatient wings within him, desperate to be sated, desperate to be released. But for this moment, it was enough for him to see the rapture in her eyes.

They had tumbled onto the bed. He had no idea when. The comforter had somehow been bunched to the side and the sheets were becoming tangled as the intensity between them heated to a temperature no gauge could measure.

He felt her fingers as they tightened on his shoulders when he brought her up and over yet another crest. There'd be scratches there tomorrow, he thought. Those would fade. The ones across his soul would last longer.

She'd had no idea it could be like this, so exhausting, so exciting. So continuous, like spun sugar trailing off forever.

Shawna sucked air into her lungs. She couldn't manage to get enough. Not enough air, not enough him. Gasping, Shawna didn't know if she could withstand any more ecstasy.

And still there was more, so much more. Layers and textures she hadn't dreamed about.

Or perhaps, in some secret compartment of her soul, she had.

She let her instincts flow and lead her. With a hand guided by a desire to reduce him to the same consistency that he was reducing her, Shawna touched him. The surprised groan that came from his lips delighted her.

Empowered, her soul swelling, Shawna glided her hand lightly along the outward sign of his desire. Murphy twisted and turned against her, making her feel that much more confident.

And that much more a prisoner of her own mounting passion.

He couldn't hold back any longer. He might have if she hadn't touched him, delighted innocence flowering on her face. But she had and it wasn't humanly possible for him to resist giving in another moment.

When he shifted his body, moving over her, Shawna was more than ready to accept him. More than ready to join in the final act that would irrevocably seal her to him no matter how much she denied it. It did no good to tell herself that it was just for now. She knew there would be consequences she wouldn't want to pay for this feeling.

Her thoughts broke like soap bubbles in the wind.

His eyes on her, Murphy linked his hands with Shawna's and crossed the last barrier. He slipped inside. Sheathed, he began to move slowly, ever so slowly, though holding back now was almost killing him.

She felt as if a torch had been put to her.

"Now, Murphy," she begged, forgetting that she never begged, never asked. "Now."

"Whatever you say."

As the rhythm increased, so did the desire that quaked and trembled within each of them. He heard her cry out his name against his ear.

When they had both finally crested, the sensation exploding in wondrous colors, drenching both of them, Murphy knew in the core of his being that there was no turning back, not for him.

The portal that he had stepped through had closed behind him forever. And nothing would ever be the same again.

Chapter Twelve

He couldn't get enough of her.

Not her scent, not her flavor, not the deep richness of her mouth, which stirred him to heights that he'd never ventured to before. It wasn't the lovemaking that left him wanting more. That was infinitely satisfying and incredible. It was her. Somehow, just by being, and by not being like the others, Shawna had managed to pierce the shield he'd slipped around his heart.

And she'd done it all entirely without meaning to.

Shawna stirred and woke up by degrees, like someone reluctantly leaving the warmth of a bubble bath to venture out onto the cold tile floor. When she finally opened her eyes she saw Murphy looking at her. He was propped up on his elbow, just watching her, as if he'd been doing that for hours. She should have felt embarrassed, remorseful. At least something grounded in contrition.

She didn't.

It would probably come later, she guessed, grateful for the respite. She stretched like a cat, then raised her head to look past Murphy's shoulder toward the window. Tiny shafts of daylight were poking through, like probing swords.

She sighed. "It's dawn."

He knew what time it was. He'd been awake for a while now, content just to watch her as she slept. "Follows night like clockwork."

She was very aware of the length of his hard body beside her. With a hand that was far more steady than last night, she ran a tentative fingertip along it and was pleased that he didn't remain unaffected. He drew her closer against him.

"I have to go home." There was no enthusiasm in her statement. No energy.

He didn't want to think of her leaving his bed, didn't want to think of anything beyond this moment. "Makes me wish for Alaska."

Shawna raised herself up on her elbow and looked at him, her long hair raining down the slope of her shoulder. She tucked the sheet around her breasts. "Alaska?"

He nodded as he began to tug at the sheet, slowly slipping it away from her body. "The nights are six months long there."

Shawna shivered as she felt the sheet sliding off, but made no attempt to pull it back. She liked the way he looked at her. "So are the days."

With enough leverage available, he worked his hands beneath what was left of the sheet and cupped her breasts. Watching her eyes, he teased the tip of her nipple with his thumb. "I'd make sure that I picked the right time."

It was hard to keep her mind on what he was saying when he was arousing her passion again. She would have sworn that her supply was depleted. She'd never even known she could be like this, feel like this, until last night.

"Yes, I'm sure that you would." She moved her head to kiss his lips and saw the flash of pain pass over his face. Concern immediately gripped her. "Murphy, what is it?"

He felt like an idiot mentioning anything about it. The sensation had passed almost before it had materialized. "Nothing."

Annoyed that he would lie to her after what they had shared last night, she sat up, the sheet falling from her completely. "I've never beaten a naked man before, but I could make an exception with you."

She was magnificent in her anger, he thought. "Ooh, you're getting me excited again." Taking hold of her waist, he slipped her onto his body so that she straddled it.

The position might have been unconventional, but that didn't stop her. She leaned forward and took a fistful of his hair as if she meant to pull it out. Her face was inches from his. "Talk."

He'd never had a threat so enticingly delivered. Murphy raised his head slightly and kissed her, then fell back. "It was nothing. It's gone now."

She wasn't about to let him off the hook that easily. She squeezed her thighs against him and smiled in triumph as she felt him respond. "But?"

The woman just didn't give up. That had its merits, but not now. He rested his hand lightly along her knee. "You make me dizzy."

She frowned as concern returned. She'd hoped, irrationally, that his dizziness would have gone by now. He was playing Russian roulette with his eyesight. "Murphy, that's not me."

Murphy slowly ran his palms up along her thighs until they rested on her hips. Humor had returned to his eyes. "Feels like you." It spread to his lips. "And I've become an expert in the past six hours on what you feel like."

The past six hours. Maybe it had been a mistake—a glorious mistake, but a mistake nonetheless. For more reasons than just one.

She tried to slide back onto the bed, but he held her firmly in place. He wasn't going to make this easy, she thought.

"Murphy, there's a breach of ethics here. I'm your doctor. I can't be your—" Shawna couldn't bring herself to say the word *lover*. It put a cheapened spin on what had happened last night. "Whatever I am right now."

Her embarrassment tickled him. He was used to brazen women, women who took to sex as naturally as they took to breathing, with as little thought behind it. It was refreshing. And just maybe, something he needed. Something that he had been avoiding because of his own fears.

''The word 'terrific' comes to mind. Also 'sensual.' 'Wonderful.' 'Hopelessly erotic.''' Leaning forward, he let his tongue tease the skin over her knee.

Unable to stop herself, Shawna squirmed as pleasure rippled through her. ''Murphy, stop. I can't think when you do that.''

He laughed softly, the sound rumbling through her body. ''That's the whole idea.''

Suddenly taking hold of her waist, Murphy brought her down, switching places. In the blink of an eye he was the one on top. His body skimming hers, he held himself above her, just near enough to activate her yearning. Very carefully he circled her neck with small, pliant kisses.

''One more for the road?'' His lips were so close she could form the words with him.

Shawna's arms were tightening around his neck as if they had a will of their own. Heaven knew she didn't have one anymore. He'd stolen it from her. ''The road doesn't need it.''

He kissed one eyelid, and then another. ''Maybe not, but I do.''

Her body, she knew, was ready to receive him. Perhaps it would always be ready. He could play her like an instrument, making every fiber in her being hum and vibrate. She and Doug has hardly paid attention to this aspect of their marriage. Lovemaking was something that was nice, but never important.

There was a whole world she didn't know about.

Her mouth curved as she moved beneath him, arousing him as quickly as he did her. ''You weren't kidding about stamina, were you?''

It was Sunday. Neither of them needed to be anywhere for at least an hour. Perhaps two. He meant to get the most out of that time. ''You bring out the best in me, Shawna.''

His words were muffled against her skin. He kissed the side of her neck, networking his way along the slim column of her throat. He felt her begin to rock beneath him, making his blood run hot. He was in awe of what she did to him. And kept on doing.

''The very best.''

A sigh of contentment escaped as she attempted to voice a feeble protest. "But I have to go." The words were all but swallowed up.

"Later," he murmured against her mouth, his hands doing wonderful things to her as they reclaimed what was already his from the first moment.

"Later," she breathed in agreement.

Or perhaps she only thought about saying the word. It didn't matter. She was falling completely under his spell.

Again.

Shawna sat very still in Murphy's car. Her hands were folded before her as she attempted to brazen out her sudden case of nerves. Second thoughts, belatedly, were multiplying within her rapidly. She had absolutely no idea how a woman behaved after a night, and a morning, of lovemaking with a man she had fantasized about.

Fantasy, she thought vaguely, didn't begin to cover it.

But this wasn't like her. This wasn't who and what she was. She had behaved completely against type and the tinges of remorse she'd known were coming had arrived, baggage in hand.

She stared straight ahead, afraid to look at him. Afraid to perhaps see amusement on his face at her expense. "Murphy, I don't know what came over me."

He smiled to himself. There were times last night when she had demonstrated an enthusiasm that totally surprised him. It was as if there had been this font of emotion that had laid dormant until the right buttons were pushed. And he had pushed them. It made him feel almost humble. And infinitely glad to be alive.

"Whatever it was, find out. I'd like to do this again."

The response was on her lips immediately. "No...."

Instinctively he knew what she was thinking. That he wanted to bed her. He did, but that wasn't the only thing at play here. There was more. Much more. It would have worried him had he let himself think it through.

"Not just the lovemaking part, although I have to admit that I may have the bed sheets bronzed as a fond reminder of my finest hour."

"Hours," she corrected automatically. He had made love to her all night. Time had stood still, and yet, it seemed to pour itself into hour after hour, until she thought she had always lain like this with him.

"Yeah." He drew the word out, grinning from ear to ear as he thought about it. "But it's not just that," he continued quickly. "I want all of it, Shawna. I want to be able to see you socially, without a tiny blue flashlight in your hand."

It took her a minute to realize what he was talking about. "That's not a flashlight." She laughed at his oversimplification. "That's an ophthalmoscope."

He nodded carelessly. "One of them. I want to see you, with or without an ophthalmoscope," he amended. "With or without your clothes." He turned to look at her as he came to a stop before a red light. "I just want to see you, Shawna." So much that it unnerved him. Maybe, if he saw her enough, this feeling would go away.

And maybe, a small voice within him whispered, it wouldn't.

Run. Now. Before you get in too deep. Shawna took a deep breath, attempting to steel herself against everything. From the hurt she knew was waiting for her. From the emotions that had run rampant through her last night and this morning.

That wanted to break loose now.

She licked her lower lip, searching for a way to say this, for a way to explain. "Murphy, what happened before was an aberration." She turned and looked at his profile as he stepped on the gas pedal again. She saw the line in his jaw grow rigid. "It's too hard for me to go down this road."

He slowed down. It was still fairly early and there wasn't that much traffic on the road. He was in no hurry to bring her home. To leave her. "I have no idea where this road is going to end."

"I do," she replied stoically. "You just said it." She could feel his eyes on her, but she didn't turn her head. She could say this best if she wasn't looking at him. "End. Things end."

He knew she was referring to the accident that had claimed her husband and child. "I'm immortal, didn't you know?"

She laughed and shook her head. "That's your problem. You think you are." She could feel the pain building even as she spoke and she struggled to shut it away. The pain of losing someone she loved. "You go racing into burning buildings and taking on spaced-out toughs, thinking nothing will happen."

He knew it had to be the agitation talking. She couldn't mean what she was saying. She couldn't mean that she wanted him to just stand back and let things happen without raising a hand to stop them.

"If I'd thought it out, a child would have died and you might have been killed."

Shawna raised her hand, shaking her head. Her thoughts were all tangled up in her head. None of this was coming out right.

"I wasn't speaking literally, exactly." She took a breath and tried again. "You couldn't have done anything differently than you did. That's you. You saved the girl, you saved me and you were wonderful," she said honestly. "What I meant was that you might think you're invulnerable, but you're not. No one is." She bit her lip. When she looked at him, there were tears in her eyes. To love meant to lose. "And I don't want to be left alone."

He wanted to pull over the car and just hold her. But that wouldn't resolve what was being said here. So instead, he continued driving. "Let me get this straight. You don't want me with you because you don't want to be left alone." He waited for a beat until his words sank in. "Is it just me, or is there something wrong here?"

Her smile was sad. But it was there, and he counted its emergence as a triumph. A point for his side.

"You make it sound ludicrous."

"That's because it is," he said gently. He grew more serious. "I don't know what there is down the road for us, but I do know that I want to walk it with you. Not because we burned up sheets but because of what happened before that. And after."

"After?"

He nodded. He could see the scene vividly and probably would for a long, long time. Shawna, standing barefoot in his kitchen, wearing only his shirt. He'd come in, toweling his hair dry from the shower and almost swept her back into the bedroom. "After. You making coffee for me, wearing my shift and nothing else."

Even the way he said it was arousing. She struggled to remember the point she was trying to make. "I was making coffee for me."

He wasn't going to be put off. Murphy raised a brow in her direction. "Did I drink a cup?"

"Yes."

"Then it was for me." He rested his case. "Leave me a few illusions." He took a left turn, passing an old Packard in mint condition. The driver was proudly taking it for its weekly run, he guessed. "Don't fight too hard, Shawna. You might not win."

She watched, fascinated, as a dimple formed in his cheek. It took all she had not to reach out and touch it. What was he doing to her? She knew she didn't want this, knew that if she opened herself up to feel something for him she'd live to regret it.

"Even if I win—" she said the words more to herself than to him "—I might not win."

He toyed with the logic behind that. "You sure you don't want to be a lawyer?"

She laughed as she shook her head, then sighed. "You make me laugh, Murphy."

"Not all the time," he reminded her with a smile that brought last night back vividly. He gestured toward the right. "Well, here we are. Want me to come in with you?"

She looked up in surprise. She had been so wound up in the discussion she hadn't realized that they had reached her apartment complex.

Shawna squared her shoulders. This was going to be a challenge. "I'd rather face my mother alone."

"Think she was worried? You are over twenty-one."

"Worried?" Shawna laughed as she repeated the word. Murphy looked at her, waiting for the punch line. "She probably has party streamers out, celebrating the fact that her daughter finally stayed out all night." Shawna looked toward her apartment door with a shake of her head. She knew she wasn't exaggerating by much.

He wasn't quite following her. "You must have done it before—"

"No." She believed in being honest, even though she knew what it must make her sound like. Like a prude. Or worse, someone no one else wanted.

He found that difficult to believe. "Never?"

"Never." She was in this deep, she might as well go all the way. "As corny as it sounds, I was a virgin when I got married." She looked down at her hands, suddenly feeling self-conscious. "Doug wasn't exactly the kind of man who wanted to get me into bed. He was more into research."

Sex and the physical side of marriage had never been a high priority with Doug. But he had been loving in his own fashion. And he had made her feel safe.

Murphy listened and wondered what sort of a man she had been married to. How could anyone be married to someone like Shawna and then turn toward his work? Her late husband must have been a hell of a dedicated man.

"There's research and then there's research." He turned off his engine. The topic fascinated him. Murphy scrutinized her as he folded his arms before him. "How about after?"

She merely shook her head.

Now, that he really found hard to believe. After Janice left him he'd forced himself to get back into the swim of things. Quickly. "You mean I'm the only other man that you ever—?"

"Yes." The word came out in a rush. She raised her eyes to his. "If you have the audacity to gloat, I swear that I won't be responsible for—"

"Gloat?" he echoed. "Why the hell would I gloat?" His mouth softened as he looked at her. Did she think that little of herself? Or him? "That's the nicest present anyone ever gave me." He nodded toward the front door. "Sure you don't want some moral support?"

The last thing she wanted was to bring him in with her. Her mother would pounce immediately. "I'm sure. I can do this alone."

He accepted her decision and started the car again. "Just don't get back into the habit of doing everything alone," he warned. She'd already opened the door on her side when he leaned over and kissed her. "I'll call you."

Shawna nodded and then got out. She knew that she would be better off if he didn't call. And wretched, too.

She walked slowly to her door, not relishing the scene that lay ahead. She knew her mother was going to attempt to pump her for details. What her mother needed, she thought, was a nice, stable relationship with a nice, stable man. That was what she had needed all along. Too bad she didn't know anyone for her.

Turning at the last moment, Shawna saw that Murphy was still sitting in his idling car. He waved and then pulled away.

Bracing herself, Shawna unlocked her front door. The sound of voices floated to her immediately. They were coming from the living room.

Oh, God, she's called the police, Shawna thought.

The next moment she discarded the thought. Her mother wasn't the type to panic that way. If she called the police, it was to buy tickets to the policeman's ball. And perhaps to snare the policeman while she was at it.

Then she was in the living room, looking at the distinguished-looking older man sitting on her sofa. He was nursing a cup of coffee and laughing. Her mother gave the impression of fluttering around him even as she sat beside him, laughing into his blue eyes.

Shawna could only stare. "Dr. McGuire, what are you doing here?"

He'd been so caught up in the conversation and the charming woman beside him that he was surprised to hear his name called. McGuire looked up and stared, amazed.

"Dr. Saunders?" She was wearing what, in his day, was described as a becoming frock. He smiled broadly. "I didn't recognize you without your lab coat." He rose slightly in his seat until she waved him back down. McGuire settled his coffee cup and saucer on the table before him. "I must say, you really look lovely." His eyes skimmed toward Sally. "Having now met your mother, I can see where you get it from."

Her mother was absorbing this like a vacuum cleaner with its suction set on high. She always came alive at compliments, Shawna thought.

Sally rose and crossed to Shawna. The smile on her face was sheer contentment. Shawna was surprised that she even acknowledged her. Being around a man tended to block most of her mother's thought processes.

Sally took her daughter's hand. "Did you have a nice time, dear?" There was what amounted to a secret smile on her mother's face that told Shawna the woman couldn't have been happier that she had waltzed in at this hour, still wearing the clothes she had had on the night before.

Her mother was one of a kind, Shawna thought.

"Yes." Shawna was more interested in what the doctor was doing here than what her mother thought. "Is there something wrong at the clinic?"

He grew serious. He didn't like having things kept from him. "Not exactly, but last night was my turn to be on duty."

"Yes, I know." What was he getting at? Had there been another break-in? She hadn't mentioned anything about what had happened at the clinic to anyone, hoping that it would all blow over. The less attention this received, the better. But if there'd been a break-in, then maybe she'd been wrong.

He rose and crossed to her, a tall man with the air of a patriarch. "I just found out from one of my patients that two men tried to rob the clinic last week while you were there." He sounded angry.

"I—" She didn't get very far.

"Why didn't you tell me?" He felt responsible. What if something had happened to her? He'd been the one to recruit her in the first place. The anger he felt was directed toward himself, not her.

"Nothing was stolen. I didn't see the point in upsetting you." She placed a comforting hand on the man's arm.

They were friends, as much as she had allowed anyone to be in the past year. If she didn't think of Murphy. "Besides, Murphy was with me." She smiled at his concern, touched. "We even got a neighborhood protector out of it. This huge man who calls himself Mount."

McGuire nodded. He had made a point of getting all the details once he'd found out about the incident. "Jeremiah Jones, yes, I know him. He has his own brand of law enforcement. The police usually give him a wide berth." He frowned. McGuire knew what it was like to keep his own counsel. But he wasn't an attractive young woman. The risks doubled. "Still, you should have come to me with this."

Shawna smiled and nodded. Maybe she should have, at that. "I didn't mean any offense, Dr. McGuire."

Sally felt she had stood on the sidelines long enough and rose to join them. Out of long habit, she positioned herself between her daughter and the distinguished-looking man who had completely captured her fancy.

"I was just telling Simon that you didn't say anything to me, either." She turned toward McGuire, simultaneously turning on a thousand-watt smile. "But then, a mother's always the last to know something."

Especially if she's not listening, Shawna thought. The next moment she relented. Sally had done the best she knew how. The trouble was, she just never knew how and never bothered to learn.

McGuire nodded his silver head. "I came by to see for myself that you were all right."

Shawna spread her hands wide and made a complete revolution for his benefit. "I'm fine."

She certainly seemed so. There was a glow about her, McGuire observed. One he'd never seen before. He didn't need a road map to tell him where it had come from. He could tell by the way she'd said Murphy's name.

"I can see that." He took her hand and held it for a moment. "Still, if you wanted to drop out, I would understand."

He might understand, but she didn't. "Drop out?"

"Yes. Stop helping out at the clinic."

Sally placed a hand on her daughter's shoulder. "Really, dear, it might be for your own good."

Shawna was surprised at the note of concern in her mother's voice. She couldn't help wondering if having McGuire here had anything to do with its sudden appearance.

She directed her answer to McGuire. "No, the thought never crossed my mind. Those people need all the medical attention they can get." Shawna thought of several of the patients she'd seen recently. "In some cases, they'd never seen an ophthalmologist, even though they needed to. And wouldn't if I wasn't there." She gained a full head of steam in case he had any ideas about refusing her help. "And if I hadn't been there, that girl I sutured up two weeks ago might have had serious complications. You know how crowded and understaffed that emergency room at Chancellor General is."

McGuire held up a hand to stem the torrent of words. "Slow down. You don't have to convince me."

He chuckled softly. He had a daughter about Shawna's age. Denise's main concern was if there were water spots on her goblets when she threw a dinner party. He wished she could learn a few things from Shawna.

"Those are all the same arguments I use when I'm recruiting other doctors." He placed a fatherly arm around her shoulders. "Still, I wouldn't want you on my conscience. I don't want anything happening to you."

"Nothing will happen. I can handle myself." She couldn't prevent the side glance she gave her mother. "I've been doing it most of my life. And what I can't handle, Mount can." She remembered how terrifyingly huge he'd seemed to her when he had lumbered into the clinic. "He promised me I wouldn't have anything to worry about, that he'd keep an eye on the place. I think just the threat of his intervention is enough to keep most everyone away."

McGuire couldn't argue with that. "You have a point. And, to be honest, I'd be lying if I said that a part of me isn't relieved to have you stay on. Still—"

Shawna cut him off with a smile. "There is no 'still,' Doctor."

Sally placed a well-manicured hand on McGuire's arm. She came up just to his shoulder.

"Don't bother arguing with her, Simon. She's a very headstrong girl. Once her mind is made up, that's it." She rolled her eyes. Shawna felt like doing the same but not for effect. "A jackhammer couldn't get through." Sally took his arm and was already steering him toward the small kitchen, commandeering his attention just as she did everything else. "Now then, can I interest you in some hotcakes to go along with that coffee, Doctor?"

Even though the back of her head was turned toward her, Shawna could visualize her mother fluttering her lashes at McGuire. *Watch yourself, Simon. Mother's at it again.*

She had to admit that this time she was rather surprised at her mother's choice. Simon McGuire was a lot older than the men her mother gravitated toward. For the first time in her life Shawna felt a nudge of approval at Sally's choice.

McGuire looked down into the oval face and smiled. "Well, don't mind if I do."

As an afterthought, Sally looked over her shoulder at her daughter. "Shawna?"

She was surprised to be included. "I've already had breakfast, Mother. But thanks for asking."

Sally only nodded in reply. "Yes, I suppose you've eaten, at that." Her eyes were almost kindly as she looked at her daughter. "Was it a good party, dear?"

Shawna was expecting a completely different sort of question and was relieved to hear one so innocuous. "Yes."

"Good." With that, she turned her attention to the man beside her and the meal she had promised. The first, she hoped, of many.

That, Shawna thought, was the longest mother-daughter conversation they'd ever had where they weren't discussing one of her mother's disastrous affairs. It was approximately twenty years late, but better late than never.

She slipped into the bedroom to change her clothes.

And to think.

She stripped off her dress and strove, in vain, not to remember the way Murphy's hands had felt on her last night when he'd performed the very same ritual. There was a lot to think about. She couldn't manage that around Murphy. Like the sun, he blotted out what lay ahead when she looked.

Grabbing the first shirt she found in her closet, Shawna shoved her arms through the sleeves of a bright green T-shirt. A pair of cutoff jeans followed. It could have been a grass skirt for all the attention she paid.

She'd never felt like this about a man. Never experienced anything close to it. With Doug her emotions had gone through a slow evolution. Love was a comfortable, warm feeling. It meant security. Serenity. There had never been this wildness that seized her breath, that dissolved her mind and knees until they became the consistency of pond water.

She knew just where she was with Doug. She hadn't the slightest idea where that was with Murphy. For all she knew, this was his standard mode of operation: overwhelm, make love and leave. When it came to experience, hers was in the operating room and the medical facility.

All this was like a jungle to her.

No, not a jungle, she amended as she picked up her dress and pressed the material to her cheek. Exciting sensations danced all through her. A paradise, that's what it had been.

Whatever happened later, this isolated evening had given her a glimpse into a place she'd never known. A glimpse of a person she had never been.

She supposed she should be grateful to Murphy for that.

But she wasn't, she thought as she let the dress fall from her fingers onto the bed.

Because no matter what she said to the contrary, what she insisted upon in her heart, he had made her care.

And she had vowed never to care again.

Chapter Thirteen

She was trying to be patient, she really was. Though it was incredibly difficult for her, Kelly was honestly trying not to meddle in Murphy's life. She wanted to give Murphy his space and not crowd him.

She had lasted three days, longer than she actually thought she would. By Wednesday the questions were multiplying within her at a prodigious rate and were fairly bursting to get out.

Curiosity was killing her.

In those three days Kelly had interacted with Murphy several times at the office. She had seen him sitting across from her during the morning briefings. At none of these occasions had there been the slightest indication that he had brought someone special with him to the party, someone who'd had a positive effect on his life.

If anything, he was more subdued, which was decidedly unlike Murphy. Had she misread signs at the party? Shawna and Murphy had seemed so right together.

Thomas had advised her to just "leave Murphy alone." She loved Thomas, but he was a man, and she firmly believed that he just didn't understand these kinds of things. She couldn't just ignore what was under her nose.

Something was up with her brother and she wanted to know what.

As casually as possible, Kelly dropped by Murphy's office right after she'd returned from lunch. Murphy appeared buried in his work. There were books spread open all over the desk. His computer droned quietly, waiting for further input. It didn't look as if he'd left his office since he'd come in this morning.

She knew for a fact that he was supposed to have been somewhere other than his desk at ten-thirty. He'd had an appointment with Shawna. One he hadn't kept. Kelly frowned. Her brother was being perverse as only Murphy could.

When she walked into his office, Murphy glanced up and then returned to what he was doing. That wasn't like him, either. Murphy always had time to stop for a few words.

"So, how's everything?"

Murphy punched a few letters into the keyboard before even answering. "Hectic."

"I see."

Kelly cast about for some way to work into the subject. This just wasn't normal, this awkward feeling she was experiencing around Murphy. This man she'd seen for the past few days in the office was a stranger to her.

He was quiet, she thought, worried. He hadn't even been like this after Janice walked out on him.

Something was definitely wrong.

Kelly fingered a leather-bound volume. Originally, she'd wanted to pump Murphy for information as to his feelings about a woman she believed was perfect for him. Now her concern reversed. Had Shawna dumped Murphy? Had she done something to hurt him? Sisterly loyalty raised its head.

Murphy made another notation on the screen, wishing he could think clearly. His brain felt as if it were in some holding tank, soaked in water. Kelly moving around the room didn't help matters any.

He glanced in her direction. "Is there some reason you're hovering around my office, Kell, or are you just practicing landing patterns?"

She stopped moving and perched on the edge of Murphy's desk. "Charming as usual, I see."

He set his mouth grimly. "Yes, everything's just as usual." No, it wasn't, he thought, and that was just the problem. *His* problem, and he would work it out.

Kelly looked at him as thoughts moved like a creeping fog across Murphy's face. He could fool a lot of people, but he couldn't fool her. She was too tuned in to him. "Is it?"

He was defensive before he could prevent it. "What's that supposed to mean?"

They both knew the answer to that, so she gave him a knowing look and let it go. She went, instead, to the heart of the matter. Shawna.

Picking up a pen from his desk, she twirled it as if it was the most fascinating thing she'd ever seen. Very carelessly she interjected, "I liked her."

He'd been hoping that Kelly wouldn't start, but he'd been braced for the past three days, expecting it. He blew out an irritated breath and returned to the Kelso file. "Yeah, well, so did I."

Did. Had he changed his mind? Why? Damn, but he was annoying.

"But?" Kelly prodded, wanting to shake the words out of him. They'd never kept secrets, she and Murphy. It hurt that he'd start now.

Impatience creased his brow. If he'd worked this out to his satisfaction, he could say something. But it was one giant knot. A knot he thought best to abandon rather than undo.

"No buts, Kell. Look, I'm busy...." He gestured toward the open books.

But Kelly wasn't looking where he gestured. She was looking into his eyes. "Is it serious?"

He shrugged, pulling the file and a few of the books closer, a settler circling the wagons against an Indian attack. "The IRS isn't investigating, if that's what you mean."

So much for the subtle approach. "That is *not* what I mean and you know it." She placed a hand over the open file, blocking his access to it. "I was talking about you and Shawna. Is it serious between you?" Because it sure as hell looked that way to her from here. If it wasn't, he would be making jokes about it, tossing it off the way he did everything.

Murphy shrugged. The denial was on his tongue but wouldn't materialize. He rarely lied and never to Kelly. "Maybe."

Finally! He was finally serious about someone. She was beginning to think the day would never come again. Eagerness began to bubble within her like soda shaken in a can. "So?"

The look he gave her had No Trespassing written all over it. "Back off, Kell."

She didn't move an inch, physically or otherwise. "You know better than that." He was her brother. She wasn't about to treat this nonchalantly. "You were supposed to see her this morning," she began.

"How would you know that?" He'd canceled his appointment. It had been the cowardly way out, but he needed time, he thought, time to piece things together. Time to get hold of himself before everything got out of hand.

Kelly indicated his desk calendar with her eyes. "I snooped while you were in court yesterday." Her voice softened as she delved for answers. "Why didn't you go?"

For more reasons than he had time to enumerate. "I broke the appointment."

"That's obvious. It's also obvious that you're avoiding the question."

He rose and shoved his hands into his pockets. The view from his window was the Pacific. It was tranquil today, so blue that it almost hurt to look at it. All he could think of were her eyes. "Maybe I don't like the question."

She saw the defensive set of his shoulders. And then it came to her. "You really care about her, don't you?" When he didn't answer, she repeated the question more doggedly, thinking that if she could get him to admit it aloud, they'd be halfway there. "Don't you?"

He might as well tell her. If he didn't, she would stay here and drive him crazy. "Yes." He realized that he'd shouted the word. Restless, he moved around the wood-paneled office feeling trapped by his own decisions.

"So?" Why wasn't he doing something about it? she thought, exasperated.

"So I'm stopping it now, before it goes any further."

He saw Kelly's mouth drop open and knew more questions were on the way. Struggling, he got a grip on his impatience. She was only concerned about him, and he shouldn't be snapping her head off.

"I have to be crazy to have gotten myself in so deep that I didn't even see the signs." His mouth quirked and Kelly had the impression that, in a way, he was talking to himself more than to her. "She has a way about her, I don't know...."

Murphy ran his hand along the back of his neck. Words ordinarily came easily to him. He found himself digging for each one.

"On the one hand, she's so damn independent it's a challenge to get close to her." That's what had started it, he told himself with little conviction. The challenge. He turned to look at his sister. "And when I do, there's this vulnerable center that needs me. Needs me while she's trying to push me away with both hands."

If she wasn't convinced before, Kelly was now. "Sounds to me like you're in the middle of a relationship."

He laughed. She made it sound so easy. But then, she had a solid marriage to fall back on. He had only one overwhelmingly shattering experience. "Or hell."

There was a glimmer of humor in his eyes, which gave her hope. "Funny, that probably would have been the way Thomas would have described our first months together."

Murphy looked at Kelly knowingly, his affection rising to the fore. "If you're anything like this at home, he's probably still describing it that way."

Kelly slid off the desk and gave him a playful shove on the arm. He might be her older brother, but she worried about him. Worried about his being hurt and, more than that, worried that because he wouldn't risk something permanent, he would wind up being alone. It was a fate she didn't want to see. "Want my advice?"

He sat at his desk again and prepared to tune her out. "No."

She ignored his answer. Like a horse, Murphy had to be led to water. And she was going to persist until he drank. Kelly flipped the pages of his desk calendar. "Make a new appointment."

"I feel fine." And he did. The dizziness had left, and there were no more bouts of blurred vision. He hadn't had an episode since that one when they'd made love. Murphy saw no point in borrowing trouble by pursuing the matter.

Kelly looked at him pointedly. She saw things that he couldn't quite manage to hide. "You never did lie very well."

She retreated for the time being, silently declaring an end to the first round. Murphy gave no indication that he was going to do anything except continue to work on the file he had open before him.

Damn. The man was stubborn to a fault, she thought with a frustrated pang. She couldn't very well call Shawna herself. That would be going too far, even for her. She just had to remain patient and hope that somehow he'd come to his senses. Other than that, she couldn't do anything except be there for him when he needed it. It didn't feel like very much.

Kelly closed the door behind her. It met the frame a little more firmly than it normally would have.

Murphy winced. Once the door was shut, he gave up attempting to make sense out of his notes. He was going through his own version of diminishing returns. The more he concentrated, the less focused he felt.

He threw down his pen and dragged his hand through his hair.

What could he have been thinking of, allowing himself to get involved this way? He cared about Shawna and he didn't want to. More than anything, he didn't want to.

He should have seen it coming. Right from the start it had been different with her. He had never pursued where he wasn't invited. And yet, something—male pride, a death wish, he thought with a cryptic smile, *something*—had urged him on until he was up to his hips in quicksand before he realized that he'd stepped over the guardrail and left the safe path behind.

Three days now she'd been on his mind, as entrenched there as ivy tenaciously growing up a trellis. There was no way he could exile her from his thoughts.

But he had to.

This time the damage might be even worse than before. He wasn't sure he could handle it. He'd been in love with Janice, really in love. He'd envisioned himself having it all as he made a bid for the American dream. White picket fence, a wife, two kids, everything.

And then Janice had knocked his foundations right out from under him. A woman he'd trusted had lied to him and humiliated him. It made a man stop and think. Made him gun-shy.

It had never happened to him before. With his outgoing, gregarious manner and good looks, Murphy had never faced rejection of any kind, much less something like this. It went beyond rejection. He felt himself deceived, betrayed. To have misjudged a person, a situation, so greatly had knocked out the underpinnings of his confidence. He'd had absolutely no idea how to handle it. How to handle the pain that came along with it. So he'd denied it all.

The women he'd seen after Janice had all been pleasant, all seeking temporary companionship. No one was hurt. No one became involved. It had worked reasonably well.

And then Shawna had come into his life, upending everything. She had said she wanted no strings, had made it clear she couldn't handle strings. He'd agreed, pleased.

But he discovered that he was lying. He wanted strings. And as soon as he realized that, he knew it was time to back off. Back off and run in the opposite direction, where tranquillity lay.

So why the hell didn't he feel tranquil?

Shawna looked at her assistant. She was attempting to sound impersonal, but it wasn't working. It was bad enough that Murphy hadn't called her in three days. Three long days while she had eyed her answering machine like some silly teenager. But canceling his appointment was the last straw.

"That was it?" she demanded, shoving her hands deep into her lab coat. "He just canceled?"

Jeanne nodded. Her heart went out to the doctor, but she knew better than to show it. "He said he was feeling better and that maybe there had been a mistake in the M.R.I."

That again. She was really hoping that they were past this point. Obviously they were back to square one. An odious square one.

She felt restless and insulted, angry and hurt. And it was all his fault. "There was a mistake, all right, but not in the M.R.I." She pressed her lips together. "I don't suppose he wanted to reschedule."

"No," Jeanne said quietly.

Shawna shook her head. "Idiot," she muttered under her breath.

Struggling with her temper, she returned to her office. She closed the door behind her, counting to ten. Shawna felt like throwing something.

How dare he do this to her? How dare he stir her up, make her feel that there was just the smallest chance that things might work out for them, and then just vanish out of her life?

Well, damn him, anyway, she didn't need this. Didn't need him.

She closed her eyes as she sank down at her desk. She had gotten to a point where she didn't need anything.

And he had messed that up royally.

Taking a deep breath, Shawna attempted to calm herself down. Wednesday was ordinarily a short day. She didn't see patients after twelve. Jeanne usually went home by twelve-thirty. This was the time she usually worked on reports, dictating them for Jeanne to transcribe later for the files. With whatever time was left, she tied up any loose ends.

Today she didn't feel like tying anything except a noose around Murphy's neck.

And then she remembered. She had promised her mother that she'd take her shopping today. It wasn't a particularly appealing way to spend an afternoon. She didn't care to spend hours browsing through clothes in department stores, but it was better than sitting here, feeling the definite sting of rejection.

She should have known it would go this way.

And yet . . .

And yet he'd been so damn appealing, so sincere, she had lost her footing without realizing it. He'd worked his way through the layers that cocooned her feelings, had shown her a glimpse of a world that took her breath away and—

The telephone rang, dissolving all her thoughts like snowflakes on a stove. Murphy? The flicker of hope danced through her even as she tried to shut it out. Her line buzzed before she could lift the receiver.

"It's your mother on one."

Shawna struggled to hide the disappointment she felt. It was her mother, impatient to get started. "Hello, Mother? I've just got a few things to clear up and then—"

"Darling, there's been a change of plans."

Shawna knew what was coming before it was said. It was an old familiar pattern. But this time she thought she actually detected a hesitant embarrassment in her mother's voice. That would be a first.

"Would you mind terribly if I canceled our shopping spree?"

Shawna leaned back and merely shook her head. She was too angry at Murphy to be annoyed with her mother, though the words *déjà vu* rolled through her mind. "No. I take it something's come up."

"Oh, yes," Sally gushed like the schoolgirl she'd never ceased being. "Simon wants to take me out for a late lunch. Isn't that wonderful?"

"Wonderful." There'd been hundreds of canceled events in her life. She'd gotten accustomed to them a long time ago. But this time she actually felt happy for her mother. Simon McGuire, while she let him, was going to make a difference in her mother's life. A difference, Shawna felt, the woman sorely needed. Maybe she'd needed someone like Simon all along. "This makes how many times?"

"Twice." The only way to have missed the pride in her mother's voice was to have been struck deaf. "I think he's getting serious."

She could very well be right, Shawna thought. Her mother was a good-looking woman, well in her prime, and McGuire needed a little companionship in his life. They were both old enough to know what they wanted, and what to do about it.

Still, Shawna couldn't help feeling protective of both of them. "Mother, Simon McGuire is a very nice man. Don't hurt him."

"Hurting him is the last thing I have in mind." Sally laughed softly, contented. "I think he's the end of my rainbow. He makes me happy, Shawna. *Really* happy." Shawna had heard that before, but sincerely hoped that this time her mother meant it. "I feel guilty, breaking our date."

Now, that *was* a first. Maybe Simon was having a good effect on her. Or maybe her mother was growing up a little at last. "Don't worry about me. I'll be fine."

"I know, why don't you have lunch with your guy?"

She felt herself stiffen reflexively. "I don't have a guy, Mother."

"Yes, you do," Sally insisted in a knowing manner. "Murphy." She paused, as if she was about to hang up, then added, "Some men just take time, Shawna. Others need a little nudge to get them on their way. Bye."

Shawna knew just where she would have enjoyed applying that little nudge.

"You broke your appointment."

The tip of Murphy's pencil snapped as he looked up and saw her standing there in his doorway. He blinked, wondering if he was now seeing things, as well.

But she was there.

And real.

For the second time in his life he felt awkward. He shrugged. "I was busy."

Shawna raised her chin. "I see."

She still wasn't entirely certain what had possessed her to come here, other than hurt pride. She wasn't the type to be pushy and certainly not the type to chase after a man.

But then, she would have bet that she wasn't the type to respond the way she had on Saturday night, either. He'd shown her a side of herself that she hadn't even known existed and this new woman had facets to her that Shawna was about to let loose.

Instead of retreating, the way she might have, she crossed to him, her eyes blazing. He owed her an explanation.

"I didn't think you were the type to just use a woman and then leave, sneaking out of her life. Especially after what you said."

Her eyes pinned him in place before he could reply. "You disappointed me, Murphy. I thought you were different." With that, she turned away, determined to make it to the elevator before she allowed the angry tears to flow. She certainly didn't want him to think they were because of him.

He'd seen the pain in her eyes, and guilt seized him by the throat. Damn, he'd been thinking only of himself, not her. "Shawna."

Very slowly, as if she could move only in slow motion, she turned around. "What?"

"Maybe you scare me." It was a sorry excuse, but it was the truth.

That was absurd. She was tempted to hit him. Something else he'd managed to unleash in her. She'd never had a temper before. "I'm five foot two. I don't scare anyone."

He crossed to her then, before she had a chance to leave him. As much as he'd wanted her, he didn't realize the full magnitude until he saw her.

Murphy took her hands in his. "Yes, you do. You scare me. Scare the hell out of me." He drew her back into the room, closing the door behind her. "I told you about Janice."

She pressed her lips together, some of her bravado winding down. "Yes, you did."

This wasn't easy. He'd never even admitted this to himself. "What I didn't tell you was how much it hurt."

She shook her head. The idiot. Didn't he think she could figure that out on her own? "You didn't have to." She almost laughed at the surprised look on his face. "Women can sense these things."

He felt himself floundering. How did he tell her that things had gotten out of control for him? "I wanted us to have a good time without strings."

That much he had made perfectly clear earlier. What he hadn't said was that he'd be out of her life so quickly. "A doctor's appointment isn't a string."

He laughed softly. "Yes, it is, when it's with you." He sat on the leather sofa, taking her with him. "I like being free." He smiled as he looked into her eyes. Because he couldn't help himself, he traced the hollow of her cheek with his fingertips. "Except that I'm not. Every time I shut my eyes I see you. When you walked in, I thought my imagination had gone into overtime."

She pulled herself free. He was doing it again, weaving a web around her. And she couldn't let him do that. She had to be able to think clearly.

"I don't understand." She pulled her head back, away from his touch, away from the warm haze he could create so easily. "You ply me with arguments why I shouldn't back away, and then you do a disappearing act." She bit her lower lip, stopping herself before she admitted too much to him, before she told him how she felt. It would only send him running back to his bunker. "Well, I won't let you disappear, not until you get that eye surgery."

He needed to know that she cared. Maybe if he did, he wouldn't feel like bolting. "The surgery. Is that the only reason?"

She fixed him with a determined look, locking away the feelings that were churning inside her. She wanted to be held, loved, wanted. He made her realize that she needed so much. But she couldn't allow herself to be a supplicant. "The only reason you'll hear from me. We said no strings, and I'll keep to that bargain if you do."

He blew out a breath. He was getting back exactly what he'd said he wanted. Except that he didn't want it anymore. And it was killing him that he needed someone.

"I have to tell you," he said honestly, "you're turning me inside out."

She measured her words carefully. It was too easy to let herself believe him. "What I'd like to do is wring your neck."

He grinned at the threat. Humor, as he'd told her, was his best ally. That and the armor plating around his heart. "Over dinner?"

He was doing it again, she thought, breaking down her defenses even though she knew what was coming. She should have her head examined. They'd probably find it empty. "Over anything you want as long as I have a clear shot at it."

He rose and pulled her up with him. Murphy felt the glide of her body against his. Yearning flared within him. He'd done nothing but want her for three days now. "I've missed you."

She wanted to believe him, even though she knew it was just temporary. "You've got a hell of a way of showing it."

She certainly had the right to say that. "Yeah, I know." He leaned his cheek against her hair. It smelled of sunshine. "So what do we do about this?"

"Beats me." She looked up at him, fear warring with desire. "And don't think I haven't thought of it. Beating you, I mean."

He liked the way humor curved her mouth. "I never realized that you had such violent tendencies."

"Neither did I." She paused, knowing she was admitting too much. "I never knew a lot of things about myself until there was you."

He knew exactly what she was saying. A shiver of fear wedged through, but he pushed it away. There was time enough for regrets later. "Happening way too fast, isn't it?"

She could only nod. Her heart was accelerating just being near him like this. "Way too fast."

He could feel a sadness as he thought of the future. Without her. "You know what they say about things that heat up so fast."

He was already laying foundations for leaving, she thought. All right, if that was the way of it, she'd enjoy what there was. "Too hot not to cool down."

In his heart he'd hoped she'd say something to the contrary. "That's what they say."

She looked at him. "So?"

Damn, he'd take what he could and tell himself it was enough. "So let's warm ourselves by the fire while it's there." He caressed her face. "I think we both deserve it."

Wantonness filled her. She was acting against type again. But she was beginning to lose sight of who she was, standing here with him. "I have the next couple of hours free. My mother ducked out on a shopping spree."

He couldn't picture her going from store to store willingly. "I didn't think you'd enjoy that."

"I don't, she does. I was doing it for her." A smile curved her mouth. "Except that she went off with McGuire."

He could see how McGuire might be attracted to Shawna's mother. "She is a femme fatale, isn't she?" Shawna nodded. Murphy tightened his arms around her. "I like the subdued type myself. They tend to be deeper."

"Nice try." She wedged a hand against his chest. "They also don't tend to be sidetracked. What I was getting at was that you could come back with me to my office and I'll give you that follow-up exam." She became serious. "I don't like you playing games with this condition you have."

"I'd rather you played doctor somewhere else where we won't run the risk of being interrupted."

She had one hand on the doorknob, determined to get him to see reason, at least about this. "Later."

"Promises, promises." He followed her out the door, trying not to make promises of his own to himself.

Chapter Fourteen

The atmosphere within the small restaurant was smoky. Voices mingled with the sound of soft, bluesy music and the noise of people enjoying themselves, falling in love, or just merely being.

Harlow's was the kind of place a man brought a woman, if he wasn't trying to overwhelm her, Shawna thought as she sipped her wine. The food was good, the service adequate and the ambience incredibly romantic.

But then, anywhere would be romantic, she mused, with him. Murphy had extracted the promise of dinner from her in trade for patiently enduring another examination in her office. Or as patiently as Murphy could manage. It hadn't taken much work on his part to get her to agree.

Murphy saw the smile rising to her eyes, the one that seemed to spread out from the core of her soul. He wondered if she knew how much she captivated him. How she kept reeling him in when he was trying to find ways to swim out to the open sea. "What are you smiling about?"

She placed her wineglass down and looked at him. A glib answer rose to her lips, one that would allow her to hide her feelings. But she didn't want to hide things anymore. Like a caged bird whose door had suddenly sprung open, she didn't want to return to her confinement. She wanted to be with him.

Shawna twirled the stem of her glass in her fingertips. "This is the way I imagined it."

God, but she did make retreat one hell of a difficult accomplishment. "When? When did you imagine this?" When they'd arrived at Harlow's for dinner she'd mentioned that she'd never been here before.

"In high school." She'd envisioned them together like this. It had never been in a specific place, just some wonderful little restaurant where the atmosphere created an aura of intimacy around them. "Being with you like this."

He'd never thought about her being attached to him then. It had been too much of an uphill fight for him to believe that she had ever really had feelings for him before.

"You thought about us?"

Her smile broadened at his surprise. "Every girl in every one of your classes thought about you and her forming an 'us.'"

He didn't want to talk about every girl; he wanted to know how she had felt. "Why didn't you ever ... ?"

There were times when men could be so thick! "*Because* every girl thought about you and her forming an 'us.'" She moved her half-empty glass aside. The flame from the candle in the center of the table shimmered within the liquid, trapped there. Just as she was, she thought. Trapped by her feelings, by her desire. But maybe it wasn't a trap at all. Not if she held the keys to the door. "If nothing else, I was always a realist." A self-deprecating smile curved her mouth. "Besides, I was getting enough rejection on the home front. I didn't need to invite it elsewhere."

"Maybe I wouldn't have rejected you." Maybe, if she had come into his life back then, things would have been different. For both of them.

Shawna shook her head. Along the way the shadow had gotten substance, but she didn't fool herself about the impression she'd made back then.

"You wouldn't have noticed." She tucked her tongue into her cheek. "It was difficult getting close to you." Not that she had tried. She prided herself on always knowing her limits.

He shifted, uncomfortable with the topic. "You're exaggerating."

She lifted a shoulder and then let it drop. "Not by much."

He wanted to pursue something she'd alluded to earlier. "Was it very hard for you, growing up with your mother?"

This time the shrug was not so careless. "I suppose no harder than it would have been with anyone else." Time had allowed her distance and the luxury of healing. "Worse than some, better than others." She took another sip before adding, "I learned to shut out the loneliness by studying. By becoming the best I could be."

Murphy leaned back in his chair and studied her. There was an unmistakable touch of class about her that went beyond the clothes she wore. It came from self-confidence. No doubt it was hard won. And was almost as appealing as her supple body. "You certainly accomplished that."

She could read his thoughts and they warmed her. Somehow, he had unearthed a touch of vanity within her, too. Vanity, temper, passion. How many more emotions were there that had been hidden until he had come along?

Shawna couldn't prevent the smile that rose to her lips. "I meant mentally."

She was pleased, he thought. A simple matter of giving her her due and she was pleased. It was endearing. "That, too." Murphy drew closer again, breathing in the light fragrance she wore. Breathing in the stirring scent that was hers alone. His eyes caressed her. "I like what you've done with your hair."

Her brows drew together, highlighting her confusion. Without thinking, she raised her hand to her hair. "I didn't do anything different."

"I know." He liked her hair, the way she laughed, the way she scowled and tried to bully him for his own good. He liked everything about her, and that made him uneasy, as uneasy as a man holding an open flame near a gas leak. An explosion was coming.

He pushed the foreshadowing away.

"You do know how to turn a phrase." And a heart, she added silently.

He wasn't giving her phrases, he thought with a sliver of anxiety. He was giving her his heart, purely against his will. *Keep it light,* he urged himself. *Keep it light.* He had Janice in his history. Once burned . . .

Murphy nodded toward the small band. "They're playing our song."

Shawna leaned back in her chair, studying him. For a man with a wicked mouth, he looked utterly guileless. That was how he did it, she decided. That was how he had disarmed her, how he had made her trust him. With that innocent look. "We don't have a song."

He was behind her, moving back her chair and urging her to her feet. "Then how do you know that this isn't it?"

Shawna shook her head, as if to clear it. She placed her hand in his, letting him lead her. "You have some very strange logic."

The dance floor was small and crowded. Yet, like everything else within Harlow's, it only enhanced the intimacy. As soon as they began to dance, as soon as he took her into his arms, it felt as if there was no one else there but the two of them.

"Don't question it," he advised softly. "Just enjoy it." Swaying to the soft, pulsing beat, Murphy laid his cheek against her hair. This was where she belonged, he thought. Damn, this was getting bad. He couldn't seem to make himself break free. Even his tongue was tripping him up. "Can I see you tomorrow night?"

She smiled against his chest. He was doing it again. But this time she meant to keep up. "Is that anything like 'I'll call you'?"

He remembered the promise he'd left in his wake Sunday morning and had the good grace to wince. "Ouch. I deserve that."

She nodded, her hair making a soft *woosh*ing noise against his jacket. "Also a kick in the shins, but lucky for you, I'm a lady."

If anyone deserved that title, she did. Which was why her sudden appearance in his office intrigued him. A lady would have told him to rot in hell for his uncalled-for behavior. "What made you come after me?"

"Pride." She looked up at him. "Hurt pride." She let that sink in for a moment, then added, "And professional concern." She was still his doctor, and she wasn't about to let the matter drop. They weren't working against a firm deadline, but she couldn't shake the feeling that there was a clock ticking somewhere. "We still have that small matter of your eye surgery to clear up."

He didn't want to spend tonight discussing his so-called condition. She was enough of a weakness for him without adding that to it. The thought of the pending surgery only compounded his feelings of vulnerability.

Murphy saw an opening on the floor and guided her toward it. Right above them a multisided ball sparkled, reflecting the thin shafts of light. It sprinkled them with moonbeams as they danced.

"Later."

She had every intention of taking him up on that, whether he wanted to or not. But for the moment she let him feel he'd pushed the subject away. There was something else she had to know. It cost her to ask.

"Would you have stayed away if I hadn't come to your office today?"

She had looked loaded for bear and utterly magnificent in her anger, standing in his doorway. Stronger men than he would have succumbed to desire.

"No."

With all her heart she wanted to believe him. Shawna leaned back and looked into his eyes. They were partially hidden by the dusky atmosphere. Yet she thought she saw something, something she wasn't sure he was aware of. Fear, just the slightest glimmer of fear. He was afraid of her, or of what she represented.

"Really?"

"Really." He couldn't admit this if she was looking at him. He pressed her to him, his hand at the center of her spine. He liked the way she shivered as she rested her cheek against his chest. His words glided along her hair. "I was just taking a little time out, trying to regain some of the control I'd lost."

It sounded as if he were talking about boardroom dealings. "Regain control? Over what?"

"My emotions." When she looked at him, he smiled at the surprised expression on her face. "You do have a way of churning them up."

"It's mutual."

He could only stare at her, mystified. Outside of Kelly, he'd never known anyone quite like Shawna. "You're the most honest woman I've ever met."

It wasn't a sensual observation, but she found it flattering. "I don't know how to be coy."

"Don't learn." Murphy threaded his fingers through hers, knowing he was sinking fast. "Don't ever learn."

He absorbed the feeling of having her nestled against him. Holding her this way, feeling her body sway into his, only made him want her in his bed that much more. She was like the proverbial potato chip. One sample was definitely not enough.

"So." He looked down at her. "You didn't answer me. Can I see you tomorrow night?"

She wanted him to. So much she could taste it. But there were responsibilities to see to. Responsibilities that defined who and what she was. "I have to be at the clinic tomorrow evening."

Another song wove its way into the first one. The band was playing a medley, he thought absently. He wanted to be with her in the worst way. More warning signs went up, but he ignored them. "I've gotten really good at filing."

He felt her smile as it grew against his chest. "Caro's been asking about you."

"There, it's settled. I'll come along."

She shook her head. "Don't you have a life?"

Murphy leaned toward her. "Yes," he whispered against her ear. "And I'm living it."

She struggled to keep her eyes from fluttering shut. But it wasn't the hour that was doing it. It was Murphy. "I should be getting home."

He nodded. She felt his hold on her hand tighten just a little. "My sentiments exactly."

Propriety dictated that she make a stab at taking a stand, though her heart wasn't in it. "My home, Murphy."

He ran his other hand lightly along her back. Shawna felt as if her clothes were being burned away, as if he'd touched her naked flesh.

"Home is a relative term," he told her. "You have a relative in yours. Mine is empty."

"I shouldn't..." There was a report she'd brought home that she wanted to look over again. And rounds to make in the morning. She had no business giving in to herself this way.

Murphy kissed her neck, a soft, small butterfly kiss that melted against her skin like a snowflake landing on her tongue. Her resolve melted just as easily. "Murphy, you're not playing fair."

"I know. I'm playing to win." At least for tonight. Doubts nibbled at him, but he refused to acknowledge them. His desire for her, his need for her, was too great.

The music stopped, but Murphy remained standing where he was, oblivious to the couples who were passing them.

"Come home with me, Shawna," he urged softly.

If she'd ever heard anything more sensual, more seductive, she wasn't aware of it. Shawna said nothing. Instead, she placed her hand in his.

She was going with him. She'd wanted nothing else for days.

"Can I get you anything?" Murphy offered as he closed the front door behind them.

His hand was on her back, a light, possessive gesture that meant the world to her. She doubted that it meant anything to him.

But it would, she promised herself.

Shawna felt her nerves knitting themselves madly into a knot. Anticipation, anxiety and intrepidity were the skeins.

She thought of the drink she'd had at the restaurant. "White wine, if you have any."

He nodded, walking toward the kitchen. "White wine it is."

She followed him, curious. "You really have some?" It didn't strike her as something a man would have in his refrigerator. Beer, yes, but not white wine.

"Sure." Murphy took out the bottle and placed it on the counter as he opened the cupboard above it. "Kelly likes it."

She watched as he poured the light amber liquid into a fluted goblet. "And all the other women you bring here, do they like it, too?"

He laughed and shook his head. "There haven't been all that many."

She arched a brow at his disclaimer. She wasn't asking for details, just the truth.

She didn't believe him, he thought. Why should she? He'd lived with a reputation for a long time now, grounded in truth but completely overblown.

"I'm not a monk, but to live up to the reputation I've somehow managed to acquire, I wouldn't have time to breathe, much less be the successful lawyer that I am." He winked at her. "And I am successful." He wasn't bragging, just stating a point with pride. Murphy handed her the glass.

She accepted it, then looked at him. "Aren't you going to have any?"

Her question brought forth a languid smile that slipped over his face like a sunbeam dancing along a garden path. "I'm waiting for my favorite drink to warm to room temperature."

She looked around, but there was no other bottle out. He'd placed the wine in the refrigerator after filling her glass. Perplexed, she took a single sip before asking, "What is your favorite drink?"

"White wine on your lips." He saw the quizzical look on her face deepen. "You drank some at Kelly's the other night. I could still taste it on your lips when we made love." His eyes held hers. "I seem to have developed quite a thirst for it."

Shawna could feel her pulse jumping. She was hardly aware of setting her glass down on the counter. Murphy framed her face in his hands. His breath caressed her skin, stirring her to incredible heights as he lowered his mouth to hers.

It was like the gate suddenly rising at the racetrack at Santa Anita. The horses took the field, pounding out of their stalls as if their very lives depended on running. On winning. As soon as his lips touched hers, a flood of emotions poured through her, surrounding her, seizing her. Drowning her.

It felt so wonderful she could have cried.

His mouth was hungrily on hers. A wildness struck. All the control, all the well-honed moves shattered as if they had never existed. He felt her hands splayed on his chest, tugging at his shirt, and something tore loose within him. He wanted to rip the very clothes off her body.

Murphy cursed the flash flood coursing through him even as he found himself being swept away by it.

He had to fight back his eagerness, afraid that he would hurt her, afraid that he would make her retreat. But the feel of her ardent hands gliding over him, pulling away his clothing, spurred Murphy on, annihilating common sense, destroying restraint. Making his desire almost uncontrollable. It was like a huge beast raging within his chest, demanding release.

Demanding her.

It was madness, sheer, compelling, mind-blotting madness. He didn't know himself.

It was like nothing he'd ever felt before. Lovemaking had always been a pleasure, a delight, stirring and hot. This was something that dragged him into the center of an active volcano, something that took control of him rather than the other way around.

He never remembered it being like this, not with Janice, not with anyone. He had never felt this way before. As if he'd go insane if he couldn't have her.

He had to stop her questing hands before he took her right here, on the floor.

Dragging air into his lungs, as if that could somehow restore his senses, he grabbed her hands and held them in his. "Whoa, Shawna, we have all night."

"I know."

Her eyes gleamed like blue diamonds before her mouth came down on his. Again and again her lips slanted over his, urging him on, driving him farther into a dark, dangerous region he'd only skirted before. His caution vanished, taking with it the last of his ability to rein himself in.

With hands that were skilled, yet trembling, he pulled her jacket from her arms. As it fell, he yanked her blouse free from her skirt's waistband. His fingers felt thick as he worked at the neat row of pearl buttons that ran the length of her body.

A *ping* told him he'd torn off a button and sent it flying to the floor.

"Damn."

The word vibrated against the sensitive hollow of her throat, burning into her skin. She felt the air sliding along her bare shoulders.

"I know how to sew," she murmured thickly, desperate to be free of the cumbersome silk that separated her from him. Desperate to feel his hands on her. Desperate to feel him.

"So do I." Pulling his head away, he had to take a breath before they both went up in flames. The only problem was, he had a feeling he was going to reap what he'd sewn.

But that was for later, not now. Fear of consequences was something that was new, even now, being quickly burned away in the heat of his desire. In the flames ignited by the sweet, tempting taste of her mouth.

He'd freed her of the last of her clothes and was quick to sample what he craved. Slowly, knowing that it drove her over the first of many peaks, he ran his tongue along her body. The taste of her skin varied, here dusky, here sweet.

He couldn't get enough of her, would never get enough of her. She tasted of every single dream he'd ever had in the deepest recesses of his heart.

Shawna's hands were steady and sure as they unnotched his belt and worked his trousers and briefs down along his hips. She wanted him.

Nothing else mattered.

Clothes were scattered, falling in tangled heaps on each other, unnoticed, unwanted. She was completely nude, completely his.

Murphy raised her up and felt a surge pounding through his loins as she wrapped her long legs around him, binding him to her more than just physically.

"Bedroom?" he whispered.

The bedroom was a million miles away and she wanted him now. "Here," she murmured against his throat. "Take me here."

If he'd had a will, she completely unwound it with those words. Like a sweater that had gotten the smallest thread caught on a nail and unraveled, she pulled his will from him. And brought them both to heaven.

Leaning her against the table, Murphy rediscovered the secrets they'd found together an eternity ago. He stroked, he caressed, he cradled. His mouth was hot, teasing, suckling, branding. Reducing her to a mindless, simpering puddle.

And reducing himself, as well.

He had to feel this. The thought broke through the haze around her brain. She had to make him feel this. But all she could do was receive and receive.

And pray for more.

His mouth trailed along her silken skin, awakening dormant infernos in its wake. Shawna cried out as his tongue slid along her belly, making it quiver in frenzied anticipation. His mouth drew closer, closer, and then he lost himself in the core of her essence.

Explosions racked her body.

Shawna cried out his name, her hands spread out on his shoulders as if she were falling, falling, never reaching an end.

Her breath was ragged, scattering the air as she forced it from her lungs. Her heart was hammering so hard she thought it would crack in two. Shawna fell back, numbed and tingling. Wanting more, not daring for more.

When she opened her eyes all she could see, all there was, was Murphy. There was nothing more.

His body gleamed of sweat and wanting. His eyes, cloudy with desire, smiled into hers. "The kitchen table's taken on a whole new meaning in my life."

And so will other things, she thought.

Arching her body, she offered herself to him. But before he had a chance to press a kiss to her flesh, she twined her arms around his neck and brought his mouth down to hers. Her body moved against his, her nipples teasing his chest. Arousing him, hardening him, making him crazy.

He couldn't hold back any longer.

Afraid that the table could give way beneath them, Murphy took her into his arms and lowered her to the floor. His eyes never leaving hers, he slid the length of his body over her, absorbing every soft nuance.

He wanted to hold back just a little longer, but he hadn't the strength, not when she flowed through his hands like hot sin.

She'd never seen the kind of passion she saw in his eyes. It made her want to weep. No one had *ever* wanted her this way. She had never wanted anyone the way she did him.

Shawna raised her arms to him, urging him forward, ready to accept him. Ready to be taken to places she'd only so recently discovered. Places that only he could lead the way to.

Murphy heard a groan ripple through the air and knew it was his. There was an ache in his body, in his very soul, and it belonged to her. As he did.

He'd pursued her on a whim and become captured of his own volition. She held him prisoner and he hadn't the strength to free himself.

He had only the strength to enjoy.

Fatal words suddenly sprang to his mind, words that would seal his fate. His doom. He kept them silent as he entered her, sheathing himself in salvation.

Unable to stop them, he muffled the words against her neck when they refused to remain confined any longer.

"I love you."

Shawna's eyes flew open. She heard, heard and hugged the words to her. Though she longed to echo them back, she understood that for now, she couldn't. Murphy would only take them back with a laugh if she did.

But they were hers and she silently rejoiced.

The tempo of their bodies increased, going faster and faster until all the barriers were broken.

Until the stardust rained on them both.

Chapter Fifteen

It wasn't cooling off, Murphy thought as he hurried to get ready. He'd overslept again and when he'd gotten up, it had taken him a few minutes to focus his eyes. It seemed to be taking longer and longer each morning, but that could just be his imagination.

What wasn't his imagination was that Shawna was lingering in the recesses of his mind, haunting his thoughts whenever he wasn't with her. No, it definitely wasn't cooling off, this feeling he had for the good doctor. This all-consuming passion. If anything, it was heating up.

Murphy broke off a piece of pastry and quickly ate it. He didn't have time for breakfast this morning. So, what else was new? He needed to get organized on the home front. In more ways than one.

More than a month had gone by and he was still putting things off. Putting off admitting that he needed an operation. Worse, putting off admitting that he couldn't walk away from his feelings for Shawna.

Both shimmered obstinately before him as he hunted for his keys, demanding attention. Demanding that he face up to them.

But how could he? To admit one was to put his mortality on the line; to admit the other was to risk everything else. His heart, his very soul.

Hadn't he already learned that to place his fate in the hands of someone else was the absolute essence of stupidity? How could he just wait around to see if she would crumple his world the way Janice had?

The answer was, he couldn't.

Shawna wasn't like Janice, but he had once felt that there was no one like Janice, either. He had trusted Janice, placed his heart into her hands. He had believed that they could have a life together that was as precious as what his parents had had. As special as what both his sisters had with their husbands.

Surprise.

Murphy lifted up a section of yesterday's paper on the coffee table and found his keys. Clutching them in his hand, he went to collect his briefcase from the hall table.

He was a shrewd lawyer, he thought as he entered the garage, but he was a lousy judge of women. Murphy tossed his briefcase into the car through the open front passenger window.

And yet, he couldn't keep away from Shawna, either. He found himself rearranging his life to make time for her, accompanying her to the clinic whenever it was feasible. It wasn't even a matter of going along to protect her. Mount had taken care of that. The man had put out the word—hands off the clinic. People came and went to the clinic in safety now.

No, Murphy went to the clinic with Shawna for the same reason he showed up at her office after hours. For the same reason he'd pick up the phone and call her at odd times during the day, in the middle of studying a brief, or after a session with a client. Just to hear the sound of her voice and have it curl like smoke in his belly.

In his mind's eye he saw her the way she'd been last night, nude and supple in his arms, flowing through his hands like quicksilver. Like a dream that would fade when he woke up.

Murphy sighed as he got in behind the wheel.

The quicksand was no longer up to his hips. It was up to his throat now, and he was sinking fast. The more he resisted, the deeper he was pulled in.

Something was going to have to be done before he made a mistake that could wind up haunting him for the rest of his life. Murphy took out the garage-door opener from the glove compartment. He aimed it at the door behind him. The wide door slowly creaked open, reminding him that he was supposed to have oiled the hinges a week ago. It sounded like someone emerging from the crypt. One hand on the wheel, Murphy turned around, prepared to back the car out.

There was a woman standing in the middle of his driveway. From the looks of it, she had been standing there for at least a couple of minutes. She appeared to be waiting for him.

Carefully Murphy eased the car halfway down the driveway. As the car idled, he pressed the garage-door opener and the door closed with a mournful protest. Tonight he'd definitely oil that thing before it set his teeth on edge.

The woman smiled at him as she stepped forward again, moving closer to his car. "Hi. I was going to ring your doorbell, but then I heard the noise in the garage and thought that you were probably leaving for work."

Murphy lowered his window farther. He didn't recognize her. "Can I help you?"

The woman, small and pleasant, looking a little like the cherub that his mother hung on their family Christmas tree, shook her head. Her brown eyes fairly gleamed. "Oh, you've already done far more for me than you could possibly imagine."

He didn't have time for this, but he didn't like mysteries and he hated to leave things hanging. Murphy turned off the ignition. Opening his door, he got out. He towered over the petite woman.

Murphy squinted against the early-morning sun and against the sharp slash of pain that was capriciously dancing across his brow.

"Do I know you?" Scrutinizing her face nudged a vague memory forward. A woman on the lawn, talking to a neighbor while her little girl played with a stuffed dog. "Wait a minute, I do. You're the woman—''

"Whose child you saved." The dark brown head bobbed up and down enthusiastically. "Yes. I'm sorry I haven't come by until now, but we've been staying in a motel, waiting for the damages to our house to be repaired." She licked her lips, pausing for air. "I know that's no excuse, but things do have a way of getting away from you."

Speaking of which, he thought, glancing at his watch, time was ticking away. He had to cut her short. "You don't owe me—''

The woman laid a hand on his arm. "But I do, I do. I can't begin to tell you how much." Her eyes suddenly clouded. "You have no idea how much."

Murphy heard the hitch in her voice. Oh, God, she was going to cry. He quickly took out his handkerchief and offered it to her.

She accepted it gratefully, looking a little chagrined. She dabbed at her eyes and then drew in a long breath.

"I promised myself I wouldn't cry, and here I am, getting mascara all over your handkerchief." Composing herself, Marion Reynolds returned Murphy's handkerchief to him. "It's just that I become so emotional whenever I think of what might have—'' Her voice broke again.

She waved away his handkerchief when he offered it again. Murphy tucked it into his pocket. "Life is full of 'might haves,' Mrs. Reynolds." He congratulated himself on remembering her name. "It's the 'what *is*' that is important." *Great philosophy,* he mocked himself, *for a man who keeps ducking out on "what is."*

Mrs. Reynolds nodded vigorously, as if she had just been privy to a great revelation. "Yes, and because of you, my daughter 'is.'" She beamed at him. "And so is my husband."

She had completely lost him. "I don't understand. I only rescued your daughter."

Her eyes shone with gratitude. "You did more than that, you rescued my marriage."

Murphy drew his brows together. "How—?"

"We were separated, Jimmy and I, and very probably on our way to a divorce." She shrugged helplessly. "You know how things can fall apart on you without you even noticing that it's happening." There was genuine regret in her voice, but in the next moment she had swept it away. "But after he heard about the fire and thought about just how close he'd come to really losing both of us, Jimmy realized how much he loved Suzanne and me."

Marion paused for a moment, wanting to get the next phrase just right. The way her husband had said it to her. 'How much he wanted to be there, to share every day with us." The woman squared her shoulders. "Jimmy said that you don't fully appreciate what you have until you almost lose it."

She looked at Murphy, her eyes bright. "That's what you've done for us, Mr. Pendleton. You've not only saved my baby, you've also brought us all together again. I just wanted to make sure that you knew. And I wanted to personally thank you for risking your life."

Touched, he smiled down at the woman. "You're very welcome."

Concern entered her eyes as she cocked her head, remembering. She chewed on her lower lip, undecided whether to mention this or not. "There weren't any serious after-effects from that bump on the head, were there?"

Lady, you have no idea.

He shook his head very slowly. There was a hazy pain setting in, red, like a blazing sunset in the western sky. 'None to speak of."

She looked relieved. "That's good, because I would have hated to think that you were permanently hurt in some way...."

So would I.

He was getting maudlin, he thought. It wasn't like him. Murphy placed a hand on the car door.

The motion wasn't wasted on Marion. "Well, I know I must be keeping you. Like I said, I just wanted to come by and tell you how very grateful I am. How very grateful we all are," she amended.

She began to back away, then stopped. "We'll be back in the house in another week, according to the contractor." She waved a dismissive hand. "Although you know how they always miscalculate. They're all probably related to weathermen. Anyway, please come by and see us when we do get back. I know Suzanne will want to thank you herself." The woman grinned. "She thinks of you as this superhero who came whooshing in to save her."

Murphy laughed at the idea.

"Well, then, I'll definitely come by to see her," he promised as he got into the car. He wondered if the highway patrol was out in force today or if he could bend the speed limit a little. He was going to need to make up for the lost time. "It's nice to have someone think of you as a superhero."

"She's not the only one," Marion assured him warmly as she waved goodbye.

"Mother, I'm going to be late," Shawna protested, hurrying into her shoes. She was holding a cup of coffee in her hand. The contents were sloshing over the side as she moved, sprinkling coffee on the kitchen floor in her wake.

She had no patients to see in the hospital this morning and no surgery scheduled until one. But there were still office appointments to keep, and her patience was running a little thin. Judging by her behavior last night, her mother had gone back to her old ways.

"Yes, I know." Sally clamped a surprisingly strong hand around her daughter's wrist, immobilizing Shawna and sending another small wave of coffee toward the floor. Shawna sighed as she looked at it. The floor was getting all the coffee that she needed.

"But I just have to tell you," Sally insisted. She looked as if she was bursting with enthusiasm. "It'll only take a minute."

Shawna sincerely doubted it, but she stopped moving and looked at her mother expectantly. She had waited up for Sally until two this morning. She'd finally given up and gone to bed, upbraiding herself for being concerned. It wasn't as if this was something new. While she was growing up there had been many nights when Sally hadn't come home until the wee hours of the morning.

It was just that this time she'd thought her mother had finally turned over a new leaf. She should have known better.

Shawna sighed as she set the now almost empty mug on the table. "All right, Mother, I'm listening. What's this big thing you have to tell me?"

Sally smiled, then suddenly looked shy as she hesitated.

Shawna frowned. This wasn't like her mother. Sally Rowen could talk the ears off a brass monkey without half trying. She laid her hand on her mother's shoulder. "Is something wrong?"

Sally shook her head, her long, dangling earrings sweeping along her shoulders, dusting along Shawna's hand. "No, everything's right. Fine. Wonderful." The volume of her voice swelled with each word, then fell. "It's just that now that you're listening, I'm not sure how to say this."

Concern tightened its grip. She scrutinized her mother's face, trying to divine the answer. "Something *is* wrong."

"No," Sally corrected gently, "I think for the first time in my life, everything's perfect."

Oh, God, not again. Shawna sighed. "You met another man." She had thought that her mother was going out with Simon McGuire last night, but she'd obviously been wrong.

"No. I met the *right* man." Sally's face softened until she almost looked like a teenager. A very smitten teenager, Shawna thought, growing anxious despite herself. "And he's asked me to marry him."

Shawna felt tension taking over and cautioned herself against it. Her mother was a grown woman. This was none of her concern. And yet, it was. It always would be. "Who?"

Sally looked confused. Hadn't Shawna been paying attention? "Why, Simon, of course."

Shawna stared. She wasn't altogether certain that her mouth hadn't dropped open. There was no "of course" about it. Simon McGuire was a respected, levelheaded, kindly grandfather. Kindly grandfathers didn't ask women they'd known a little over a month to marry them. Did they?

"Dr. McGuire asked you to marry him?"

If Sally noticed the note of incredulity in her daughter' voice, she gave no indication. "Yes. Last night. This morn ing, really."

Shawna could tell that her mother was far and away b the dreamy look upon her face.

"We were sitting in that lovely little gazebo overlookin the ocean." Her eyes turned toward Shawna, as if trying t pull her into the scene. "You know, the one in Lagun Beach. The really romantic one." Her sigh underlined he description. "I was chilly, so he slipped his arm around m to keep me warm. He really can keep a girl warm, yo know," she confided.

Before Shawna could answer that, no, she didn't know Sally had sprinted down another length.

"That's when he said that I made him feel so young, s alive again." To Shawna's amazement her mother actuall blushed. "And he told me that he didn't want to ever los that feeling. Or me."

Sally was twisting her hands together, her fingers knot ting as if she were pressing the sensation back inside her afraid that it would escape. She looked down at them as i she'd never seen them before and whispered softly, "I sai there was no chance of that."

Her head shot up as if she'd suddenly been injected. An she had been, with joy. Sally took both her daughter's hand in hers, attempting to transfuse the sensation. Everyon should feel like this. All of the time.

Sally couldn't remember when she'd been happier. "An then he said he wanted to be sure. *That* was when he aske me to marry him."

Odd, but she was already getting used to it. "And yo said yes."

A wide grin split her mother's carefully made-up face The answer had been a foregone conclusion. "I said yes."

Her mother had been down this path several times, an though Shawna thought that McGuire was a wonderfu man, doubt nibbled at her. This woman, flighty, impossi ble, nomadic, was still her mother, and she cared about he a great deal. Shawna didn't want to see Sally hurt for any reason.

"Are you sure, Mother? Are you very sure?" She held up her hand as her mother opened her mouth. "Before you answer, remember your track record."

A self-deprecating smile curved her mouth. "Not a very pretty one, is it?"

She'd been the one to raise the point, but now that it was out in the open, Shawna felt a twinge of remorse. "That depends on your point of view. Compared to a couple of well-known movie stars, you're a piker."

But there was another way to look at it. "Compared to the average woman, I'm a loser."

Shawna took hold of her mother's shoulders. There was compassion in her eyes as well as love. "You could never be compared to the average woman, Mother."

Sally came to life like a newly watered flower. "That's what I like about you, Shawna, you're so loyal." Her expression sombered around the edges as realization entered her eyes. There was so much to make up for. A whole lifetime. "Oh, God, Shawna. I did make such a mess of my life. And yours. You were always the one who could pull all the pieces together, not me." Holding Shawna's hands in hers, Sally stood back and admired what she had had only a small hand in creating. "Although I have to say, you turned out beautifully despite my influence."

Shawna wouldn't have said she was shocked, but she was very close to it. "Do you mean that?"

"Yes."

A smile slowly lifted the corners of Shawna's mouth, as slowly as the beam of light filtering through her being. She would have thought herself beyond that. But parental approval at any age, she thought, meant a lot. "You know, that's the first time you ever told me you were proud of me."

Sally began to deny it, then realized that Shawna was probably right. Her daughter kept better track of things than she ever could. "Is it?"

Remorse was in her eyes. Seeing it startled Shawna. And it went a long way in erasing a lengthy list of hurts.

"I should have said it a long time ago." Pride swelled within her breast as she looked at her only child. Pride and love. "Because I have been, for many years now. I've done a lot of foolish things in my life that I really regret."

Her voice filled with emotion when she thought of all the missed opportunities, the times she'd allowed to slip through her fingers because she'd been so busy with her own life.

"The only thing I never regretted was having you, even if I didn't know how to show it. I guess I always thought that you could take care of yourself, so it was all right for me to be the way I was." There was no way to go back and fix any of that. She could just go forward and try to make amends.

Sally embraced her daughter. "But I've always loved you, Shawna. And I'm sorry I wasn't the mother that you deserved."

"Don't be sorry." Shawna smiled at her. "You were a very interesting mother, not to mention beautiful. You were the princess, and I was the enchanted frog."

Sally was quick to deny the assessment. "You were never a frog."

"Close. Back then. But it all worked out," she continued before her mother could argue with her any further. "If I hadn't had to raise myself and look out for you, I wouldn't have turned out so stubborn—"

"So tenacious," Sally corrected. "So much more able to withstand the curves that life throws." Sally blinked back tears as she cupped her hand along Shawna's cheek. "You're the best part of me, Shawna. You always were."

Sally blew out a breath, embarrassed as she sought to shake off the somber effects of her emotions. There was a wedding to think about. She took on a fresh head of steam.

"So, after I said yes, we went to his house and made love." She shut her eyes as she remembered, missing the expression on her daughter's face. "He really is very creative—"

There was no changing the woman. Shawna could only laugh. "Mother, I don't think I need to hear this about Dr. McGuire."

Sally looked at her in surprise as her reverie was cut short. "Oh. All right. I just wanted you to know that I'm going to be very, very happy. He makes me feel good. And safe." She almost sighed the last word. She had never felt safe before.

"I can gather that without going into the minute details." Shawna kissed her mother's cheek. "Be happy, Mother. You deserve it."

Shawna looked at the clock on the kitchen wall. God, but she was running behind schedule. She started for the front door.

Sally followed her. She wasn't finished. "Be my matron of honor?"

Matron. It sounded so old. And her mother seemed so young. But then, love could do that to you. This time, with luck, her mother had finally found the pot of gold at the end of the rainbow. "You got it. Now I really have to go."

Sally nodded. "When you come home, we'll work on the wedding plans."

And for the first time, Shawna realized as she left her apartment, she would like nothing better than to see her mother married.

The news bubbled within Shawna like a precious secret, warring with another one, a secret of her own that she was holding back until the right moment came.

She went from one examining room to the other, seeing patient after patient, counting the minutes until she had a free moment to call Murphy.

He called her first. Trust Murphy to be faster, she thought, settling into her heavily padded chair. She lost no time in telling him the first of her news.

Murphy's reaction was pure astonishment. "You're kidding?"

"No, I'm serious. My mother's getting married. To Dr. McGuire, of all people." She sat back, rocking. "I never pictured McGuire as the kind of man to get swept off his feet. But if anyone could do it, my mother could."

It probably ran in the family. "Maybe he swept her off hers," Murphy suggested.

Shawna laughed. Jeanne poked her head into the office, motioning toward the report she held in her hand. But

Shawna waved her back. Whatever it was, she'd get to it in a few minutes. She had a conversation to finish first.

"She alluded to that, but Mother is deceptively fragile at times. What she wants, she usually gets." Shawna thought back to the first time she had seen them together, her mother fluttering her lashes at the distinguished man, curling up to him on the sofa. "I don't think Dr. McGuire had a snowball's chance in hell."

He could tell by her tone that she was pleased with this match. "I think Dr. McGuire is a very lucky man to find love at his age." He was attempting to find a way to work up to the question burning in his mind.

Shawna took a deep breath, preparing for a plunge. She picked up on his cue and hoped she could dovetail into her own news. "I think that people are lucky to find love at any age."

The long pause on the other end of the line gave her an uneasy moment. But it was nothing compared to what she felt when he spoke.

"Move in with me, Shawna."

For a minute she couldn't even think. He was asking her to share his bed in a temporary arrangement. Not his life, but his bed. While he was giving her something with one hand, he was tearing away something far more precious with the other. Shawna unconsciously placed her hand over her flat stomach and felt a pang.

Using the tool he'd once showed her, she tried humor to talk him out of this before he pressed the matter too far. Before he hurt her too much. "Bad timing. I'm finally getting my bed back."

A wave of foreboding filtered through him. It had taken him time to conquer his demons, to finally admit to himself that Shawna was the best thing that had ever happened to him. That because of her, he could actually feel again. She'd reassembled him and made him whole. He didn't want to lose her. "Fine, we'll christen it just before you move in."

Shawna sat up, steeling herself against the pain his words had generated. He wanted to keep this temporary. "No. It's not an option."

He didn't understand. Wasn't this what she wanted? he'd been so adamant about no strings. Having her move 1 kept the path open for her. Murphy was confident that ith that step taken, he could eventually wear her down to he point where she would agree to marry him.

"Why? You care, Shawna. I know you do."

She could feel the tears rising in her throat, clawing to be ree. "Yes, I do." She bit her lip to keep it from trembling. 'It's too complicated to explain."

She wanted him to ask her to marry him, not to move in. he wanted him to care enough, to love her enough to take risk on forever. The way she was ready to risk it with him.

Murphy backed away before her rejection could sting, but .e wasn't fast enough.

"I don't need an answer right away," he cautioned. 'Take your time. Think about it."

If he'd been in front of her, she would have thrown omething at him.

"I don't need to think about it." Her voice was sharp to ide the fact that it had cracked. "The answer's no. No now, o later."

She wasn't going to sell herself short, to slide into a relaionship and just let it drift. She knew exactly what she vanted. Marriage. To him. If he couldn't give her that, she vasn't going to accept half measures.

Besides, she wasn't just thinking of herself anymore.

Murphy resisted the temptation to slam down the telehone, to back away now before she knew how much she'd urt him. "I think we have something good."

"We do." A tear fell on her desk, spreading out like a lear ink blot. "The answer's still no." She barely whisered the refusal.

"Why?" It didn't make any sense to him. He felt as if he vas hitting his head against a wall. It wasn't in his nature to eg, and yet here he was, hanging on, hoping she would hange her mind.

She let out a ragged breath slowly, praying he wouldn't .ear. Praying she could keep her voice steady. "I can't exlain it if you don't understand."

He could feel his temper rising. Damn her, why was she turning him inside out this way, making him think that there was a chance, then pulling away like this?

"That's a cop-out."

"No, that's the truth. It doesn't mean anything if I have to explain it to you." Her fingers feathered along her desk calendar. She blinked twice to clear away the tears so she could see. There was a notation next to one o'clock. "I have surgery in an hour. I can't afford to be upset."

So, it was over, he thought. "I'll call you later," he said stonily.

"Sure."

She placed the receiver back into the cradle and knew he wouldn't.

Chapter Sixteen

Shawna rushed through the clinic's doorway, her stomach churning. Passing the row of patients in the waiting room, she nodded mechanically at several faces she recognized. Her target was the back of the clinic. She wanted to get there before it was too late.

Caro had looked up the moment the door to the clinic opened. A cryptic smile curved her mouth when she saw Shawna.

"Well, hello. We were beginning to worry about you." To her surprise, Shawna didn't stop at the desk to exchange a few pleasantries. She didn't even slow down to answer. Caro rose, turning as Shawna passed her. "Are you feeling all right, Doctor?"

Shawna merely nodded, afraid that if she opened her mouth to reply, there might be dire consequences. She could feel her stomach rising to her mouth. Like a homing pigeon, she glued her eyes to the rear of the clinic, determined to reach the tiny bathroom.

She just made it in time.

When she slowly reemerged a few minutes later, Shawna felt better. Not great, she thought ruefully, but at least partially human. At this point, it was the best that she could hope for. Telling herself that she didn't feel as if she could sleep for a week given the slightest opportunity, Shawna walked into the small office next to the bathroom.

Simon McGuire was just getting up from behind the desk. She flashed an apologetic smile at him as she reached into the battered locker for her lab coat. He should have been on his way home by now.

"Sorry, I know I'm running behind schedule. There was a traffic jam on the freeway."

He crossed to her and held her coat as she put her arms into the sleeves. "That's all right. There's no time clock to punch here. I can't very well dock what comes from the generosity of your soul, now, can I?"

She turned to face him. Scheduling conflicts had prevented her from seeing or talking to McGuire since her mother had told her the good news. That had been almost a week ago. Her life had been one whirlwind of work since then. She'd made sure of it. But it had taken its toll.

"So, I guess that congratulations are in order." She forced a smile to her lips as she shoved her hands into her pockets. It was mind over matter, she thought, telling herself that her stomach *was* settling down and didn't feel like a tidal wave about to pound on the beach. "Mother told me that the two of you were getting married."

He beamed like a young bridegroom instead of the wise general practitioner his patients sought out.

"Yes." He scrutinized her face for her reaction. "Approve?"

"Approve?" How could he possibly think otherwise? He was a kind, caring man with an excellent reputation among his colleagues, and her mother was crazy about him. "I'm absolutely delighted! You're the best thing that ever happened to my mother."

He regarded her thoughtfully. She appeared rather peaked around the edges. "No, you are. But I'd like to make a stab at being a close second."

His words took her by surprise. "Me?"

McGuire nodded. Casually he draped an arm around her shoulders, delaying her return to the waiting room. The clinic was full, but it was a rare occurrence when it wasn't. He wanted a few minutes alone with his future stepdaughter.

"Sally's told me a great deal about you, a great deal that I'm sure wasn't in the letter of recommendation that came from New York Hospital."

Sally had been honest with him about her own failure as a parent. She'd told him that Shawna had taken care of both of them ever since she was a little girl, acting more like a mother than Sally had. She'd told him, Sally said, because she wanted to be sure that he knew exactly what he was getting into. Her honesty only made him love her more.

The admiration in McGuire's eyes warmed Shawna. Now if it could only settle her stomach, she mused.

"Funny, until recently I never thought of my mother as being aware of anything that was going on."

"She was, Shawna. Believe me, she was."

Words of praise always made her fidgety. The focus belonged on her mother and McGuire, not on her. Shawna spread her arms to him. "Well, at any rate, welcome to the family, Simon."

He appreciated her easy acceptance and hugged her. After a moment he stepped back. His eyes were kind as they gently swept over her face. "So, are you going to tell him?"

Shawna stiffened. She felt as if a pail of cold water had been thrown at her. She looked toward the front of the clinic, anxious to start working. Anxious to put distance between herself and the questions. "Him? Tell who what?"

The hand on her shoulder was gentling, the look in his eyes understanding. "Shawna, perhaps I'm overstepping myself as your future stepfather, but I've had a soft spot in my heart for you from the first day I saw you."

She raised her eyes to his face warily. "Really?"

He nodded. "You looked needy. And as you know, I'm a sucker for needy cases."

She'd always prided herself on hiding her feelings, though she would have been the first to admit that when she came to Harris Memorial her emotions were in complete upheaval. Still, she hadn't thought that a stranger would have detected that so easily.

"I don't think that I looked particularly needy, Doctor, just—"

"It wasn't in your clothes, Shawna, it was in your eyes. You were hurting. Now, as your almost stepfather, I think that there's something you should know about me," he continued. "I don't get sidetracked very easily." McGuire's manner grew serious as his concern became evident. "Shawna, I've been a doctor for twenty-eight years, and I have three daughters of my own. I know a pregnant woman when I see one."

A whimsical smile played on his lips. "And if I didn't, the episode in the bathroom would have given me a rather nice-size clue. We have sinfully thin walls in this clinic." His eyes indicated the bathroom.

Shawna shrugged carelessly, though she knew it was useless to continue the pretense. "I ate something that didn't agree with me."

He saw things in her eyes that she wasn't telling him, no matter how well she thought she masked them. "More like you had a relationship that didn't agree with you. At least temporarily," he added. He, like Sally, had his hopes about the situation. "Sally tells me that you've stopped seeing Murphy."

She felt restless, as if she was getting in her own way. Why not? Everything else was. "I wasn't seeing him exactly. We had a few dates and then decided to go our separate ways, that's all."

It was far from all, McGuire judged. "So, he doesn't know."

She looked down at the floor. The black-and-white checkered linoleum was yellowed with age and cracked in a few places. She stared at the crack, following the zigzag pattern. "No."

He felt the urge to hold her, the way he would with his daughters whenever they'd had a heartache. But he knew that Shawna wouldn't appreciate it right now. She was too busy struggling with her independence. "Are you planning on telling him?"

"Eventually. Maybe." She shrugged, feeling completely helpless. It wasn't supposed to have turned out this way. But then, she thought, her initial reaction had been right. Keep a tight rein on your heart and nothing can hurt it. The trouble was, she had forgotten her own rules. "I haven't thought things out that far."

"Far," he repeated, a smile lifting the corners of his mouth. "Then you've decided to have it."

She looked at him in surprise. Not to have the child had never entered her mind. "Oh, yes. Yes," she echoed more firmly. "I could never think of— No, it's a baby. How could I—"

McGuire raised a hand. "Easy." His voice was soothing, patient. "I knew the answer to my question before I asked, but I wanted to hear you say it." He studied her face. "Maybe you needed to hear it, too." He didn't want her to feel that he was pressuring her. Just that he cared. "You owe it to all three of you to tell him, you know."

She didn't relish the idea of seeing Murphy. There were too many emotions churning within her for her to face the matter rationally.

Shawna blew out a breath. "Yes, well, if I find some time where I'm not throwing up or going from patient to patient, I'll give him a call." *Maybe.*

McGuire nodded, knowing that for the time being she wasn't about to do anything of the sort. He wondered if Sally knew that her daughter was pregnant. Shawna didn't strike him as the type to volunteer this sort of information on her own.

"You do that." He glanced at his watch. He had just enough time to go home and change before he went to pick up Sally. "Now, if you'll excuse me, I have to see a beautiful woman about dinner."

Shawna was glad to give up center stage. She grinned fondly at the man. From the little interaction she'd had with her mother, Sally had told her of an extensive itinerary. They were behaving like two energized teenagers. Shawna was thrilled for both of them. "You're spoiling her."

He laughed. "Yes, and I fully intend to go on doing it. It's about time someone did."

Though her knees felt a little wobbly, she hooked her arm through his and accompanied him down the small hall. "You're going to make a terrific stepfather."

He stopped and looked down into her face. "I also make a terrific grandfather. I even know all the verses to 'Rock-a-Bye-Baby.'"

She raised her brows in mock surprise. "There's more than one?"

McGuire rolled his eyes toward the ceiling. "Oh, you younger people, always in a hurry. There are three."

His eyes twinkled, and had he had a beard, Shawna would have said that he could easily have substituted for Santa Claus. Maybe he had, at least in her mother's case.

Congratulations, Mother. You "done good." Finally.

McGuire's eyes shifted toward her stomach before lifting to her face. "Don't forget our little talk, all right?"

She nodded as she walked out with him. She wouldn't forget, but for the time being she had no intention of saying anything to Murphy. Not unless she had to. She refused to have him think that she was using the baby as a way of getting what she wanted.

Maybe she didn't even want it anymore, she told herself.

The hell she didn't.

Caro shifted in her seat as McGuire and Shawna walked out. She nodded goodbye toward the man and looked at Shawna, her manner uncharacteristically solicitous. "Ready for your first patient?"

Shawna forced a smile to her lips, though the last thing she felt like doing was smiling. "Ready and waiting."

Caro nodded and picked up the file closest to her. She pushed the chair away with the back of her legs. "I'll get you some tea in a minute," she promised.

Shawna stared at her.

"Always worked for me when I had a queasy feeling." Caro winked as she passed. "Mrs. Fuentes, the doctor will see you now."

As she retreated to the back and the office for a moment, Shawna was vaguely aware of a heavyset woman rising in reply. How had Caro figured out that she was pregnant?

There was definitely no mistaking the knowing look in the woman's eyes.

There was a chipped mirror hanging within her open locker and Shawna glanced at it.

That's how, she thought. All Caro had to do was look at her. Her complexion was no longer translucent. It appeared almost pasty, but maybe that was just the light. The light, however, didn't give her those dark circles under her eyes. Maybe that had been Caro's clue.

Pretty soon no one would need any clues. The evidence would be right out front for everyone to see.

God, what a mess, she thought in a moment of despondence.

The next moment she banished it. She'd handle this, just as she had everything else. The one thing she knew for certain was that this baby would never lack for love.

Shawna had absolutely no idea when or how she was going to face Murphy with this. She didn't need or want his financial support. She didn't want anything from him that he had to be forced to give.

She didn't want him there because he had to be, she wanted him there because he *wanted* to be.

What she wanted was his heart. Willingly tendered, out of love, not out of a sense of responsibility or duty. Nothing else mattered but that, and that had been denied.

She sighed as she splayed a protective hand over the baby that was no larger than a pinprick within her. Well, if her mother had gone through this thirty years ago, she could certainly go through it now. If nothing else, she was far more resilient than her mother. And far more logical.

Some logic, she thought disparagingly.

A font of empathy suddenly surged in her heart, one that had never been tapped before.

"I understand, Mother," she whispered softly. "I think I finally understand how you felt."

Taking the file that Caro had left for her right outside the door, Shawna squared her shoulders, fixed a bright smile on her face and opened the door.

"Hello, Mrs. Fuentes, what seems to be the trouble?"

* * *

"Where is she, Jeanne?"

Jeanne looked up from her computer and smothered a gasp. The face of the man who stood in front of her was a mask of barely controlled fury. For a moment, stunned, she didn't recognize him. When she did, her mind blanked out his question. All she could think of was that she had never seen anyone so angry before.

Murphy had just gotten off the telephone with Shawna's mother. He'd taken the call in his office politely enough, thinking that the woman was attempting to mend the rift between her daughter and him like some budding matchmaker.

He hadn't been prepared for the bombshell she had dropped on him with no foreshadowing. He also hadn't been prepared for the sheer wave of grief that he'd experienced because the news had come to him from someone other than Shawna.

Hadn't he meant anything to her? Had it all been just in his mind? She'd not only turned her back on him, pushing him out of her life, but now she was going to cut him out of his child's, as well.

He'd driven like a man possessed to get here.

"Is she in her office?" he pressed when Jeanne made no answer. There was no one sitting in the waiting room, and it was just before noon. He assumed that she was in her office, going over reports. Hiding from the world.

Hiding from him.

Jeanne felt as if she'd been sealed to her chair. Murphy's eyes were intense. "No, she's in one of the examining rooms." Somehow, she managed to gain her feet. "I'll tell her you're here."

"You do that." The words were so low, so dangerous, they sent Jeanne hurrying from her desk. "You tell her I'm here. I'll be in her office."

Reining in his anger, his hurt, Murphy walked to the end of the hall.

It had rained earlier today. Now the sun was splashing light on everything, embracing its warmth. It broke through the window in rainbows.

He felt only darkness.

How could she? How could she try to keep this from him? Anguish rattled the steel bars of his resolve as he picked up the multicolored cube she kept on her desk. The colors were all arranged in a pattern that had to be matched in order for the puzzle to be solved. He twisted it, impotent anger flowing through his fingertips. Murphy had no interest in occupying his mind, he only wanted something to do with his hands. His mind wasn't up to functioning analytically.

The cube broke apart in his hands.

Disgusted, he dropped the pieces on the desk. They bounced once, then fell onto the floor just as someone entered the office behind him.

He swung around, knowing who he would see before he did so.

Shawna's throat was dry. She moved as if her knees were welded together. She'd hurried through the remainder of the exam when Jeanne had told her that Murphy was here. She owed Mr. Dembrowsky a thorough exam and asked him to reschedule. All she wanted to do was run from the office as fast as possible.

From him.

To him.

God, but she was confused, and it was all his fault.

She saw the pieces lying on the floor. "You broke my cube."

He stepped away from it, and from her, afraid of what he was capable of doing. "I'll buy you another."

She had no idea where her courage came from. She'd felt drained only a moment ago.

"I didn't know you had an appointment today." Shawna fisted her hands inside her pockets, struggling to keep her voice level.

She had raised her chin defensively, and he had the overwhelming urge to clip her one. "I didn't know I needed one to see the mother of my baby."

It felt as if someone had siphoned off her air. "Who told you?" Even as she asked, she knew. Damn Simon for sharing this with her mother. When she'd left the apartment this morning her mother had begged her to call Murphy. Obviously, she hadn't waited for her to do it.

It's my baby, Mother. I'm carrying it. I'll tell Murphy when I damn well please.

A sense of betrayal choked Murphy as he looked at her. Even now she was being defiant. Damn her for ever stirring him up this way. "Your mother. At least she had the decency to call me and tell me."

She bristled at the accusation. "Decency?"

"Decency," he snapped. It was indecent to hide this from him, this child who was a part of him. "She called me half an hour ago. She thought I should know." He pinned Shawna with an accusing look. "She said she didn't want you making the same mistakes that she did by running away."

The words passed through her heart like a knife. So that was it. Her mother had run away from the father of her child. From her father. Maybe he had never even known that Sally was pregnant. "I'm not making a mistake. I know exactly what I'm doing."

Murphy threw up his hands, still careful to maintain his distance from her. He'd never felt fury like this before. He'd never felt any of the things that he'd felt since she'd come into his life. And then left it.

"Well, that makes one of us, because I haven't got a clue in hell what you're doing or why you're doing it."

Belatedly she realized that the door was still open. She closed it behind her. "Lower your voice."

He wasn't about to take orders from a woman who'd treated him with no more concern than she would a rodent. Less. "I'll shout if I want to."

She matched him tone for tone, her eyes blazing. "Not at me, you won't."

"Who am I supposed to shout at?" he demanded, crossing to her. He gripped her by the shoulders, clenching his teeth together to refrain from shaking her. "It wouldn't be the same shouting at Jeanne. She's not the one who walked over my heart with spiked heels."

His retort stunned her into momentary silence. She looked up at him and thought she saw something flicker in his eyes amid the fury. Pain? Why? He'd been the one who had hurt her. All he was displaying now was wounded macho pride. "Getting it backward, aren't you?"

What was she talking about? He saw her wince and released her, knowing he'd squeezed too hard. "I don't think so." He moved around, trying to find a way to vent his feelings. "I asked you to move in with me and you acted as if I had the plague." He turned to look at her. His eyes were accusing. She'd led him on. "I thought you were above game playing."

She had no idea why she suddenly felt like crying. Damn those hormones for kicking in at the wrong time. "So did I, until the stakes got too high."

He had no idea what she was talking about. "What the hell is that supposed to mean?" he shouted.

She shouted right back at him. "I fell in love with you."

"And I fell in love with you." Her words sank in and he lowered his voice. What had he missed? "So what's the problem?"

Half her unborn child's genes were coming from an oaf. "The problem was what to do about it."

He still didn't understand. "You said no strings. I was giving you a relationship with no strings. Wasn't that what you wanted?"

"No." She blinked, cursing tears that wouldn't evaporate, but shimmered on her lashes. "I lied."

He stared at her, incredulous. He had to be hearing things. "What?"

"I lied, all right?" Embarrassed, angry, she turned away. "I wanted strings. I wanted packaging, bubble wrappers, tape. Everything. I wanted to be wrapped up so tight with you that neither one of us could ever get free." She glared at him. "Or want to get free."

He reached for her, but she pushed him back. This wasn't going to be solved with a kiss, or by allowing herself to slide back into the passion she so desperately craved. She couldn't just think of herself anymore.

"And I knew when you asked me to move in with you that you wanted to stay free. I couldn't do that." She searched her heart and knew that she'd lied again. "Well, maybe I could," she amended, "but I didn't have only myself to think of anymore. I had a baby."

Suddenly as restless as he, she began to roam around the office like a trapped animal searching for an escape route. Only there wasn't any, not for her. She'd never escape the love she felt for him. But he didn't have to know that.

"A baby who wasn't going to grow up the way I did, aimless, rootless, belonging to no one, while her mother looked all over the country for someone to love her."

Murphy shook his head. She was rambling. "You're not making any sense, you know."

She let out a frustrated sigh. "I don't have to make sense, I'm pregnant. I made sense for thirty years and look where it's gotten me."

It was beginning to gel. He reached for her again. "You're still babbling."

This time she pushed him away with less energy. "It's my office." She sniffed. "I can babble if I want to."

The light that materialized at the end of the tunnel was a bright one. "Let me get this straight. If I had proposed to you, you would have said yes?" To think of the hell he'd gone through for nothing.

"Yes." She said it as if she expected to be challenged.

He grinned. His anger vanished like a puddle of water in the desert. "Then I really don't think we have much of a problem. The baby can have a complete set of parents."

She was still leery of his reasons. "I don't want you to marry me because of the baby."

When he took her into his arms, the struggle she offered was only minimal. "All right, I'll marry you despite the baby. How's that?"

She started to laugh as she shook her head, tears gathering again in her eyes. But this time they were tears of joy. "Are you serious?"

"Yeah, for once, I am." It felt like heaven to hold her in his arms. He indulged himself and kissed her before continuing. "I've barely been able to function since we stopped seeing each other. I need you, Shawna—I have since the very beginning." He smiled into her face. "You're the only one who can pull all my pieces together and make me feel whole.''

He framed her face and kissed her again. ''I was going to accept you on any terms you wanted, just to have you in my life. Marriage'll do just fine.''

He released her, knowing that to hold her like this would only create yearnings within him that he would be unable to do anything about in her office. ''Tell you what, I'll come by after work tonight and we'll celebrate. I'll take you to my place and cook dinner for you.'' And after dinner they would really celebrate.

''You cook?'' She tried to picture him moving competently around in a kitchen. It didn't seem to suit him.

''Better than Kelly,'' he assured her. Moving forward, he kicked aside a piece of the cube. Embarrassed now at having broken it, he bent to pick up the pieces. When he straightened, his face was pale, his fingers tightening around the broken cube.

''Shawna?''

The strange note in his voice caused a ripple of unease within her. ''Yes?''

''I don't mean to alarm you, but I can't see. Out of either eye.''

Chapter Seventeen

Shawna leaned against the locker where she had hastily thrown her jacket and purse earlier and sighed.

It was over.

She had just spent the longest two and a half hours of her life and it was finally over. She closed her eyes. Almost against her will, the whole ordeal materialized again.

The first part had almost streaked by. Trying not to let his words panic her, she had taken Murphy's hand and guided him into a chair in her office, where she'd examined him.

The worst had finally happened. And she had to do something quickly before it became permanent.

He knew she was shining a light into his eyes. He had heard the click. But in the world he'd tumbled into, there was nothing. Absolutely nothing.

"It's not going to pass, is it?" Murphy asked her.

The restraint in his voice amazed her. Setting aside her ophthalmoscope, she gripped his hand in hers.

"Damn straight it's going to pass." In contrast to his, her voice was brimming with emotion. "But only if I make it pass."

He smiled then, squeezing her hand and clearly fighting the fear that was attempting to overwhelm him. "Make it so."

If he could be brave, so could she. "Just what I need. Jean-Luc Picard."

She kissed his forehead, her heart wrenching within her breast, then called for Jeanne. The woman was loyally waiting in the reception area, ready to spring into action in case Shawna needed any help.

"Get me an operating room scheduled, Jeanne," Shawna called down the hallway. "Now." There was no questioning the urgency in her voice.

Shawna crossed back into the office. The sight of Murphy sitting there, staring into nothingness, clawed at her heart. Hurrying to the telephone, she tapped out the number of a colleague. She was going to need an assistant for the surgery and fast.

She misdialed and swore. It was only the urgency for speed, she told herself, that was making her fingers fumble this way, not fear.

But fear continued to ride shotgun beside her, anyway.

Jeanne came into her office just then to tell her that her bid for an operating room would have to wait until later that afternoon. Jeanne slanted a curious look toward Murphy, wondering what was happening.

"What line are you on?" Shawna demanded, irritated at the stumbling block.

"Two."

She depressed the second button on her telephone and started talking as soon as she heard a response on the other end. Using everything she had at her disposal—bravado, pull, fear—she wormed her way into a slot within the hour. An elective surgery was bumped up to two o'clock. This was an emergency.

"You're magnificent when you're in high gear," Murphy told her as she urged him up on his feet. His manner belied the apprehension she knew was cloaking him.

"Flattery isn't going to get you anywhere. If you'd listened to me in the first place," she retorted, guiding him into the outer hall, "this kind of hurry wouldn't be necessary."

She realized he hated this dark world he was in. He had hoped that the fluid behind his eye would dissipate naturally. But it hadn't, and now he was suddenly plunged into the center of a sightless region. Shawna knew that Murphy was scared, really scared, and he was fighting not to show it.

"And if you'd listened to me, I wouldn't have had to come in here, raving like a maniac."

"We'll talk," she promised. And they would, once this was over....

And now it was.

She felt as if she'd just run the Boston Marathon on her knees through broken glass. God, but she was exhausted. The fluid buildup had been greater than she had anticipated. The bloated dural sheath of the nerve had capriciously shifted when Murphy had bent down for the pieces of the cube. The resulting shift in pressure had rendered him blind. It could have happened at any time.

Thank God it had happened when she was there.

"Nice job." Dr. Alex Mead nodded at Shawna as he stripped off his green livery and tossed it into a laundry receptacle. "Made me feel rather useless, just standing around there."

He'd come through for her at what amounted to a moment's notice, shifting his patients around to accommodate the surgery, and she was extremely grateful. She owed him one. Big time.

"You wouldn't have been if I'd suddenly had to go running off to throw up."

Mead stopped rebuttoning his hand-tailored shirt. He'd assisted Shawna during other surgeries and been duly impressed with her technique. "Since when do you get a queasy stomach during surgery?"

She was about to tell Mead that she was pregnant and then stopped, surprised that she'd admit something so casually to someone who wasn't related to her. She hadn't even told her mother—Simon had. Maybe more than just Murphy's sight had been corrected in that operating room. Maybe the way *she* saw things had, too.

But before she could say anything, Shawna felt a large, comforting hand on her shoulder. "Since she was operating on someone she cared about."

Shawna turned to see that McGuire was standing beside her. "What are you doing here?" It wasn't as if he had to walk through the locker area to get to another part of the hospital. He had sought her out.

"I came to give you moral support, in case you needed it, which I see you don't. Word got out." He nodded toward the operating room. "You caused quite a ripple in hospital politics by bumping that nose job." He could see by her expression that she hadn't the faintest idea whose surgery she had had postponed, only that it had been necessary. "Seems the nose belongs to Heather O'Greer, daughter of a well-placed councilman."

Was that all? "Her nose'll keep."

McGuire laughed as Mead left the room. "How's Murphy doing?"

She realized that she still had her gloves on and began to strip them off. "He's going to be just fine."

McGuire had expected nothing less. "I had my suspicions he would be. He has a terrific surgeon."

Shawna tried not to let the praise matter too much. But it did. She unknotted the tie at the back of her gown, then slipped it from her shoulders. The gown joined Mead's in the laundry receptacle. "I'd better go and tell his family the news. I had Jeanne call them."

It had been a complete afterthought. All she could focus on at the time was Murphy and the horrid feeling of urgency that was pounding through her.

McGuire had passed by the surgical waiting room on his way over. "There's a cluster of people in the lounge who might fit the description of worried family members."

She nodded her thanks and went through the swinging operating-room doors into the corridor.

Shawna had no sooner crossed the threshold to the lounge than she saw Kelly springing to her feet. Within a moment she was at her side.

Kelly grasped Shawna's arm. "Is he—?"

It always felt wonderful to be able to give a patient's family good news. This went far beyond that feeling.

"He's going to be just fine."

Shawna's eyes swept over the collection of faces. She recognized Kimberly and her husband, Adam, and Thomas. The petite white-haired woman holding on to Thomas's arm was Murphy's mother. The thought that it must be nice to have a support group echoed in Shawna's mind.

Within a few months they would become hers, as well.

As succinctly as possible she tried to explain the procedure she had performed on Murphy. "I did what's called an optic nerve decompression to drain the fluid from behind his eye. The swelling had gotten to be larger than we thought. Murphy's lucky. We got it in time before there could be any permanent damage."

"He always was lucky," Thomas said, holding Kelly to him.

Mrs. Pendleton looked at Shawna, gratitude shining in her gray eyes. "Can we see him?"

Shawna nodded. "When he's in his room. He's in recovery now. They'll be bringing him up to his room in about an hour." She pointed down the hall to the front of the building. "You can check with Information to find out the number. Until then, relax. It's over."

Kelly squeezed Shawna's hand and spoke for all of them. "Thank you."

Shawna returned the smile. "Just doing my job. If your brother hadn't been so stubborn, there would have been no reason for these theatrics." A whimsical smile lifted the corners of her mouth. "And Heather O'Greer wouldn't have had to live an hour longer with a nose she hated."

She didn't bother explaining, knowing the others were too overjoyed to pay much attention to her last comment.

Nausea notwithstanding, she was feeling pretty overjoyed herself.

There was a noise buzzing somewhere around him. Murphy felt as if he were swimming up from the depths of a lake, up to the top. To where the noise was.

To where the light was.

He had to find Shawna.

The single thought beat in his brain like the rhythm of the relentless rain as it fell against a window.

He had to find her. Before he lost her. Forever.

With what felt like supreme effort, Murphy swam to the top, urgently calling her name. It felt as if he was swimming for hours. And still he couldn't reach the top.

"Right here, Murphy. I'm right here."

Pressure. A hand. There was someone holding his hand. Murphy forced his eyes open. It wasn't easy. Each eyelid weighed close to a ton, and his view was obstructed by the bandage.

The room was swaddled in cotton. There was a face shimmering above him. A woman's face, fragmented. He blinked twice before the fragments formed a whole.

"Shawna."

The idiot was trying to raise his head, she thought in exasperation. She laid a hand on his shoulder, urging him back down. "Shh. Lie still, you're in recovery."

It took him a moment to make sense of what she said. "No, I'm not." His tongue felt thick, too big for his mouth. "I've mended. You said yes."

He took a breath and appeared to have fallen asleep. But when she attempted to move her hand away, his eyes fluttered open again, his fingers tightening on hers. "You did say yes, didn't you? Or was that a dream, too?"

If he hadn't just had surgery, she would have hugged him. As it was, she had to restrain herself. At least, for a little while.

"No, it wasn't a dream, and yes, I did say yes." Her smile contrasted with the tears that sparkled in her eyes. "But, you know, I might be taking unfair advantage of the situation."

He struggled to understand. Thoughts moved through his brain like the giant wheel of a steamroller. "Why?"

She felt her heart warm just at the sight of him. She'd been so frightened when she had seen his face pale in the office. "Well, it's a known fact that a lot of patients fall in love with their surgeons."

A very weak smile curved Murphy's lips. At least, h thought it did; he wasn't completely sure. "I did it before th operation. I wanted to beat the rush." A wave of need cam over him as he felt her drawing her fingers away from hi hand. "Stay with me, Shawna."

She had an afternoon full of patients. "I—" For once she thought, they could wait, or be rescheduled. Her ba by's father needed her. And she needed him. She hadn't re alized just how much until the past few hours. "Yes, I' stay."

He knew she would, but he wanted to make sure. "For ever."

She laughed softly. Forever had a wonderful ring to it She looked down at their linked hands. For a man just ou of surgery, he had a good grip. "As long as I get bathroor privileges."

The smile on his lips was fading into his dreams. "Yo can have anything you want, just stay."

Before she could answer, the blanket of anesthesia re claimed him and Murphy drifted off to sleep.

Shawna nodded gratefully at the nurse who scooted chair over for her beside the bed. Sitting down, she smile at Murphy as she brushed the hair away from his forehead As if he could get her to leave. She'd subconsciously sense almost from the beginning that he possessed all the neces sary pieces to make a good husband. He just needed a littl work, a little prodding, to get those pieces to assembl themselves into a wonderful whole.

"Yes, I'll stay, Murphy," she whispered softly. "For ever."

* * * * *

A Note from the Author

There wasn't a time, ever, when I wanted to be a boy. I have always enjoyed "being a girl" (even before Rodgers and Hammerstein wrote the song in *Flower Drum Song*. When I was a little girl, the only role models I had were Sheena, Queen of the Jungle and Annie Oakley. They were enough. I liked their style and their independence. In some manner, shape or form, all my heroines have had their roots in Sheena and Annie. They've all been very independent women.

I felt then, as I do now, that being female automatically means you're special. We've had to be strong, yet feminine—and usually, twice the man any man is. For me, being female meant I had to try harder to prove I was just as good as any guy, in school and in the work world. I think it helped me achieve my goals (marrying the man I set my sights on, having the children I desired, and, finally, becoming a writer, the way I always dreamed).

From the beginning, Shawna Saunders was very special to me. She survived a difficult childhood in which the roles of mother and child were, for the most part, reversed. Rather than feel sorry for herself, Shawna gave her mother emotional support and went on to make something of herself. As an adult, when double tragedy struck, Shawna survived that, as well. Instead of withdrawing from the world, she dedicated herself to helping others. It takes a very special lady to be that selfless. It was that quality, and her independence, that Murphy Pendleton found so appealing. I hope you will, too.

On a final note, I'd like to thank you for making *me* feel special by reading my stories.

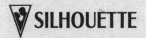

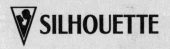
❤ SILHOUETTE

⟨ SPECIAL EDITION ⟩

COMING NEXT MONTH

SAME TIME, NEXT YEAR
Debbie Macomber

That Special Woman!

One unforgettable night with Summer Lawton had James Wilkens vowing to meet her at the same time, the same place, the next year…

A FAMILY HOME
Celeste Hamilton

The sexiest man in Tennessee had proposed to Lainey Bates, but he'd done it to give his son a family home. Lainey wanted her husband's heart…

MARRIAGE ON DEMAND
Susan Mallery

Hometown Heartbreakers

Amid countless adoring females, Rebecca Chambers hadn't expected delicious Austin Lucas to notice her, but he had. Now he was planning on giving his child his name; would he also be giving Rebecca everlasting heartache?

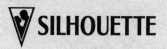

❖ SILHOUETTE

SPECIAL EDITION

COMING NEXT MONTH

THE REAL ELIZABETH HOLLISTER...
Trisha Alexander

The search for her true identity led Grace Gregory to a family of great wealth and power, to Paul Hollister, a naturally suspicious man. Was she the woman he'd been waiting for?

JENNI FINDS A FATHER
Brittany Young

Alec Devereaux and Tess Parish both could achieve their dreams if they were married for one full year. Tess's little sister, Jenni, and Alec's daughter wanted to make it permanent...

HEARTH, HOME AND HOPE
Kaitlyn Gorton

Cooper Sanford was back—but a lot had happened since Coop had broken Hope's heart. What was the secret she wasn't telling him?

SILHOUETTE
Desire

FROM HERE TO MATERNITY

Beginning next month a new mini-series from Elizabeth Bevarly celebrating the many joys of motherhood—and fatherhood!

Three single women each meet the man of their dreams…and find themselves expecting a surprise package. Watch these soon-to-be mums as they are swept off their feet and into the maternity ward!

In July:
A DAD LIKE DANIEL (Desire 908)

In September:
THE PERFECT FATHER (Desire 920)

In November:
DR DADDY (Desire 933)

FROM HERE TO MATERNITY: Look what the stork brought—a bundle of joy and the promise of love!

GET 4 BOOKS
AND A MYSTERY GIFT

Return this coupon and we'll send you 4 Silhouette Special Editions and a mystery gift absolutely FREE! We'll even pay the postage and packing for you.

We're making you this offer to introduce you to the benefits of Reader Service: FREE home delivery of brand-new Silhouette romances, at least a month before they are available in the shops, FREE gifts and a monthly Newsletter packed with information.

Accepting these FREE books and gift places you under no obligation to buy, you may cancel at any time, even after receiving just your free shipment. Simply complete the coupon below and send it to:

HARLEQUIN MILLS & BOON, FREEPOST, PO BOX 70, CROYDON, CR9 9EL.

No stamp needed

Yes, please send me 4 free Silhouette Special Editions and a mystery gift. I understand that unless you hear from me, I will receive 6 superb new titles every month for just £2.20* each postage and packing free. I am under no obligation to purchase any books and I may cancel or suspend my subscription at any time, but the free books and gifts will be mine to keep in any case. (I am over 18 years of age)

1EP5SE

Ms/Mrs/Miss/Mr _____

Address _____

_____

_____ Postcode _____

COMING NEXT MONTH FROM

 **SILHOUETTE**

Intrigue

Danger, deception and desire—
new from Silhouette...

FREE FALL Jasmine Cresswell
THE WAINWRIGHT SECRET Margaret Chittenden
SILENT SEA Patricia Rosemoor
STREET OF DREAMS Lynn Leslie

Desire

Provocative, sensual love stories for the
woman of today

COWBOYS DON'T CRY Anne McAllister
A DAD LIKE DANIEL Elizabeth Bevarly
A MAN OF THE LAND Carol Devine
TRUTH OR DARE Caroline Cross
ANYTHING'S POSSIBLE Judith McWilliams
HIS BROTHER'S WIFE Audra Adams

Sensation

A thrilling mix of passion, adventure
and drama

LOST WARRIORS Rachel Lee
BIRTHRIGHT Julia Quinn
ONCE MORE WITH FEELING Nora Roberts
PASSION'S VERDICT Frances Williams